OB

By the same author

THE INSTITUTE
PARADISE BAY

OBSESSION

Maria del Rey

First published in Great Britain in 1993 by
Nexus
332 Ladbroke Grove
London W10 5AH

A catalogue record for this book is available
from the British Library

ISBN 0 352 32853 3

Typeset by Avocet Typesetters, Bicester, Oxon
Printed and bound in Great Britain by
Cox & Wyman Ltd, Reading, Berks

This book is a work of fiction.
In real life, make sure you practise safe sex.

OBSESSION

1

It began with a telephone call, the shrill electric tone shattering the silence of the night like a dagger through the heart. Jonathan swore under his breath, the sleep taken from him by the startling explosion of sound. Blindly he reached across the bed, fumbling to lift the crying phone from its cradle, wishing the damned thing had never been invented.

'Yes?' he asked wearily, lying back, peering at the clock next to the phone. It was four o'clock in the morning.

'I am sorry, master, but my mistress has a call for you,' a softly spoken woman said, sounding as if the idea of a pre-dawn phone call horrified her as much as it did him.

Damn, it was a wrong number, it was always a wrong number at that sort of uncivilised hour. 'Look, this is a wrong number,' Jonathan snapped angrily, peering at the clock again, knowing that he wouldn't be able to get back to sleep again.

'I'm sorry ... ' the woman said, pausing momentarily. He could hear the doubt in her voice. 'Master?' she repeated hopefully.

'Look, who do you want?' Jonathan demanded, sitting up on one elbow, preparing to hurl the phone back across the room.

'Jonathan de Molay?' the voice asked tentatively, the tone becoming nervous and quiet.

It was his turn to pause, to wonder what was going on. 'Yes, that's me,' he said, trying to place the woman at the other end, trying to put a name and a face to the soft nervous voice. It had to be a wrong number, or some kind of very unfunny joke. The voice was strange, the woman sounded strained, uncertain, agitated. It was no one he knew, he was certain of it.

'I am sorry, master, but my mistress has a call for you,' the voice said again, rewinding and repeating the same words — the same words and with the same tone of voice, as if reading from a script, with the words and inflection down on paper to be repeated until the correct response was elicited.

'Who is this?' Jonathan asked. If this was a joke, and he could think of no other possibility, then it was a strange one. Who could it be? He didn't even know anyone with that weird a sense of humour; he didn't know anyone with any sense of humour. Nobody sprang to mind, he knew that the woman on the other end of the line was a total stranger. And not just any stranger; there was something strange about her too, something that he could pick up in the voice, and in her odd choice of words.

'I shall put you through to the mistress,' the woman said, an obvious note of relief in her voice.

'Who are you? Give me a name at least,' he pleaded. The line went dead, there was a moment of sharp static and then the line sprang back to life. He sat up and leant over to put the bedside light on, catching a glimpse of his pale reflection in the mirror across the room, a quizzical look on his face.

'Have I woken you, darling?' a new voice asked. Another woman, but this time with no hesitation, no nerves. She sounded confident, relaxed, slightly amused. Her aristocratic voice was distant, echoing tinnily on the line, as if she were away from the handset, speaking across a room.

'I think . . . ' Jonathan started to say, thrown off balance by the woman's voice.

'Quiet, darling,' the woman said, cutting him off at once. 'I saw the way Naomi looked at you today, looking up at you with her cry-baby eyes. Don't think I didn't notice, nor the way you looked back at her. I watched the two of you, saw your charming smile and the way she looked away after holding your gaze for a second too long. All day I waited for you to say something, to remark on her behaviour at the very least. I was so disappointed in you darling, making eyes at one of my girls like that.'

'Look, I really . . . '

'Silence, darling!' the woman snapped, her voice loud and clear, as if she had walked right up close to the telephone. 'Quiet. Just listen, darling, I just want you to listen.'

The woman was obviously used to being listened to, and with a voice so achingly pure he could understand why. Every word sounded perfect; he could see her lips forming the sounds, opening and closing seductively, the words leaving her mouth like a lover's kiss. He shrugged inwardly and lay back on the bed to listen.

Straining hard he could hear the sharp tip-tap of heels on the floor. She was walking away from the telephone again. He tried to picture her, to see her in his mind, tall and elegant, undeniably sexy.

'I was so terribly disappointed, darling,' she continued, sounding amused again, he could imagine her smiling, or pursing her lips in a seductive pout. 'But then I realise that the fault is entirely mine. Imagine my lack of diligence. I think, darling, that I have been guilty of the most awful neglect. I have been so besotted with you that I've let my duties as a mistress go to seed. It's

11

high time that I rectified this terrible state of affairs. I'm going to punish Naomi for you, darling. For you.'

Jonathan caught his breath. The talk of masters and mistresses was strange enough, and with her accent the words sounded so anachronistic, straight out of another age.

'Are you comfortable, darling?' the voice asked softly.

'Yes,' Jonathan said, unwilling now to interrupt the strange flow. Every time the woman spoke, every time she called him 'darling', he added a detail to the picture forming in his mind. She had to be beautiful, stunning in every sense; her voice was a projection of her, an aural embodiment of her essence as a person.

'Naomi, apologise to the master.' Her voice was cold and stern.

'I'm sorry, master, honestly, I am,' another woman said, sounding afraid, a slightly pleading tone to her voice. She sounded distant, far from the microphone or telephone or whatever else was hooked up at the other end.

'You've been a bad girl, haven't you?'

'Yes mistress, I'm sorry, I'm sorry . . .'

There was a sound of shuffling, the snap of heels on the floor again. 'Stop that! Honestly girl, it's too late for that. The stupid girl's only just remembered to kiss my heels,' she said dismissively.

'What . . . ' What was going on? It sounded so weird, so totally weird. He looked around the room, at the reflection of himself, bathed in pale orange light, sitting up in bed with the phone in his hand. Everything was normal at his end, everything as it should be. The other end of the call was another world, some other planet. If it was a joke it had to be the most elaborate and surreal joke he'd ever heard.

'Quiet, darling,' mistress chided softly. 'Naomi is on

12

her hands and knees, sitting at my heel, shivering like the bad girl that she is. She knows that it's time for her to be chastised, punished for her impertinence. What shall it be? Paddle, strap, birch or cane? You choose, darling. Let it be our punishment, from both of us.'

It was the perfect time to break in, to call a halt to it all, to explain that it was a wrong number, that he was just some poor soul pulled from sleep by mistake. 'Strap,' he whispered, closing his eyes to see this beautiful mistress dressed in black − it had to be black − standing over the other woman, clutching a leather strap in her elegant white hand.

'Excellent choice,' mistress agreed, sounding for all the world as if he had selected the finest wine for a meal, and not an implement for punishment.

'Please, master . . . ' Naomi wailed pathetically, real fear and anguish in her voice.

'Silence!' mistress snapped, and Naomi fell silent. 'She's kissing my heels again, running her tongue up and down the shiny black spike, kissing the leather all over. She knows I like that, stupid girl, but it won't do her any good. Enough, girl, enough.'

Jonathan pulled the covers aside. He was naked, his body reflected in the mirror. He was excited; there was something about the woman's voice, something beyond the bizarre situation being described, that made his prick go hard. His breathing had become more rapid and his heart was pounding in his chest.

'Pull your skirt up,' mistress commanded, and Jonathan thought he could make out the ruffling of clothes, a whisper of sound at the very edge of perception. 'And your panties down.' Again the faint ruffle of clothing. 'She has exposed her backside for me, darling, she's on all fours down in front of me. Her backside's pressed high in the air, her pretty buttocks slightly apart. I like Naomi, she has such lovely soft skin, and so pale, so beautifully pale. Oh darling, if only you could see her, she looks so lovely. Her face is all screwed up, biting her lower lip, looking up at me with those same cry-baby eyes that she flashed at you. It's the anticipation, that lovely feeling of waiting for it all to happen.' She laughed drily, an innocent kind of laugh without malice or anger, so at odds with the situation she was describing. 'I almost feel jealous of her.'

He felt it too, a pent-up feeling of expectation. A woman, Naomi, was going to be punished for real, beaten with a leather strap, and he was doing nothing to stop it. He had even chosen the implement instead of calling a halt to the whole shocking thing. It had to be a dream, a strange kind of dream that felt so real, more real than real life itself. His prick twitched again; a faint jewel of fluid was seeping from the eye in the glans.

'I'm going to punish you for being so impertinent, do you understand? You must never forget your place, never forget your natural station in life. You will never look any master or mistress in the eye again, never. Is that clear?'

'Yes, mistress, yes . . . ' Naomi wailed again.

'Are you comfortable, darling?' mistress asked, her voice clearer for an instant, as if she had turned to face Jonathan.

'Yes,' Jonathan croaked, unable to break the spell, feeling the expectation rising within, the excitement welling in the pit of his belly. It was for real. There really was another world at the end of the telephone line, with a beautiful and elegant lady about to beat another woman with a leather strap.

'Are you excited?' mistress asked him.

'Yes.'

'Is your delicious cock hard? I bet it is, so lovely and

hard. If only you were here, darling, we could punish Naomi and then make love while she tended us. Would you like that?'

'Yes,' and it was so true, so absolutely true. Jonathan smoothed a hand down his body, and then, almost surreptitiously, took his prick in his hand. He squeezed it, felt his excitement swell even more. He closed his eyes, wanting to see everything in his mind, to see his mistress in every gorgeous imaginary detail.

'How many strokes, darling? Shall I beat her six times, or more?'

'Six,' Jonathan said. Part of him was repulsed by what was going on, disgusted by the spectacle of some poor soul about to be beaten for his gratification. But the feeling was weak, overwhelmed by the excitement of what was happening.

The telephone was cradled under his shoulder and it was uncomfortable, and becoming more so. He leaned across the bed quickly and pulled the phone towards him. There was only one thing to do. It was a gamble, he risked losing the voice, the voice of his beautiful mistress, but he took the chance. In a split second he pressed a button on the keypad and rested the handset gently in its cradle. He held his breath and listened.

'She's still on her hands and knees,' mistress said, sounding so far away, so faint. Jonathan scrabbled under the phone, almost knocking it over, suddenly afraid that the experience was going to fade into silence. He found the volume control and turned it to maximum.

'Are you ready?' mistress asked patiently.

'Yes,' Jonathan sighed with relief. She was still there, the mysterious woman on the other end of the line. He lay back on the bed and closed his eyes again.

'I've put a knee on her back, to keep her in place, and to remind her how powerful her mistress is. Her backside is sticking up even more, so sweet and inviting.

I can see the pinkness between her thighs, peeping between the lips of her sex. How lovely she looks.'

The first blow snapped suddenly, echoing through the room like a gunshot. Jonathan opened his eyes, startled, heart pounding. Naomi wailed and cried out. He moaned softly, rubbing his hard prick up and down softly, shivering with pleasure.

'I can see the welt, it's a vivid scarlet stripe down the side of her left buttock. The contrast is so striking. Darling, that was a joke,' she said, sounding disappointed that Jonathan had made no response. 'It feels hot to my touch, and it feels different too, I can feel the skin rising. Stop it girl, or you'll get more than six. She's rubbing herself against me, trying to rub the heat out of her backside no doubt.'

Again there was a snap, a sharp retort around the room. He closed his eyes again and imagined it was in his room, in front of him, not in some unknown place far away. He rubbed himself harder, letting the dreamy sensation merge with the dreaminess of his imaginary world.

Another snap and more muffled wailing from Naomi. She was obviously trying to stifle her cries, trying to keep her mouth shut in case mistress decided that six was too lenient.

A fourth snap, and this time a louder moan from Jonathan, the breath escaping from him involuntarily.

'Her backside is crossed with lovely red strap marks now, an x on each buttock,' mistress explained proudly. 'She keeps biting her lip, her lovely pretty little face is all screwed up. You should see her eyes, so lovely, so wide. If only you were here, darling. I feel so hot, so excited, if only you could fuck me hard right now, to press your hard cock into me. Oh darling, I do love you.'

Snap – a much harder stroke, the sound louder than

16

ever before. Naomi couldn't stifle her cry this time, and let out a howl, her cry taking a second to fade to silence.

'That's better,' mistress said coldly. 'Without you here, darling, I'll have to get this little bitch to look after me with her mouth. She can do me well, but it's not the same as having you inside me at the same time. I'm so excited now, I can feel my sex becoming moist, and my nipples are pressing against the silk of my blouse. Are you hot, darling?'

'Yes.' Jonathan wanted to say more, to tell her how much he wanted her, to do all the things that she desired, but was afraid to. If he spoke for too long she would realise the mistake, and that would be the end.

Snap, the last stroke, the final note in the rhythm. Naomi's wail of anguish filled the room.

'She's wet,' mistress explained matter-of-factly. 'I'm pressing my fingers into her sex and I can feel how wet she is. And hot, I swear that the heat from her backside has burned into her tight little hole here. Stop it girl,' she warned coldly. 'She's rubbing herself again, wanting me to press deeper into her. Honestly, Jonathan she looks divine like this, now she's ready to do anything.'

Jonathan was breathing fast, his prick throbbing under the gentle steady rhythm of his hand. It felt good, the sound of her voice washing over him like the purest water, invigorating and refreshing, sensual and alive.

'Pull my dress up girl, now suck me well or there'll be more. That's it, oh that's good, lovely . . . ' mistress moaned softly, her breathy voice entwining into Jonathan's fantasy. 'Deeper, that's it, suck me hard, good . . . Ohhh, that's good . . . '

Jonathan's moans became mixed with hers, their breathing matched in tempo, swirls of sensation and sensual pleasure became transformed into something electric that passed over the wire linking their two worlds.

17

'So deep . . . So . . . lovely . . . Jonathan . . . I . . . love you . . . darling . . . '

Jonathan cried out once, his body shook spasmodically, seized by the force of orgasm. For one moment he was there, with mistress, beside her, at her feet, his mouth buried deep into the exquisite moistness of her sex. The thick cream from his prick burst out over him, smearing on to his belly, flicking on to his hands. It felt so good, so electric, so bloody unbelievable.

The telephone died and came to life with the harsh buzz of the dialling tone. It took him a moment for him to find his bearings. He leaned across and lifted the receiver and then dropped it, cutting off the dreadful tone that signalled a return to dull normality. As he moved, the thick globules of semen dripped down his belly and on to his thighs.

Jonathan closed his eyes and shook his head, trying to snap out of whatever had overtaken him. The picture of mistress, an image that he had put together from the sweetness of her voice, was burned indelibly into his mind. He could see her still, and hear her voice, so clear and refined. She was perfection incarnate, mind, body and soul.

The questions were there, but there was no rational explanation. It hadn't been a joke or an extravagant put-on. They had called him by name, both mistress and the other woman, so it couldn't have been an accident.

Only now did he realise how keyed up he had felt, so wound up in the experience. His climax had been ecstatic, a moment of release and not the bare fulfilment of a biological need. It had never felt that good before, never that powerful.

After wiping himself with some tissues he lay back on the bed, dazed and confused. The reflection in the mirror was just as it always was, a dull bedroom, with book-lined shelves and white furniture, nothing at all out of the ordinary. He looked at himself, tired eyes staring back, wondering what in hell was going on.

Everywhere Jonathan looked he thought he saw Mistress, but it was only ever a pale shadow of what she was like. Mistress, and now in his mind it was Mistress with a capital M, was perfect, and nowhere did he see perfection. Her voice had insinuated itself deep into his mind, her words echoing around and around inside his head. Like a song that lodges in the brain. She called him 'darling', drawing the word out, her voice slightly low and breathless, touching a raw nerve somewhere.

He woke late the next morning. His prick was hard and in his mind he could picture Mistress. He reached down instinctively and touched himself, squeezing the reassuring hardness, a ripple of pleasure pulsing through him. He glanced at the clock; it was late, and that left him with even less enthusiasm for work than usual.

That first day had been awful, frustrating, dissatisfying in every sense. It had been hard to concentrate on anything, the usual hectic chaos of work was nothing but an annoyance. He felt withdrawn and unaccountably angry. His mind kept wandering, all he wanted to think about was Mistress and what she had said, and the effect that she had had on him.

The pages of figures that he had to turn into a report refused to gel, the number blurred and made no sense. It was boring and meaningless, just another report like a million other reports he had drafted and delivered. It meant nothing, that was the worst of it, for the first time it struck him that it was all meaningless. That was a terrible thought, a sudden realisation that he was wasting time, time that he really didn't have to waste.

At one point the phone had startled him, snapping him out of the dreamy reverie that he had slipped into. He snatched the receiver and held it close to his ear, wishing fervently that Mistress would breathe her silken words to him. It had been a vain hope, the talk had been of work, and delivered in the dull clipped tones that passed for polite conversation between colleagues.

Would he ever hear from Mistress again? He had to talk to her, to find out who she was, to meet and make love to her. He had to see her, simply and absolutely had to.

Rather than go out for a drink that evening, he returned home directly from work, unable to face the false jollity of drinking with people he didn't really like. It was always the same, the hard drinking into oblivion, the vicious back-biting of colleagues jockeying for position. If he had to laugh one more time at some puerile joke or barbed comment he felt he'd explode. Even his early departure didn't go unnoticed; the faintly jeering laughter of the crowd leaving for the bar echoed in his ears as he headed for the station.

It was a terribly existence, hard in its own way, soulless too. There was nothing in it, no focus, nothing of value. There was only a kind of trenches camaraderie, the machismo hard-drinking, hard-playing, hard-working culture that they were all supposed to share. And at times, when he'd had too much to drink and the world lost its shape, it seemed wonderful, as if he were forging a brand new world out there. But then he'd black out and feel so sick he wanted to die.

It was empty, but there was nothing else. It hadn't mattered before; Jonathan had hardly articulated the things he now felt. It was so much easier not to think about it, to let himself flow with the crowd, until he didn't care any more or couldn't think any more. But now, somehow, it did matter.

He showered as soon as he got home, letting the streaming jets of water wash over him, washing away the frustrations and anger. The flat was empty, but for a change it seemed warm, the antiseptic atmosphere, so typical of a fashionably furnished but unlived-in flat, was muted. He flopped into an armchair with a drink and let the silence absorb him. It was peaceful, the ambience soothing away the last of the day's worries.

Even if Mistress never called again, and that was the most likely eventuality, his life had changed. He couldn't tell why, or in what way things had changed, but he felt certain that they had. Perhaps it had just been the intrusion of the unexpected, the sudden and unexplained irruption of the bizarre into his dull and monotonous existence.

The drink began to take effect, the warmth spreading through him, making him feel human again. Sometimes it was too easy to feel sorry for himself, to just sit down and let himself bask in the wonderfully selfish feelings of self-pity. He poured himself another drink, telling himself to snap out of it. He had to do it sometimes, scold himself, force himself to snap out of whatever was biting him. There was nobody else to do it, he had only himself to depend on.

If Mistress were around she would scold him, he was sure of that, her voice forcing life into him, urging him to be a man, to be human. She would do that for him, making him confront the world, so that he could face up to anything. It was a lovely fantasy, borne of the memory of her voice and the dreamy feeling of intoxication.

He went up to bed, taking the bottle with him, cradling it in his arms. He let the bathrobe fall to the floor around his ankles, stood naked, his body reflected in the mirror. He stood for a moment, looking at

21

himself, then slipped into bed, placing the bottle on the pillow beside him.

He flicked the television on, turned the sound down and watched the images dance in front of him. Without words it was meaningless, a mad dance of people and places, as disconnected as the vivid images of a drunken dream. How could anyone hope to understand anything, anything at all? Another slug of whisky, the delicious feeling of lava down the throat, the heat oozing through him like a twisting, turning monster.

Another flick of the remote control and the lights faded slowly until the room was illuminated only by the dancing colours from the television set.

If only she would call, if only. He could hear her voice, like a siren song, whispered in his ear so that only he could hear it. She would whisper to him, call him by name, her sweet voice winding down into his brain. The memory of it made him go hard, his prick twitching to life. He touched himself again, rubbing himself gently. It was her, that was all it took; the simple memory of her voice was enough to excite him.

He lay back in the darkness, eyes closed, breathing hoarsely. She was standing over Naomi, black leather strap held tightly in long white fingers with painted scarlet nails. Her lips were red against her pale skin, dark eyes made up to look darker. She was dressed in black, a tall slim figure, her body outlined in a slinky black dress. Naomi was at her feet, kissing and sucking at the spiked black stilettoes, her body in a posture of fervent worship.

'Darling . . . ' Mistress said, her voice like the softest breeze of the night. The sharp snap of the leather strap on bare flesh echoed through the room, accompanied by the breathless cries from Naomi. Cries of pain and pleasure, of refusal and desire.

Jonathan felt lost, spinning out of control,

overwhelmed by the conjunction of memory and reality. His hands were playing up and down his prick, moving in rhythm with the dream playing so vividly in his mind's eye.

'Now suck me . . . ' Mistress whispered, and he opened his mouth and sucked from her sex, tasting the sweet bouquet of her, taking her essence deep into his mouth. 'Jonathan, I love you . . . ' she cried, as if she were falling through space with him.

He cried out, his cry at one with hers, their pleasure carrying them over the edge. They were together, one and the same person, the pleasure, pure and ecstatic, binding them through space and time.

It didn't take long really. The snide remarks and barbed comments were doing the rounds after only a couple of days. Jonathan was withdrawn and not at all interested in the office gossip, their equivalent of losing all interest in life. The fact that he dropped out of the nightly drinking parties meant that he was fair game of course. It was a tight little fraternity, a band of young men and women devoted to their image of the work-hard, play-hard, do-it-all winner. And if you weren't part of the team you were a loser.

Increasingly Jonathan felt a loser. He kept dreaming, imagining that Mistress miraculously appeared before him, whispering into his ear, touching him with her elegant fingers. But it was only a dream, and he wasn't so far gone as to forget that. Work had turned from an exciting battleground to an annoying irrelevance, an irrelevance that he put up with only because of inertia. The dream of success, the thing that had kept him going for so long, was dead. Whether he succeeded at work or failed dismally was no longer of any real interest.

His new routine was established in a matter of days. The first train home from work, then to curl up with

23

a bottle and his brooding thoughts. It took a while before he realised what he was doing, but once he saw it he knew that there was nothing else to do. He lay in bed, cradling a drink, the flashing colours from the TV bathing his naked body, waiting anxiously for the telephone to ring.

It had happened once, it could happen again. Mistress could call.

He shifted uneasily, turned over, slowly opened his eyes. The border between sleep and wakefulness was still blurred, there were no hard and fast boundaries. Was it a dream? Something was nagging, something insistent in the back of his mind.

'Fuck.' He stretched out at once, grabbed the phone, knocking it to the floor with a crash, the empty glass falling with it, splintering into a thousand crystals. He scrabbled for the receiver in the darkness, his knuckles registering the sharp stab of broken glass.

'Master?'

'Yes?' he cried urgently. Vaguely he was aware of the blood pouring from his hand, the warm trickle slipping down his arm.

'Mistress wishes to speak with you,' the voice said, the same voice as before, nervous and feminine.

'Yes, good . . . ' His heart was thumping and his throat felt dry. It was the moment he had been waiting for, and now he felt unprepared for it. His hand was stinging painfully, little rivulets of blood cascading down his arm to the elbow. It didn't matter.

'Darling, I have to speak to you,' Mistress said, breathless withe excitement, her voice as warm and familiar as a lover's touch.

'No, I have to speak to you.' He sat up in bed, hands shaking.

'Who is this?' Mistress asked coldly.

'Please don't hang up,' Jonathan begged, raising his

24

voice with the sudden fear that he would lose her. 'My name's Jonathan de Molay, you called me several days ago.'

'Jonathan?'

'Yes, you called me by name. You called me to tell me you were punishing Naomi . . . '

'You're not Jonathan, what's going on?'

'Yes, I am. My name really is Jonathan de Molay, but I guess you were looking for someone else.'

'There's been an awful mistake, a terrible mistake . . .' Mistress sounded distant, and Jonathan guessed that the call had been passed into another room, hooked up to a microphone as before.

'I have to meet you,' Jonathan blurted out, unable to stop himself.

Mistress laughed. 'What a ridiculous idea,' she said disdainfully.

'Please, I have to see you. I just have to.'

'Why on earth would I possibly want to see you?'

'You don't understand, I have to see you. I just have to see you. Ever since I heard your voice I haven't been able to get you out of my head. Please . . . '

'Go on,' Mistress said, her voice giving nothing away.

'I keep hearing your voice, it's in my head. You sound so . . . so . . . And I keep imagining you . . . And . . . '

'I see.'

'Please, let me meet you, just once. That's all.'

'And your name really is Jonathan de Molay?'

'Yes, I swear it is.'

'How very interesting,' she said, though she didn't sound it. 'What do you do? Who are you?'

'I'm a business analyst for one of the banks in the City.'

'One of the old banks?'

'No, for one of the new American banks.' He felt

25

the disappointment at the other end, as if he had let himself down.

'This is boring,' Mistress said. 'So you imagine me, I am in your thoughts constantly. Describe me.'

'It's your voice,' Jonathan began. 'You sound perfect, beautiful, intelligent, classy. You sound like a dream.'

'A dream? I like that. But what if I were a fifty-year-old frump, overweight and bored, with all the breeding and finesse of an African rhinoceros?'

'But you aren't, are you?'

'No.' She laughed again, relaxed, in control. 'I'm wearing a black evening dress, tight black silk, a slit down one side. I am wearing a diamond-studded choker, long gold earrings. My hair is long and dark, but tonight I wore it high. I have nothing on under my dress, nothing at all. When I move I reveal glimpses of my smooth bare thighs. I make grown men dribble into their soup. I make their wives dribble too. Is that how you imagine me?'

'Yes, that's exactly how I picture you.' Her words danced around him, drawing the picture in his mind, making him excited again.

'I have very firm high breasts, the nipples are pressed against the sheer silk of my dress. I like to walk across a crowded room and watch the eyes follow me, eyeing my breasts or my long legs. Would you do that? Watch me with hungry eyes?'

'Yes, I'd watch you every inch of the way.'

'Is your cock hard? Do I excite you?'

'Yes. You made my prick go hard with the very first words you spoke. I'm hard now.'

'Good. I have Naomi at my feet, on her hands and knees, looking up at me. What would you do in her position?'

'I would . . . I . . .'

'Yes?' Mistress snapped impatiently.

'I would kiss your feet, and then kiss your ankles and calves and the inside of your thighs.'

'Are you touching yourself?'

'Yes,' Jonathan admitted, feeling embarrassed but unable to deny the truth. It was what she wanted though, he was sure of that.

'My dress opens quite a way. Naomi can look up at my sex, she can see me where I'm wet. What would you do then?'

'I would take you in my arms and smother your body with kisses.'

'No,' Mistress said adamantly. 'You do not take me in your arms. You are at my feet, on your hands and knees. I'm in control, you are at my mercy. I lift my foot and press my heel into your shoulder, I press down digging into you. What do you do?'

'I suffer it, I let you dig your heels into me. God, at least I can look at you, maybe even feel your leg against my face. I'd kiss your calves and ankles and thighs. I'd look at you and that would be enough.'

'I press my heel into your mouth, what do you do?' Mistress sounded taunting, a note of challenge in her voice.

'I take your heel into my mouth and suck it, I let my tongue play up and down it. Anything, I'd do anything to be near you.'

'I force you on to your back, you're lying flat on your back staring up at me. I stand astride you, looking down on you because you are beneath contempt. Insect. I step on you, press my heel flat on your cock. What now?'

'I accept it. I can look up at you. Your shoe is going up and down my prick, even if it hurts it's still you.'

'That's right, my heel is digging into your cock, and your cock is still hard. Up and down, rubbing up and down, my sharp heel pressing painfully into your flesh.

27

Up and down. It hurts, I want it to hurt. My heels are hard, and sharp, just so they can hurt.'

Jonathan moaned softly, his eyes were closed and he could see it all. Her long limbs up above him, her bare thighs white and perfectly shaped, her sex obscured by the tight dress. Her heels masturbating his prick, sending spasms of sharp pain through him, the pain turning into pleasure, only more intense than any pleasure he had ever experienced.

He tried to control it but he'd gone too far. He gripped the base of his prick and felt the thick cream forced out in delicious pleasurable spurts. He couldn't stifle his cries of pleasure and relief.

'Darling, is that what you want?' Mistress mocked him.

'Please let me see you . . .' Jonathan whispered, but Mistress replied by putting the phone down. The harsh whine of the dialling tone mocked him, in its way as cruel a rejoinder as any that Mistress could make.

2

There was a flutter of paper on the desk and Jonathan looked up at the door. He smiled and sat back in his seat, putting the document he'd been working on face down on the desk.

'Hello stranger,' Caroline said, smiling. She breezed into the office and sat in the seat on the other side of the desk, making herself conspicuously comfortable.

'Hi, and to what do I owe the honour of a visit?' Jonathan said, picking up the document just as Caroline reached out to take it. She looked lovely; she had the power-dressing routine down to a fine art. Short checked skirt, black high heels and stockings, smart red and black jacket, the thick slabs of strong colour sending out all the right signals. She was beautiful, smart and intelligent. And that was where she was different, and far too good for the reptiles she mixed with. Everyone else was either smart or intelligent, but she was definitely both.

'Oh, nothing much. Just being sociable that's all.' She reached out and grabbed the document from Jonathan's hands, smiling mischievously.

'Is that all?' he asked suspiciously. He leaned back in his seat and looked at her warily. There had been a time when he and Caroline had been inseparable, but that time had gone, and now he rarely even thought of it. When they had started out together they were a team, part of the same crowd of bright young things and conquering heroes on the floor of the London financial markets. They had celebrated the start of their relationship with champagne and oysters, flamboyantly and extravagantly announcing their union to all their friends and colleagues.

Then they had ostentatiously flown to Paris for a long weekend, and on the night following their return they had gone out with friends to get gloriously drunk. The night had finished with them giving the other marks out of ten, to a drunken chorus of cheers and jeers and adolescent innuendo. She had given him a nine. He had given her eight. He would have given her ten but it wasn't the done thing, giving a ten meant you were in love. And that was a social disease that smacked of other times and other generations. So he gave her eight marks to keep her on edge, introducing an element of uncertainty in order to hide his true feelings. And even though it had long passed, he often regretted not giving her a nine as well. But that would have been too easy and too honest.

Caroline waited for the suspicion to melt from his eyes. 'Of course it's true,' she said. 'Why else would I come down? Certainly not to look at this.' She gave him back the paperwork with a playful and exaggerated look of distaste on her face.

'I thought only Soapy Patterson had the honour of being graced with social calls.'

'Forget Soapy,' Caroline said, just a little too vehemently.

'I see,' Jonathan said, and he couldn't help smiling. So that had finished too. He was glad, she was too good for a second-rater like Soapy. The problem was that she was far too good for him too.

'God, you're out of touch,' Caroline said, leaning

back in her seat, crossing her legs elegantly. Jonathan smiled, he knew what that meant — anyone not part of the scene was suffering a lingering social death. 'Is everything okay, Jon?' she asked on cue. 'Is there anything wrong?'

'No, I'm fine really,' Jonathan said, thankful that she was concerned rather than just prying. If he could talk to anyone it had to be Caroline, but there was no way that he could even begin to talk to her about Mistress. It was too strange and bizarre, beyond her understanding just as it was beyond his.

'There's an awful lot of money riding on your back, and a fair sum of it is mine.'

'What's the betting?'

'It's split down the middle at the moment, half says you've found love and the other half says you've found God.'

Jonathan laughed. 'And where have you got your cash?'

'Well, I suggested that you had found a social conscience or were suffering some form of existential angst,' she smiled. 'But Gardner ruled that as finding God, and though the odds are good it looked like a ringer to me. So I'm gambling on love. Not good odds, but the only other choices are mid-life crisis or impotence.'

'I see.' Jonathan paused for a moment, as if weighing up the choices himself. 'And have you been delegated the job of finding out which it is?'

'Not really,' she said, and she sounded more serious, leaning across the desk and looking him directly in the eyes. 'I'm just a bit worried about an old friend. But does that mean I'm going to enjoy an unexpected windfall?'

Jonathan shook his head. 'None of the above,' he said finally. But he could see that in a way she was right. Mistress wasn't love, but it was closer to love than religion.

She sat back in her seat, a relaxed smile on her face again. 'Gardner also suggested that I get down on my hands and knees and do a penis health check,' she said. 'Just to rule out the impotence. Though I think it's something he'd rather enjoy doing himself.'

'Why do you still hang around with them, Caroline? Why don't you just tell them to drop dead?'

'You mean sit in my poky little office all by myself? And then finish an exhausting day's work and go home to an empty flat? No thanks. If I wanted that I'd go the whole hog and really get religion.'

'Is that what you think's wrong with me?'

Caroline stood up. She looked pained, her eyes, always dark and intense, seemed to glow with an added sadness. 'All I'm saying, Jon, is that if you need a shoulder to cry on, then I'm here. You need your friends, don't forget that.'

'Do you ever think of Paris?' Jonathan said suddenly. At that instant he really wanted to take hold of her and put his mouth to hers and just suck the breath out of her. For a single moment she had looked the way he felt, and he was so glad for it, grateful that she still felt for him. Grateful, and excited, something inside him came to life again, a twisting mixture of love and desire that made him feel glad to be alive. God, it was enough that it reminded him that he really *was* alive.

'Yes, I think of it a lot.' She looked at him for a moment, their eyes locked together. Something happened, something indefinable, they paused, not breathing, not moving, just looking at each other as if for the first time. Then Caroline breathed, and the feeling dissolved. 'I used to think of it a lot when I was with Soapy.'

Jonathan detected the change of mood, he realised that he had been holding his breath too. 'Did you think of it when you and Soapy used to . . . ' he said, finally dispelling the unspoken tension.

'Especially when Soapy used to do his duty,' Caroline said, her face twisting into a smile.

'That bad was it? I never understood what you saw in him.'

'That's funny, he said the same thing about you. My offer stands, if you want to talk, or you want help, you know where to find me.'

Jonathan watched Caroline go, knowing that he'd missed his chance again. She was gone, and only the faint trace of her scent remained to tantalise. He'd been an idiot, she was waiting for him, it couldn't be more obvious. But he'd sat in his seat, relying on old memories instead of building new ones. Stupid, stupid.

He stood up and went over to the window, to look down at the bustle of the city traffic, waves of people passing through the narrow cobbled streets. It was a sight that had once inspired him with ambition and excitement. Now he was thankful that it provided a distraction.

'It can't work with Caroline,' he told himself, only half believing it. It was too complicated, they were too much alike. It was over, it could never start again.

But there had been that moment when he felt a stab of fear and excitement in the pit of the belly, like the world turned upside down, when he felt like an all-conquering hero again. That's what Mistress had made him feel like. And it was only her memory that had made him hold back.

On the way out from work Jonathan had seen Caroline with two or three other colleagues, crossing through the heavy traffic and then disappearing down the stairs into one of the cellar bars that became the *de facto* office when business hours were over. For a moment he debated joining them, knowing that in minutes he would be bantering and laughing with them, fighting his battles after hours, with cutting words and sharp sarcasm as his weapons. Caroline would join him, and together they would be a team again, taking on the whole world. He had paused, caught in a moment of indecision, but then a sharp gust of wind cut across his face and he was moving again.

The journey home was filled with the memories of Paris. They had spent the entire weekend making love, repeatedly coupling wildly, passionately, then again slowly, languidly. He could see her so vividly, lying back in the bath, her skin wet and glistening, the water lapping at her lovely breasts, her dark nipples bobbing just below the surface. He had joined her and together they made love in the bath, the water splashing with the rhythm of their bodies. She felt so good, soft and warm in his arms, her body slipping and sliding under him, his prick entering deep into her sex.

And she had surprised him too, with her daring and imagination. They had made love in the bath, and then she had called one of the hotel chamber maids to clean up. And while the maid did her work, Caroline had taken his prick in her mouth and sucked it to life again. She had sucked him deliciously, hedonistically, using her lips and tongue, gently biting his hard prick so that he moaned and cried with pleasure. She liked to hold the tip of it with her lips then swoop down to the base, taking it deep into her mouth, running her tongue under it.

The maid had remained perfectly composed, not lifting an eyebrow or saying a word, though she certainly didn't pretend not to look. And when it was over, when he had come in a breathless climax,

Caroline had asked the maid for a tissue to wipe the thick smear of semen that trickled from her pretty lips.

The memory was torture. On the crowded train his hard prick had pressed painfully into his clothes, and he had been unable to make himself comfortable. But it was also torture because he knew that he could have it all again. If he had followed Caroline to the bar, or had taken her again in the office, then it would all come back. The gloriously sexy lovemaking, the feeling of companionship, the unspoken feeling of having someone else to share with.

But it wasn't to be. It had failed once, and it could fail again. Because the feeling wore off, the lovemaking wasn't enough to last forever. Everyday life intruded, like conflicts at work, the demands of friends, and the fact they were two different and strong-willed individuals.

That was where Mistress was going to be different. He was sure of it.

Once home the memories of Caroline and Paris faded. Already home was associated with Mistress and not Caroline, the flat had been bought after he had moved out of Caroline's flat by the river. She hadn't even visited him since. When he had hosted a house-warming party their feelings for each other were still raw and confused and she had petulantly refused to attend.

He showered quickly, feeling cleansed of the day's frustrations and worries. And then he had something to eat, a quick microwave meal, and then to the bedroom. A new phone had been installed, with hands-free calling and a good speaker. He had also added a cassette recorder to it, ready to capture forever Mistress's words when she called. Everything was as he wanted it to be, in perfect readiness for her call.

And then he waited.

Time passed quickly. It didn't hang heavy, the hours did not drag on endlessly. There was no feeling of boredom or anger. The sense of anticipation was all, the sure and certain feeling that Mistress was going to call.

He had faith, he felt it inside him, like a living, breathing entity. There could be no doubt, none at all. He knew that if he doubted even for one second, then the pure futility of it all would suddenly overwhelm him. No, he waited with infinite patience for the call that had to come.

Most nights he would drift off to sleep in the early hours, not even noticing the time, and without disappointment either. Some nights the memories would be too vivid, the images would crowd into his mind. And then he could do nothing but replay the events as they had happened. The voice would be so strong and clear, she spoke to him like a hypnotist leading him into trance. And then he would masturbate, just as he had done when she had called.

He would be at her feet, kissing her shoes, or pressing his mouth into her sex. It felt real, more real than anything else in his life. The sharp tip of her heel would spark electric currents through his body, so that his prick ached for release. 'Darling . . . ' she would say and he would come, shooting thick white cream on to himself. It was the holy water of his worship for Her, for Mistress; evidence of her divine power.

'Yes?' Jonathan said anxiously. The reflex had been automatic. A single tone from the telephone had been enough. He was up close to the speaker, almost standing over it, his heart beating wildly.

'Master?'

He recognised the voice at once. 'Naomi?'

'Yes, Master. I have instructions for you.'

'From your Mistress?'

36

'Yes, Master.'

'Her name, what is her name?' Jonathan asked desperately.

'You are to follow these instructions precisely, Master. That is all I can tell you,' Naomi said, sounding nervous.

'I'm listening,' Jonathan flicked a switch and the cassette began recording. The most he had hoped for was for Mistress to call him, but now this sounded better. Naomi gave an address in London, in the West End somewhere. 'Yes, I've got that,' he said noting it down.

'Be there in precisely one hour. Formal dress. If you are not there at the precise time, then Mistress instructs me to tell you that all further contact will cease.'

'Tell her that I'll be there, I promise I will. Thank you, Naomi.'

The phone went dead.

Formal dress? Jonathan was flustered, what the hell did that mean? How formal was formal? A suit and a tie wasn't good enough. He dressed quickly, silk shirt and the stylish dinner jacket he'd last worn to the firm's annual ball. Caroline had been on his arm. He'd felt like a king. He had the same feeling now, but magnified and intensified a hundredfold.

He looked up the address on a map, it was an avenue at the southern entrance to Regent's Park. It was an hour's drive, but by the time he was dressed he had less than that.

The drive was hectic. He swore blindly at the traffic that seemed especially malicious. Every other driver was intent on getting in his way, blocking him in or cutting him up. The traffic lights were conspiring against him too, changing to red every time they saw him. But he ignored them, accelerating across the junctions with manic abandon. He had to get there,

37

even if he had a couple of near-misses that were too close for comfort.

It started to rain, a light drizzle that got heavier with the traffic. The city lights turned fluid, sliding down the windscreen in sparkling rivers of radiance. Jonathan's hands were sweaty, gripping the steering wheel with white knuckled tightness. He felt like he was floating on air, yet mired in mud. He wanted to go faster, to cut through the traffic with a lightening stroke that would land him at the right place and at the right time.

At last he was there. A long curving avenue round a small square. Tall Regency houses, architecture that embodied money, class and power, sat on every side of the square.

Jonathan parked the car in a street nearby that was noticeably more downmarket than the avenue, and hurried out into the rain. The house loomed over him as he stood at the heavy black door. Automatically he checked his tie, brushed a hand through his hair, then rang the door-bell. No first date had ever been so nerve-racking; in fact no date had ever been so nerve-racking.

The door was opened by a young woman. She looked to be in her early twenties, quite pretty with intelligent eyes. 'Please follow me, Master,' she said, opening the door fully for Jonathan.

He entered, peering round nervously. The hall was rather grand, a flight of stairs curved up to the left, several doors to rooms all around. A number of portraits hung on the walls, lit by soft orange lights, their distinguished features looking down on him with studied arrogance. They were guardians, demanding a respectful bearing that would not ripple the surface of the stately silence or disturb the icy atmosphere.

The young woman shut the front door and led the

way across the hall towards the stairs. Jonathan followed close by, intimidated by the quiet opulence of the surroundings. 'You're not Naomi, are you?' he asked quietly.

'No, Master.'

She was dressed in a long dark skirt and white blouse, with flat brown shoes. Jonathan wasn't sure whether the clothes were a domestic uniform or not and didn't know how to ask. 'Is the Mistress here?' he asked instead.

'Yes, Master, she is here.'

'Can you tell me her name? I need to know so that I don't look a complete idiot when I meet her,' Jonathan explained anxiously.

'I'm sorry, Master,' the young woman stopped at the top of the stairs and faced him, 'but I have my instructions.'

She turned and led the way into one of the rooms on the first landing. Jonathan followed obediently, swallowing hard to quench his sudden dry thirst.

'What's this?' Jonathan said, unable to conceal his disappointment. He had expected to be led into a grand dining room, to finally meet Mistress, or at least some of her guests. Instead he had been shown into a small drab bedroom.

'Please wait here.' The young woman backed out of the room and closed the door behind her.

Jonathan walked to the window. It was still raining hard, in the square below the trees were swaying with the wind. The rain, driven by the wind, tapped hard against the window.

If it had been a hotel room Jonathan would have demanded a change, or he would have booked himself into something better. There was a single bed, a small bedside cabinet. A wardrobe opposite the bed, next to the window. An old armchair on the other side of the window, a footrest in front of it. A dull room, and a disappointment after all the psyching up.

He waited by the window, checking his watch several times. It wasn't what he had imagined. He had imagined something lavish, perhaps an impromptu dinner party where one of the guests had dropped out at the last minute. Or that Mistress had been as intrigued by him as he was with her and had invited him for an intimate dinner. She had called him by name, he was convinced that she had to know something of him.

The door was locked when he tried it, which was disconcerting. He hadn't heard it lock, but then the rain on the windows and the sound of the wind were loud enough. There was nothing to do but wait.

The old armchair was comfortable. He put his feet up and waited, hands together, fingers under the chin. The feeling of excitement was there again, like a fire that flared with a sudden draft. It couldn't be far away, the moment he had waited for. If she called him darling to his face he was going to climax, he was sure. But it didn't matter, she would know then just how much he wanted her.

The door opened and the young woman walked in again. Jonathan didn't move.

'I have someone to see you, Master,' she said, opening the door fully and standing to one side.

Jonathan jumped up. 'Mistress?'

The woman who entered was masked. She had long blonde hair that was pulled back tightly and tied in a thick tail, as if she had been horse-riding. She had pale skin and a long thin face, and her lips were painted glossy red. The black mask obscured the top part of her face, from the bridge of her nose to her hairline. Her dress was similarly remarkable. She wore a very tight shiny leotard that seemed moulded to every

40

contour of her body, from the firm breasts to the slight roundness of her stomach and the bulge of her sex. Her legs were bare, smooth long thighs down to knee-length boots, made from the same glossy black material as the leotard. The boots were tipped with sharp heels that snapped like fire crackers on the polished floor. Her hands were similarly gloved, the glossy black material stretching tightly from her fingers to her elbows.

'Undress,' the young woman said, allowing herself the merest hint of a smile. It didn't sound like an order, but neither was it a request.

Jonathan waited for a second then began to undress slowly. He had never imagined anything so wild, anything so obvious. It was coming true, she was going to dig her heels into him, to walk on him, because he was dirt. The thought made him strangely excited, his prick was hard, and he could feel himself starting to lose control, his prick throbbing dangerously.

'I'm ready, Mistress,' he said, standing naked in front of the armchair. He couldn't take his eyes off Mistress, she looked divine. The nipples of her breasts were like buttons against the glossy material, rubber or plastic or whatever it was.

'On your knees,' the young woman directed, motioning with her hand for him to kneel. The smile on her face broadened, and she stepped closer to him.

He knelt down on all fours, just as he had in his fantasy. The floor was cold, and it was uncomfortable, his knees hurt on the hard polished wood. But when he looked up everything was as he had imagined. Mistress towered over him, her face impassive, her lips pursed tightly. But the eyes behind the mask, piercing blue eyes, were sparkling crystals shining down on him. 'I'm ready, Mistress,' he whispered.

The young woman stepped closer and pushed the

footrest in front of him. 'Lean on this,' she ordered. 'Put your arms behind your back.'

'Is that what you want, Mistress?'

The masked woman made no response. She just stood still, legs parted, glaring down at his naked body. Jonathan obeyed, crawling forward and resting his chin on the footrest, placing his hands together behind his back. He twisted his head round and looked up plaintively at the impassive woman.

The young woman stepped forward quickly and snapped something on to his wrists.

'What the . . . ' Jonathan was about to swear when Mistress moved. He fell silent, aware that his hands were cuffed together with cold steel bonds. That wasn't part of the fantasy, but it had to be what Mistress demanded.

The young woman moved away, and as she did so she passed her hand up Jonathan's thigh and over his balls. She cupped the heavy ball sac for an instant and then firmly squeezed his prick. He responded with a sigh, understanding that he was now at their mercy. Bound as he was, there was nothing he could do to resist. It was an odd feeling for him; he'd never felt so helpless before, but paradoxically it also felt reassuring.

The young woman let his prick go and then withdrew from the room, giving Jonathan a last smile before closing the door.

'From the moment that I first heard your voice I've been dying to meet you,' Jonathan said nervously. Now that he was alone he realised that in his fantasy he had never really spoken, and neither had Mistress. Sure, in his fantasy she called him 'darling' or made him kiss her shoes, but they were unreal words, fantasy-speak.

Mistress moved across the room like a goddess. Her heels cracked like thunderbolts in his ears, her body was lithe and she moved like silk blown by the breeze. Her breasts jigged tightly, trapped under the glossy second skin that gave her an unreal perfect sheen. She stopped in front of him so that when he looked up he was looking almost directly at the bulge of her sex.

'I don't know what it is . . . ' he said, even more nervously. His throat was parched, and his body shaking. He moved, stopped. His hands were held fast, the chains were cold against his skin. The feeling of vulnerability grew stronger.

Mistress walked round him, looking down at his naked body, checking him over. He tried to follow her, twisting one way and then next. She stopped behind him, where he couldn't quite see her. The light was behind her and her shadow fell over him.

He sighed when she touched him. Her gloved fingers felt smooth and cold against his skin, he shivered with pleasure. She traced a finger from his knee up the inside of his thigh, she cupped his balls in her fingers, squeezing softly so that he held his breath. She let go and turned her attention to his prick, touching it and squeezing just as the other woman had. He tried to move round, to see her but she put a hand out and stopped him.

'It's your voice, it's the most perfect voice I've ever heard,' he continued. He closed his eyes and let a spasm of pleasure pulse through him. She had rubbed a finger from the tip of his prick right down and across the crease between his buttocks. She was exploring him, touching him everywhere with the same delicate touch. It felt ecstatic, heaven on earth. For the first time he realised that someone was really looking at him rather than looking through him. The aphrodisiac effect was strong. His prick flexed, he could feel that the glans was smeared with sticky fluid.

Without warning Mistress pressed a gloved finger

43

against his anus, and let it rest there. Jonathan held his breath, trying to calm himself, afraid that she would press her finger into him. He waited, his eyes closed tightly, pleading with himself to relax. Mistress seemed to be toying with him; she let her finger rest for a moment then stood up.

'I've been waiting for your call for days now,' Jonathan said, thankful that he could see her again. She walked past him and he could see her back. The leotard was pulled up tightly into her rear cleft, her backside fully displayed by the high cut of the costume. He longed to kiss her, to press his lips against her firm flesh, to taste her in his mouth.

She stepped across the room to the bedside cabinet, and looked back at him without smiling. He smiled to her nervously. Why didn't she speak? Did he displease her in some way? He wanted to please her, it immediately made him feel anxious. She had explored his body, examined him with surgical detachment. Had he failed her?

She opened the drawer and then straightened up. In her hand she held some kind of whip. Its black handle matched the black glove, the longer lash hung stiffly. His eyes met hers and for a moment he thought she smiled, but then it was gone and he couldn't tell whether it had been real or part of a fantasy.

'Let me kiss your heels, let me show you how much I worship you,' he said, and his voice was thin. He didn't want to be beaten. He had ached to kiss her sex, to kiss her heels, to humble himself before her, but not for anything more.

She marched back towards him, and this time he was sure that the menace he saw in her half-obscured eyes was not imagined.

'Please,' he whispered, looking up at her with fear in his eyes. 'Please don't do this to me.'

44

She stood over him and pressed her knee into his back, holding him in place. She had done it to Naomi and now it was his turn.

He screamed. The first blow hissed through the air and snapped firmly into his left buttock. It was a deep biting pain, a sharp stab of burning sensation. A second blow, he looked up and saw her bringing her arm down with a flash of the whip. It stung with the same intensity on the other buttock. His prick ached, throbbed. He still felt hard, almost breathless with sexual excitement. It hurt, but it felt so good. Her knee held him down, adding to the feeling of containment.

Mistress shifted slightly and began again, this time the blows cutting across his backside. She beat several rapid blows in succession, burning deep red scars across his backside. The sensation was hot, pulsing through him, surges of excitement. He felt dizzy, catching his breath and exhaling with each impact. His senses were aflame, and confused by the onslaught. It felt hypnotic, a derangement of the senses that caused a sweeping ecstatic adrenalin rush.

Mistress moved around to the front. She lifted her foot and placed it by his head. He turned and began to kiss her heel, kissing it with more passion than he had ever kissed anything. He smothered her boot with loving kisses, pressing his lips against the cold leather, lapping at it with his tongue. He felt delirious, out of control.

She reached down and grabbed him by the hair and forced his face flat on the footrest and then pressed the heel into his mouth. He opened his mouth, let her press her boot into him. He licked at the steel tip, closed his lips over the smooth leather. He could hardly breathe, his body was alive with sweat and pain and pleasure. He wanted to find release, to orgasm, the pressure building in the pit of his belly was becoming unbearably ecstatic.

She snapped the whip again, flaying the stroke against the length of his back. He cried out, a strangled scream that was stifled by her heel in his mouth. He gasped, felt himself falling through space, burning out of control. He was out of himself, outside the body squirming under Mistress. Then thick squirts of semen pumped out of his prick and on to the floor.

He seemed to black out for a moment and then he was flat on the floor looking up silently at Mistress. When he moved he realised that he was lying flat in his own semen, smeared over his body. His backside stung, a burning painful reminder of what miracles Mistress had performed. His mouth was warm and he tasted blood from his lip. She stood over him still, cold and impassive, looking down through her mask with nothing but idle curiosity.

'Speak to me,' Jonathan pleaded quietly. He tried to get up but slipped again, writhing in the mess on the floor. Something clicked at that instant, something terrible.

Mistress turned away, smiling for the first time.

'Who are you? You're not Mistress, are you?' Jonathan screamed after her, he tried to get up again. He managed to sit up on his knees, his eyes were wide with a look of slowly dawning horror. Mistress turned and walked away from him, her beautiful body so graceful in its black shiny skin. She turned back for one last disdainful look then walked blithely out of the room and left him there.

It wasn't Mistress. He had been humiliated and degraded by a perfect stranger.

3

Jonathan sat naked on the footrest, arms still bound tightly behind him, shivering and growing colder as the semen caked on his skin dried slowly. His body ached, the lattice of red welts that crossed his lower back throbbing painfully as he sat.

The room closed around him, like a seedy motel room cast in a dim orange light to hide the cracks in the walls and the filth on the floor. His head was lowered, and he stared into space down at his feet. It was not how he had imagined things, not at all like the vivid fantasy that he carried in his head. This was real, there was no blurring at the edges as the focus of the fantasy moved. The floor was cold, his arms were stretched uncomfortably around his body and his backside was scored with painful reminders of the beating that had been inflicted.

It wasn't Mistress. The thought circled in his mind, round and round, looping endlessly. He felt an empty disappointment, right down in the pit of his stomach, like a hollow void inside him. His excitement was gone, the thrill of submitting to Mistress had been illusory. It wasn't Mistress.

But the excitement had been real while it lasted, the pleasure he had felt had been powerful, and so very different from anything he had ever experienced before. It was confusing. The fact that it hadn't been Mistress, and he was more certain of it with every moment that passed, seemed on the one hand to invalidate the experience, and on the other to add to it.

He looked up when the door opened, keeping his shoulders hunched over and staring up at the woman who entered. 'Naomi?' he croaked, finding that his throat was as dry as dust.

'Yes, master,' she replied. She closed the door and walked slowly across the room, carrying a silver tray. Her face was calm, almost serene. She had greengrey eyes that regarded him soberly and wide lips slightly parted but without smiling.

'That wasn't Mistress, was it?' he said hopelessly.

Naomi shook her head, her long brown hair cascading over her shoulders. She wore a smart navy jacket over a white blouse and matching navy skirt. It looked a little like a uniform but he couldn't be sure; there was the same ambiguity about her dress as with that of the woman who had led him to the room. The way she walked, tall and elegant, made it look even more as if she was in uniform, but then he saw a thousand women a day dressed in the same way without concluding that they were all in service.

She knelt down in front of him and placed the tray at his feet. Jonathan looked at her. She was so close he could breathe her scent, and feel the warmth of her body next to his. Her face was lightly made up, a touch of colour on her cheeks, her eyes delicately flicked with mascara.

He looked at himself and felt sick. He was still shivering, the thick film of semen that coated his icy skin was drying up. 'I don't know what to say to you,' he said finally. 'I've never been in this sort of situation before.'

'You don't have to explain to me, Master.' Naomi

48

picked up a damp face towel from the tray and began to gently wipe Jonathan's body.

'Why do you call me Master?' He closed his eyes to enjoy the soothing warmth of the towel on his skin. She was wiping the filth away, holding the towel with both hands and rubbing it softly up and down his body.

'Etiquette. You are a guest of my Mistress,' she said.

'How did you ever get involved in all of this?' he asked, wondering how he had got himself into such an awful situation. Already he felt that he knew Naomi, that she wasn't a stranger like the other women. But that only made him feel worse.

Naomi paused, holding the damp towel in the centre of his chest. He opened his eyes and looked at her for a second, meeting her calm gaze with a half smile. She smiled back, her lips parting over bright even teeth. 'It's a long story,' she said, wiping him again. 'I used to be an air hostess for one of the big airlines. At first it was an exciting kind of life. But then it wore off. You get tired of all the travelling, physically tired. And then bored by the dull routine of it.'

'But aren't air hostesses fantasy figures that men drawl over?'

'Perhaps, Master. But then that changed suddenly. I was asked to steward a private flight to Paris. I accepted and it was the wildest thing I'd ever seen. I don't know what it is. Maybe people think that because they've defied the laws of gravity then they can defy every other law. There's something about planes and sex that attracts people. I thought I'd seen everything, every possible combination of bodies in midflight, but this was so different. I didn't even have the vocabulary to describe it, it was so utterly extraordinary.'

'Maybe it's because people feel so close to heaven that they want to fly in other ways too,' Jonathan suggested.

'I don't know what it is. But that was where I met Master de Molay and Mistress. And I've been with them ever since.'

Jonathan sat back and let Naomi wipe him between the thighs, her hand brushing softly against his prick. He looked at her, opening his thighs wider, but she seemed to be concentrating purely on cleaning him. 'What is it about her? And him?'

'I think you know that already, Master. Please stand.'

'I can't.'

She stood and pulled him to his feet. He fell, pressing his naked body against her. She seemed to linger for a moment, letting him rest his body against hers, then she steadied him and dropped to her knees before him again. The towel was cold and she put it down and took a second one, pressing the soothing warmth under his balls.

He parted his thighs, aware that her touch, delicate and calming, was starting to excite him. He was looking down at her, sitting on her knees in front of him. Her hair had fallen to one side and he could see the soft skin of the nape of her neck. Her face was close to his abdomen, her soft breath was caught in the tight curls of the hair between his thighs.

'Please turn, Master,' she said quietly, glancing up at him. Their eyes met and he smiled nervously. His prick was hard, standing stiffly inches from her mouth. Was he really her master? Her lips were close, they looked so soft and sensitive, capable of giving the most exquisite feelings of pleasure with the simplest of caresses.

He turned round slowly, making sure that her eyes were on his prick as he moved. 'Are you with Mistress all the time?'

'Yes, Master.' She began to wipe his back with the towel.

'What's she like?'

'How do you want her to be?'

Jonathan looked down at Naomi, on her knees behind him. She smiled and continued to wipe his back, occasionally running her fingers down his back. 'Do you love her?'

'I'm not sure. I worship her, I'd do anything that she asked without even thinking about it. But that's not love. At least that's now how I felt when I've been in love in the past. This is stronger than love.'

'What's that?' Jonathan looked down at Naomi. She was rubbing something into his skin, something cold but which seemed to take the edge from the stinging pain he still felt.

'It's OK, it's just some balm for your wounds. Your body will be marked for days. Every time you look at yourself you'll know that you've suffered for Mistress. It'll remind you of her.'

'Is that how you feel?'

Naomi smiled. She spread some more of the cream into her fingers and then applied it to his lower back and buttocks. Her fingers pressed firmly and smoothly on his skin, sliding slowly up and down, tracing invisible patterns on his backside. The pain was receding quickly, turning into a creeping warmth spreading over his body. Her fingers were exciting him again, moving over him tantalisingly. She began to press her fingers down between his buttocks, gently exploring him under his balls, rubbing between his arsecrack where the whip had left its mark.

'That feels good,' he sighed, parting his legs and bending forward a little.

Naomi stopped suddenly and stood up.

'Please . . . ' Jonathan looked at her imploringly. She couldn't stop, it felt too good, he wanted her to carry on. His prick was rock hard and aching for her

51

touch. He wanted her to kiss him on his prick, to take it into her mouth and smother it with loving caresses.

'I have to prepare you for Mistress,' Naomi explained. She reached down and flicked some kind of catch that released the cuffs on his wrists.

He rubbed his arms and wrists, glad that he was free again. His shoulders ached, it felt as if he had been locked tight. Naomi stood by, watching him. 'Will I really meet Mistress this time?'

'I have to prepare you,' she repeated softly.

He looked at her and realised that she was excited too. Her breath was running a little faster and he could see her skin flushed pink. Her eyes were on him, sparkling with an intensity that he hadn't detected earlier. He took her hand and put it on his prick, holding it there for a second. She moved her hand up and down, stroking him softly, her fingers running down into the dense bush of hair and up again over the bulbous glans. 'Am I really your master?' he whispered into her ear, taking hold of her shoulders.

Naomi squeezed his prick, closing her hand tightly over the hardness. 'If my Mistress commanded I would do anything you desired, gladly. But I have my instructions, Master. You must be ready for her.'

Reluctantly Jonathan let go of her. He was torn now, between desire for Mistress and desire for Naomi. There was a difference. Naomi was real. But the lure of Mistress was stronger, looming powerfully in his imagination, her intangible presence colouring everything.

Naomi bent down and picked something up off the tray on the floor. As she stood up she brushed her face against his prick, kissing the tip of it very softly, dabbing her tongue into the opening and drawing out a silver bead of fluid that stretched out like a long fine chain.

'You want to, don't you?' he said hotly.

Naomi nodded, her face reddening slightly. She held a collar in her hand and reached up to put it around him. He bent lower and she carefully placed it around his neck. Already it felt so natural, as if he had done it a million times before. She buckled it quickly and then he straightened up.

'Is this how she wants me?' he said, rubbing the stiff leather collar with his fingers.

'Yes, Master.' She bent down again and this time picked up a long chain, with tight oval links and a clip at one end and a leather handle at the other.

'Mistress wants me on a chain, like a dog?' he said, half smiling to himself. The idea was exciting in an oddly disturbing way.

'Mistress ordered that you be prepared in this way. To be brought to her on your hands and knees like a dog.'

'I ought to be disgusted by this. I'm a grown man, this is so . . . so . . . '

'Degrading?'

'Yes. God, what am I doing her? What the fuck am I doing here?'

'You know, Master. You know the answer to that.' Naomi ran her hand down his back, lingering momentarily over the lash marks, then around to caress his erect prick again. The glans was liberally covered with sticky fluid, which she rubbed on to her fingers. She looked him in the eyes and then brought her fingers, visibly wet with his prick fluid, to her mouth.

'Jesus . . . ' Jonàthan felt a surge of excitement pulse through him. Watching Naomi suck his seminal fluid into her mouth like that, her eyes fixed on him, a look between lust and absolute innocence on her face, made him feel weak with excitement.

'It's time now,' Naomi whispered and tugged at the lead around his neck. 'Follow me, master.'

Jonathan followed a few steps behind, suddenly very nervous. He stayed close to Naomi, the chain swinging gently between them, her shadow falling across him as they climbed the next flight of stairs. The portraits on the wall, haughty and disdainful, seemed to be looking directly at them. The house was silent apart from the click clack of Naomi's heels on the stone steps and the soft padding of Jonathan's bare feet.

They stopped at the next landing and Naomi lead him across to a white door. She turned and looked at him for a second, brushing her hand through his hair and adjusting the collar slightly.

'God I'm nervous,' Jonathan admitted quietly.

'Yes, I always feel the same way when Mistress calls. It's like walking on pins. It's a delicious feeling, isn't it?'

'No.'

Naomi smiled and kissed him on the lips, pausing to let her breath mingle with his before pulling away. 'On your knees please, Master.'

'Now?'

'Yes. Mistress is waiting for you.'

Jonathan fell reluctantly to his knees. His heart was pounding and he could hear the blood rushing in his ears. For the thousandth time he asked himself what he was doing. It all seemed so strange and unnecessary. It was different with Caroline, so very different. And suddenly he wanted Caroline, he wanted to be with her, away from the cold house and the icy atmosphere and all that it represented.

Naomi opened the heavy white door and strode into the room, tugging the chain sharply to force him after her. He crawled in, looking up expectantly. It was a dining room, very long, with crystal chandeliers hanging from the high ceilings. It was still raining outside, the rain was drumming in waves on the windows on one side of the room. For an instant the rivulets coursing down the glass reminded him of the beads of water sliding down Caroline's glistening skin. Where was Caroline? What was she doing?

Naomi tugged again and Caroline was gone. Jonathan crawled after Naomi, crossing the room in parallel to the long oak dining table that dominated the space. He struggled to keep up, shuffling along uncomfortably, trying also to peer round Naomi to catch a glimpse of Mistress, if she was there. The room appeared to be empty; glancing up at the table he could see that none of the places had been set, the polished surface reflecting back the crystalline light from the chandeliers.

Halfway along he caught sight of Mistress, or he assumed it was Mistress. It was hard to see from his position so close to the ground, but he could see that a woman was seated at the head of the table. Her long pale legs were partially obscured by the table and chairs, but whoever she was she wore no glossy black boots like the woman that had beaten him.

Naomi stopped and pulled the chain up sharply, suddenly choking him and pulling him to one side. His eyes filled with tears and he cried out from the pain. Instinctively he tried to loosen the tight collar, to fight the claustrophobic feeling rising from his chest.

'Stop that!' Mistress snapped, and Jonathan looked up at her.

Mistress was beautiful. She had medium-length brown hair tinged slightly with red. It was immaculately coiffured with layers of wavy hair falling on to her bare shoulders, catching the light and holding it like an aura around her. Her face was pale, long, with a straight nose and high cheek bones. But it was the eyes that made her face so stunningly beautiful, dark eyes that looked down on Jonathan with an intense expression that hovered between outright contempt and sardonic amusement.

Jonathan looked at her, watching the way the expression in her eyes seemed to be changing, evolving second by second, then turned away. She knew him, she could see right through him, right down into his soul.

'And you really are Jonathan de Molay?' she asked, her voice as clear and as pure as spring.

'Yes, Mistress,' Jonathan said, his voice sounding pitifully weak beside hers. He glanced up at her again, caught her half-smile then turned away again.

'How very odd,' she said, speaking perhaps to herself or perhaps to Naomi. 'It must be some bastard line that managed to keep the name. There's certainly none of the breeding there.' She put a finger under Jonathan's chin and lifted his head, looking at him critically, turning his face from side to side. 'No family resemblance, none at all. Not even the de Molay nose. How very disappointing.'

'I'm sorry, but my name is de Molay,' he said quietly, meeting her eyes for an instance. As she was leaning over towards him he could see the generous swell of her breasts cupped tightly by the silky material of the dark cocktail dress that she wore.

'Quiet! You'll speak when spoken to, understand?'

'Yes, Mistress,' Jonathan said falteringly. Part of him wanted to get up off the floor and put a stop to it all. But another part of him responded to her harsh words, finding her harsh tone, and his demeaning position on the floor, secretly exciting. It was that part of him, the hidden part that he was only half aware of, that she could see, he was certain of it.

'Has he been insolent? Or disobedient?'

'No, Mistress,' Naomi replied quietly.

'Why did you come here?'

'To see you, Mistress,' Jonathan said humbly.

'To do what?'

'I don't know.' He looked up at Naomi and then at Mistress.

'You've been beaten already,' Mistress said coldly. 'Now, why did you come here?'

'Honestly Mistress, I don't know. To see you, to see if you matched the woman I had built up in my fantasy. I wanted to find the source of the voice that wouldn't get out of my head. And you do, Mistress, you are everything I imagined you to be. No, even more beautiful . . . '

'Shut up! What makes you think I'm at all interested in what you think? You're nothing to me.'

'Yes, Mistress,' Jonathan said, his heart racing. Her voice, her effortless tone of unbridled contempt, was arousing, a knot of excitement forming in the pit of his stomach.

'From now on you address him as Dog,' Mistress said, looking at Naomi.

'Yes, Mistress,' Naomi said obediently.

'Did Dog enjoy his beating?'

'Yes, Mistress, Dog enjoyed it very much I think.'

'Did he climax?'

'Yes, Mistress, all over himself,' Naomi said calmly.

Jonathan felt the shame rising up, his ears and face burning red with embarrassment. He glanced at Naomi but she was expressionless, her eyes fixed on Mistress, her body held stiffly, nervously.

'Had you ever been beaten before?' Mistress asked, smiling now. She put out a hand and took the lead from Naomi.

'No, Mistress,' Jonathan mumbled. He felt sick, his stomach turning ominously.

'A bad dog must always be beaten, and a bad dog

57

will always love a master that beats him. Isn't that right?'

'But I was beaten by a perfect stranger,' Jonathan said quietly.

'But you responded, didn't you, Dog? You responded in perfect Pavlovian fashion to your perfect stranger . . . '

'But it wasn't you,' Jonathan said, daring to look Mistress in the face, meeting her eyes head on.

'Silence!' she snapped, her voice echoing through the room, she tugged sharply at the lead, causing Jonathan to wince with pain and to clutch once more at the tight collar. 'Never, ever interrupt me, is that understood?'

'Yes, Mistress,' Jonathan whispered.

'A perfect stranger? What does that mean? Was she perfect in her strangeness? Was she perfect and a stranger? Aren't I your perfect stranger? People say such stupid things, things that don't make any sense at all. I think you must be the perfect stranger. You allow others to treat you like a dog, yet your only complaint is about the identity of the person that beat you. That's strange, very strange indeed I think. Aren't I correct, Dog?'

'Yes, Mistress.'

'What are you?'

'I'm a dog, Mistress.'

'Good boy,' Mistress laughed, stroking her hand through his hair. 'You're a good dog, aren't you. Good dogs are such friendly creatures, so trusting, so simple.' She moved round in her seat and crossed her legs over in front of Jonathan. Her long thighs were bare, the pale white skin looking so soft in the dim light. She stretched out her hand in front of him.

'Lick Mistress, Dog,' Naomi said quietly.

Jonathan looked up at Mistress, her eyes were on

him, looking at him with an expression of icy disdain. He edged forward on his hands and knees, the chain hanging loosely over his shoulder. Her hand was so small, a thin delicate wrist and long elegant fingers with long red nails. He kissed her fingers softly, touching her with his lips, then licking softly and slowly with his tongue. She pressed her fingers into his mouth and he sucked them in, sucking and kissing, letting her caress the inside of his mouth with her fingertips.

'Good boy,' she said softly, moving her hand towards her, making him crawl after it.

Jonathan inched closer, eyes half-closed, licking and sucking at Mistress's fingertips. She stroked her glistening fingers up and down her knee and he followed, kissing her there, licking his tongue over her warm smooth flesh. He moved closer still, on hands and knees between her thighs, her dress stretched tight over her body. He kissed and sucked at the soft glassy flesh, his mind blank but for the pleasure of being close to Mistress. She lifted herself for a second and pulled her dress up and then sat down again, lifting a leg over his shoulder.

He looked up at Mistress and saw her eyes were half-closed and her red lips open. He could feel her catching her breath, sighing very softly. She was naked under the dress, her white skin in contrast to the dark triangle of hair at the join of her thighs. He closed his eyes and moved closer, guided by her legs closing around him, drawing him to her sex. He could breathe the subtle perfume of her body, feel the warmth of her thighs against his face.

She parted the lips to her sex and he saw the glistening folds of pink flesh. He moved closer and kissed her softly, reverently on her apex. She sighed and he kissed her again, harder, deeper. With her free hand she pushed his face down and he began to suck and lick and kiss, mouthing her deep in her sex. Her taste was honey in his mouth, sweet nectar on his tongue. His prick was hard, aching, but all he wanted to do was to suck and kiss Mistress. He pressed harder, tonguing her as deep as he could, moving back to lick her pussy lips then plunging deep into her again.

'Good boy . . . Good boy . . . ' Mistress whispered, clutching his hair tightly, pulling harder and harder. She leaned forward and pressed herself up against his hungry mouth. She let go of his hair and dug her nails deep into his shoulder, crying out louder and louder. Her eyes were closed and she was thrashing her head from side to side, digging her heels into his lower back. She cried out, froze, then fell back limply.

Jonathan was pulled back, the lead jerking painfully at his neck. He looked up and remembered that Naomi had been behind him all the time. His face was damp with the thick creamy juices from Mistress's red sex, the mark of her essence on him, like a mark of ownership. His breathing was unsteady, but he felt a kind of pride flowing through him. Pride and a certain indefinable pleasure. He had brought Mistress to climax, he had served her well.

'Sit back now,' Naomi said quietly, touching him on the shoulder. It stung, he looked round and saw the impression of Mistress's nails marked red on his skin. His lower back ached with the twin imprint of her heels.

Mistress sat up slowly, adjusting her pretty dress once more. Her skin was flushed pink, her eyes a little unfocused. Naomi moved forward and helped to fix her appearance, brushing her wavy hair into place, adjusting the ruffles at the hem of the dress. In a few moments Mistress looked as calm and as cold as she did when Jonathan had first set eyes on her.

'Please Mistress,' he said quietly, his voice a little shaky, 'will I see you again?'

'What do you mean see *you* again? I granted you an audience, that's enough. Be thankful for that, Dog,' she said frigidly.

'But . . . '

'Enough!'

'Lie down, Dog,' Naomi directed. Jonathan looked at her blankly. He had given Mistress such pleasure, was she really so ungrateful? He wanted some sign of gratitude, some signal that she had enjoyed it, that he had given her pleasure. 'Do it,' Naomi said, and this time he lay flat on his back.

He looked up at Mistress towering above him. She was looking away from him. The dress wasn't very short, but he could see a fair way up her thighs, at the darkness that he had so lovingly mouthed. Her breasts jutted forward, wrapped delicately in the black dress. How he longed to kiss her there, to make love to her properly.

'Please Mistress . . . ' he begged forlornly. Her smell was around him, on his face, her taste strong in his mouth. Why was she doing this to him?

'Turn over,' Naomi said, rattling the chain to catch his attention. He looked at her and saw that her eyes were glittering, with the same look of desire that he had seen earlier. Obediently he turned over on to his stomach, his hard prick pressed flat on the floor.

He cried out suddenly. Mistress stepped on to him, planting herself halfway down his back. Her heels were like needles sinking into his flesh, the flat of her shoes pressing down. She stood steadily, perfectly balanced, an elegant lady in every sense.

'Call the others,' she said casually, her commanding voice as cool as the night. 'I think it's time we were going.'

'Yes, Mistress,' Naomi said, glancing down at Jonathan. 'What about Dog?'

'Tie him up,' Mistress said dismissively.

Jonathan watched Naomi go, walking smartly out of the room, her backside swaying gently as she went. He was in agony, suffering the searing pain of the heels boring into him. Mistress seemed so confident, so perfectly balanced. She shifted, pressing her weight from one foot to the next. Jonathan was pinned down completely, he couldn't move, could hardly breathe. But his prick was hard. Mistress was right, he was strange. She stood on him, hurting him unbearably, and yet he found pleasure in it. He wanted it. He wanted her to stand on him.

Naomi returned with the two other women. The masked woman smiled when she saw him.

'Time to leave, we have to be at Joanne's party in an hour,' Mistress said and stepped off Jonathan.

He sighed, felt relief tinged with disappointment. She was going to leave. He waited on the ground, still flat, waiting for instructions. His body ached all over, from the beating, from her heels, from her nails.

The masked woman came and pulled him up by the lead. Very roughly she pushed into the chair that Mistress had vacated. She took his arms and pulled them behind him, snapping on the same cuffs as before. In a second, before he really knew what was happening, he was a prisoner again.

'Please Mistress . . . ' he begged, his voice full of pleading, quivering tearfully.

'Poor stupid darling,' Mistress said softly, she came close and took his face in her hand, her fingers tight over his mouth. She looked at him pityingly. 'Is this really what you want?'

'I want you . . . ' he said, looking into her eyes,

searching for the special look that would be for him. He wanted her, he wanted her more than anything else in the world.

'Poor stupid darling . . .' she whispered, drawing out the word, letting it fade with her breath so close to his lips. She bent down and he saw the look in her eyes, the look that was for him. He saw it. 'Darling . . .' she whispered, and let her fingers move over his prick.

She kissed him softly, pressing her lovely lips against his. He closed his eyes, and her voice was in his head again, whispering like the soft breeze on the horizon of his dreams. He froze, gasped. He opened his eyes and already Mistress was marching away, her heels cracking like gunshots in the silence, her entourage following like ladies-in-waiting.

His belly was wet with thick cream. He had climaxed with a kiss.

Jonathan woke up just as the first light of dawn touched the room. He moved to one side and realised that he was still naked, alone in the deserted house. His body ached all over, his arms felt as if they had been welded into place. Very stiffly he tried to move, lifting his arms over the back of the chair. When he looked down he saw that the cuffs weren't locked. He hadn't even tried to escape; he had so completely accepted his position that the thought of escape hadn't entered his mind.

He shook the cuffs from his hands and stood up. In the distance he could see the sun peering over the horizon of trees in the park. It was cold and he was shivering. He bent down and picked up the cuffs before heading out of the room.

The house looked empty, the silence was so absolute that there could be no doubt. He peered into the next

63

room and saw the furniture covered in dull grey dust covers, a layer of fine dust around the room.

He ran down the stairs, suddenly afraid that he had been set up in some devious way. There was no way he could explain himself if someone should suddenly appear. There was no way he could explain it to himself.

He found his clothes and pulled them on quickly, using a handkerchief to wipe himself clean first. The room looked small and dingy in the early morning light, and only a faint stain on the floor by the footrest gave any hint of what had happened. He raced downstairs, ignoring the splendour of the house, shattering the silence with his footsteps. He reached the front door and stopped, he glanced round at the paintings on the wall and stepped out, slamming the door behind him, the house reverberating with its force.

And then he was out. The air was crisp and fresh and he filled his lungs as if it were his first breath. The white exterior of the grand houses shone like gold in the brittle sunlight.

Jonathan ached all over, his tortured body protesting every step. It was pain, but his body also tingled with a new feeling of vitality. It hurt but he knew he was alive, he felt like he was walking on air. The light seemed clearer, the air fresher. Everything looked different, he had forgotten what the world looked like and now it was fresh and new again.

Life had changed and it felt good.

4

Jonathan squeezed into the lift just as the glass doors closed with a sliding pneumatic whisper. It jerked into motion and he shuffled into a corner to rest against the glass, looking down sullenly at the world receding below.

'Well, it looks like it was a rough old night for you.'

Jonathan looked up with a terrible sinking feeling, the obscenely cheerful tone could only be Gardner, the last person in the world that he wanted to see. He looked purposely away, concentrating on the world continuing to fall away, the elevator moving smoothly up the side of the building on an exposed steel and glass vein. In the distance the Thames sparkled in the early morning light, a motor launch skimming the surface, cutting a long wide gash in the gold-brown waters.

By the time the elevator had reached its halfway mark it was almost empty, and, without looking, Jonathan was aware of Gardner staring at him.

'Still got to give it to the old girl,' Gardner said in the overly clipped public-school accent that he affected, 'she was right. It was love after all.'

'Look, give it a rest,' Jonathan said wearily, looking up to see Gardner smirking like an emotionally under-developed adolescent.

'My, my, we are moody, aren't we. You've cost me

65

a mint. I had good odds on you and the old girl getting back together again. I know, call me an old romantic, Mills and Boon if you must, but I was convinced you two would hitch up again.'

'Gardner, for fuck's sake shut up,' Jonathan hissed, wishing for all the world that the elevator floor would open up to deposit Gardner hundreds of feet below.

'Touchy, touchy.' Gardner backed off a few feet, bouncing from foot to foot, his face beaming with excitement, like a boy with a big secret that he can't wait to share with everybody else.

Jonathan stepped out at the next floor, suffocated by Gardner's larger-than-life presence. He was the sort of man who lived his entire life as if he were at a minor public school. Everything revolved around a kind of cloistered lifestyle that denied the existence of an outside world, and where the only currency of value lay in gossip and scandal. Gardner was a sad case; it was said that he had never even been to a public school, that the over-affected voice and the mannerisms were all some smart put-on, a kind of private joke that enabled him to laugh at everybody else. It was crap, Jonathan was certain of it.

He climbed the next couple of flights to his office, staring without enthusiasm at the glorious views of London spread before him. The reflection in the tinted glass looked tired, the sad face and lined eyes staring back at him blankly.

The computer room was the usual hive of activity, monitors blinking red and blue, phones and faxes screaming in the background, voices raised above the clamour. Jonathan walked through, glad that the noise and activity gave him the chance to go unnoticed. Once in his office he shut the door and slumped into his seat, letting his body go at last.

He ached and stung all over, with his fingers he could

feel the tiny horse-shoe imprints where Mistress had stood on his back. He closed his eyes and saw her, legs parted, her tightly bound breasts jutting against her dress, her face aloof, undeniably sexy. And she was standing on him, pressing her heels into him viciously, wearing a look of cool superiority that made his heart beat faster when he thought of it.

It had been a strange and intense experience. And then it had ended, she had humiliated him and then was gone, rushing away into the night like a Cinderella who had contemptuously scorned Prince Charming. He didn't even have a glass slipper to find her with; all he carried were the scars of a beating and her heel marks embedded in his flesh. He had to find her. Had to.

The phone rang and he picked it up and put it down again. He didn't want to talk, he didn't want to do anything. Outside he could see the bustle of the computer room, and across the way a huddle of analysts talking excitedly by a coffee machine. It was meaningless, none of it mattered, not really. What was he to do? Far from curing his infatuation, meeting Mistress had only intensified it.

The phone rang again; this time he listened, agreeing and disagreeing with the voice at the other end in all the right places. It was automatic, like reading a book when his mind was somewhere else. He was reminded that he had a report to deliver that morning, but the urgency of it failed to really get through. He put the phone down and reached into his desk for an electric razor, still going over all that had happened.

Caroline burst into the office minutes later, while he was still shaving. 'I've just seen Gardner,' she said, and Jonathan knew what that meant.

'What did he say?'

'Oh Jonathan look at you, you're a mess,' she said,

coming round to his side of the desk. She took the razor from his hand and put it down, sitting herself on the edge of the desk.

'I'm all right,' Jonathan said softly, almost apologetically.

'Who is she, Jon, is it anyone I know?'

'No, there's no one.'

'Don't lie to me Jon,' Caroline said sternly. 'I know you well enough. Look at you. Bags under the eyes, your face is pale, you've not had any sleep have you? Is she someone here?'

'Would you be jealous if she was?' Jonathan asked, smiling for the first time.

'I might be, but then again I might not care at all,' she smiled, shifting closer to him. She was wearing a smart red suit with a short skirt and dark stockings, the vivid colours lighting up the office.

'There's no one, I just had a drink with some friends, that's all,' he said, picking up the razor and clicking it on again.

'Then what's that?' Caroline said coldly. She reached out and pulled his shirt collar back to reveal the deep scratches in his shoulder, the long red finger marks distinct against the pale skin. She touched him and he winced, pulling away from her.

'It's nothing.'

'Cut yourself shaving? Or were you visiting a maiden aunt?' Caroline said, her voice brittle and her face suddenly hard.

'Please Caroline, it's not what you think . . . '

'Like fuck it isn't,' she snapped. 'At least have the decency to tell me the truth.'

'But . . . Really I can't explain.'

'Forget it,' Caroline said furiously. She turned and left, slamming the door after her so that everyone turned to look at her.

68

It was Gardner's fault, the bastard was like a spoilt kid. On impulse Jonathan got up, wanting to go upstairs to punch him in the mouth. He walked to the door and looked out, glaring at the people looking back at him. His hands were clenched tightly and he was breathing hard. The bastard, the fucking bastard. He half-hoped that Gardner would happen to pass by, then he'd go out and smack him in the mouth in front of everybody, nothing would give him greater satisfaction. But he knew that Gardner would keep out of the way, laughing at the trouble he'd caused, but hiding nevertheless.

The phone rang again and Jonathan ignored it. Gardner was the least of his worries. He glanced at his watch, he had a meeting in an hour and he had nothing prepared. He had upset Caroline, not so much because he'd gone with someone else, but because of the way he'd done it. And he had to find Mistress.

Jonathan sat at his desk, head in hands trying to clear his head, glad that at last the meeting was over. It had been dismal, there was no other word to describe it. With everything else on his mind he had no time to prepare, nor had he any real interest in what he was saying. The only saving grace, and it was little comfort, was that the meeting had been an internal presentation, no clients had been present. It wasn't much to cling to, but he knew that if he'd acted that badly in front of people from the outside he would have found himself with an empty desk and someone else's name on the office door.

At one point he had looked up and had realised that he had lost coherence, he didn't know what he was saying or where he was. The faces around the table looked either shocked or were smirking with self-satisfied glee. And it had dragged on and on, stretching interminably while he struggled to regain some control. Every time he moved he could feel his body ache, the heel marks were hard black bruises under the skin, and each twinge of pain took away from the present, taking him back to Mistress and his humiliation.

Eventually the meeting finished; he looked around the room and knew that coming in to work had been a bad move. He should have gone straight home to give himself some chance to recover from the experience. He stood alone at the head of the table, packing away his notes, aware of the cold distance between himself and the others in the room. They were deliberately keeping their distance, waiting for him to leave so that they could begin the post-mortem. He left alone, knowing that his reputation would be pulled apart, and that like vultures they would strip the carcass bare with ruthless precision.

'What in the hell is going on, Jonathan? What is it?' Caroline demanded angrily, bursting into the office in a fury, slamming the door behind her and standing in front of him with her hands on hips.

'I thought I was *persona non grata* at the moment,' he said, sitting back in his seat. She was the last person he expected to see. A director perhaps, down for a close personal chat, man to man, but not her.

'Forget that,' she said sombrely. 'That doesn't matter, this does. I don't care what you do Jon, I'm being honest now. But this counts.'

'Don't you think you've got your priorities wrong?' he said. He didn't believe her, she did care what he did, and with whom he did. But he was glad that she still cared, to have hurt her would have been terrible and he would never have forgiven himself. He smiled, she looked so serious, her eyes wide, breathing fast, angry because he had failed himself and not her.

'Don't talk nonsense,' she said dismissively.

'No, you've got your priorities wrong. So I screw up at an internal meeting. Big deal. Does it really matter?'

'Of course it matters,' she sighed, relaxing a bit. She sat down opposite, brushing a hand through her long black hair. There were tiny wrinkles around her eyes, little lines in the skin that made her more attractive. 'You're very well spoken of, people are watching you. It's only a matter of time before you move upstairs. Don't mess it up now.'

'Is that true?' Jonathan looked unconvinced, smiling lopsidedly. It was the sort of thing that Caroline would make up if she thought it would do him some good.

'Well if you didn't persist in your sojourn in the wilderness you'd know these things,' she said, smiling.

'You mean hang around with Gardner and his little gang?' he said scornfully.

'Gardner's got nothing to do with this and you know it. He's got his uses, he's tolerated, that's all. And what I've just said is true, you are on your way up. You've worked hard enough, don't you think you deserve it?'

He got up and walked to the window. The whole of London lay around him, stretching for miles, from the towering steel and glass monoliths close by, to the distant trees and greenery of the suburbs. 'Something's happened to me, Caroline,' he said at last. 'It's not that I don't want you to know, it's that I don't know how to tell you.'

'Try me.'

'I can't, I don't even know myself what's going on.'

'What is it? From the beginning.'

'This is going to sound weird, I mean it is weird, very weird. I got a phone call, in the middle of the night, for someone with the same name as me. It was

71

a woman . . . ' he broke off and turned to face Caroline, she was sitting at the desk, hand under her chin, looking at him expectantly. 'Well, there was something about this woman, something different. She sort of clicked. Not . . . not in the normal way . . . '

'You mean you fancied her?' she said, smiling knowingly.

'No, not exactly like that. Not the way it was between the two of us. No, this was different, you see, I can't explain it.'

'You're doing fine, carry on.'

'Well, to cut a long story short I got to meet her last night. Don't ask me to explain what happened.'

She smiled more broadly. 'I'm a big girl now,' she said. 'Judging by her paw marks on your back I think I know what you mean.'

Jonathan shook his head. 'That's just it,' he said quietly, slumping back into his seat, 'it wasn't like that at all. This was different, very different. And now she's gone and I don't know what to do.'

'So I was right all along,' she said rather sadly, as if talking to herself, 'it is the dreaded L-word.'

'Honestly Caroline, it isn't. It's not love, I don't know what it is. I don't know who she is or where she is. All I know is that I have to see her again.'

'That sounds suspiciously like love to me. And I suppose that she's more important than your career?'

'To be honest Caroline, I don't give a damn about work. I need to get her out of my system, to flush out whatever it is from my bloodstream. Then I can think about work and . . . ' he looked at her closely, ' . . . other things.'

'Take time out,' she said, standing up. 'Fix up a sabbatical of some sort, three months, six months. Do it now, before you screw up any more. If you go now people'll just remember the good things you've done, hopefully today will be forgotten.'

'But I don't even know where to start. I haven't got a name, or a proper address or . . . '

Caroline sighed heavily. She walked round to him and bent down low. She touched his face with her hand and then kissed him gently on the mouth, their lips pressing close. 'I must be mad,' she said, standing up straight. 'You have got a name, your name. You said that she was looking for someone with your name, that's all you need to start with.'

'Thanks. You're not mad, you're just very, very smart,' he said gratefully.

'Six months you said, to wash it out of your system, right?'

'Yeah. Six months.'

'Let me sort this out,' she said walking to the door. 'I'll have your sabbatical arranged by the end of today. Then you'll be as free as a bird for half a year. And at the end of it you'll be able to think about other things, won't you?'

'Yes. Is it that simple? Just a couple of words from you and then I'm free?'

Caroline smiled. 'If only you'd pay attention,' she said, standing by the door. 'I'm moving in higher circles now, how do you think I know that you'll be moving up soon? We could go a long way together.' She was still smiling, but her eyes were suddenly nervous, looking directly at him. 'Six months, right?'

'Yes, six months. I promise,' he said. She paused in the doorway for a moment then turned and left. He watched her go, unable to quite believe that it was going to be that simple. Just a few well-placed words from her and then what?

He felt exhausted, he rubbed his eyes with his fingertips, the colour behind his eyes fluorescing orange

73

and yellow. Caroline's scent lingered around him and he could taste her lipstick on his lips. He felt like a bastard, a cruel ungrateful bastard. What had she done to deserve him? She had everything going for her and yet she was throwing herself away on him. Six months he had promised, and it had been a heartbreaking lie. He knew there was no way that he could get Mistress out of his mind, the poison was too deep for that now.

Caroline was even going to arrange time for him, letting him loose to pursue Mistress, in the vain hope that it was a minor infatuation that would fade and die in a matter of months. Poor Caroline, Jonathan thought, she really didn't understand.

Jonathan woke up and realised that he was free. For the first time in years he knew that there would be nothing else to claim his time or his energy. This wasn't a holiday or an all too short break, this was the real thing, life without work and it felt wonderful.

He showered lazily, examining the marks on his body. The whip marks were fading fast, the heel marks were black bruises slowly turning yellow. She had marked him out, and he knew then that what Naomi had said was true — he carried the marks with a feeling akin to pride. He was proud that he had served Mistress so well. The memories were close to the surface, always there when he closed his eyes, a permanent mental distraction. Everything reminded him of what had happened; a well-shaped thigh, the snap of high heels, a softly spoken voice, rain on the window.

The first thing he did was to drive out to the grand house, wanting to revisit the place where it had happened. He felt drawn to it, like a thief returning to the scene, or an arsonist wanting to watch the flames he had set. It was bright and sunny, the white exterior of the house catching the sun and flaring yellow in the brightness. He sat at a bench in the green, in the shade, looking up at the window that he had looked out of.

The house still looked empty, it had the lonely air of desertion about it. He saw people come and go in the houses around it, but their presence was unfelt there. At one point he walked across the road and rang the door bell, hoping that Naomi would answer and lead him up the curving stairs and past the arrogant portraits hanging on the walls. But nobody came, the house was as deserted as he remembered it to be, the grand furniture hidden under the grey dust covers.

Finding Mistress was never going to be that easy, which is why she had probably used the old house. Jonathan knew that he could try to trace the owner, but that route seemed even less direct than chasing up his namesake. He took a long leisurely stroll through Regents Park before leaving for home, enjoying the air and the pleasure of walking across the grass.

Finding the other de Molay was an exceedingly simple business. It took Jonathan half a morning to come up with an address, several addresses in fact. The other de Molay was the sort of man who got himself noticed. He was rich – the list of addresses was evidence enough of that; he was in his prime, his family had the history to go with the money; he mixed with all the right people. In fact he and his friends *were* the right people.

Jonathan took an instant dislike to him, just from the information he had gleaned from the magazines and the gossip columns. The whole aristocratic milieu went against Jonathan's meritocratic instincts. It was distasteful, conjuring up images of an alien world of unearned wealth and privilege. He had met people like that before, people who felt they had a right to everything because of who they were rather than what they'd done. They were like Gardner but a thousand times worse.

Mistress wasn't like that. She was from the same background, Jonathan imagined, but she was different. For her all pretence and affectation were stripped away. She knew where she stood and where people were in relation to her. There was something about her that marked her out from the rest of her class, something special, something that set her apart from everyone else, rising above them naturally.

Sometimes he caught himself making little stories in his head, deciding that Mistress was this or that. It was silly, he really had no idea what she did or what she thought, just as he had no idea what his namesake was really like. Maybe he took a dislike to him because he was her lover, and that everything else was his way of rationalising the jealousy. But Jonathan couldn't help it. Mistress was as much a product of his imagination as she was of real life, she was only partly human.

He had the addresses for de Molay but no phone number. It would have been easy to get one if he really wanted to. Jonathan's own social scene intersected with theirs; the border between old money and new money was blurred, and becoming more so. He knew enough people to begin fishing for the number straight away, and guessed that it would only take a couple of days to pull it out of the hat. But something made him hold back for the moment; perhaps he feared arousing too much attention. He didn't want his namesake to discover what was going on.

There was no definite plan, no well-thought-out route to Mistress. Jonathan hoped that he would find de Molay, follow him for a while and then catch him going to Mistress's house. And that would be it. What he did from then was hardly worked out either, he didn't dare to think about it, afraid that if he did the ridiculousness of it would suddenly overwhelm him. He was an analyst, it was his job to be clear, logical and always rational. This was none of those things, and it was all the stronger for it.

He spent the next few days visiting the addresses that he had, working down the list in alphabetical order. He would draw up in his car and wait, parking on the corner of the street or across the road. And then he would wait, eyeing everyone who came and went, making notes furtively. A couple of times the police stopped him, demanding to know what he was doing and who he was. He lied, telling them the first thing that came into his head. Both times it worked, maybe because his own expensive car didn't look too out of place in the surroundings.

It was on the evening of the fourth day that he first saw de Molay. Jonathan had spent all day waiting outside a smart riverside house near Chelsea, driving around every few hours to avoid the attention of the police. The morning had been bright but as the day drew to a close it had become grey and dark. The change reflected Jonathan's mood, the early morning optimism turning to doubt as the hours dragged on.

It was a hell of a place to spend the day; there was nothing but his thoughts to occupy him. Everything reminded him of Mistress; there were too many smart attractive women there, tall and elegant, dressed in the most stylish of clothes, stalking the streets with the kind of feline elegance that Mistress possessed. Looking across to the other bank of the Thames he could see the smart new riverside apartments, airy-looking penthouse suites with balconies opening high above the river. It was a kind of fantasy landscape, beautiful palaces looking purposefully away from the grey surroundings behind them. It was the sort of place that he imagined Mistress could inhabit, a queen above her subjects, rising majestically above mundane reality.

It was in the early evening, as he was about to leave, when he saw the sleek Jaguar car pull into the street, its gleaming surface catching the dying light of the day. Jonathan knew it was him at once, even before he saw the car come to a stop outside de Molay's house. The sight of the driver confirmed it. She emerged from her seat and stepped round to open de Molay's door. She was very tall, a striking blonde with long flowing hair, wearing a chic grey jacket and short grey skirt with black high heels that glinted like the silvery-black surface of the car.

She was the sexiest chauffeur that Jonathan had ever seen. There was something familiar about her, something that struck a chord, but Jonathan's attention was immediately diverted by de Molay as he emerged from the car. He was dressed casually but with style, wearing a deceptively simple blue jacket and contrasting grey trousers. The photographs that Jonathan had seen had given the impression that de Molay was tall and thin; in reality he was of average height, but the confident way he stood, with his back straight, looking straight ahead did seem to add inches to his height.

The photographs were also wrong about the face. Gone was the rather vain expression that had stared back from the black and white magazine photographs, and instead he looked relaxed, though rather serious. He had greying hair swept to one side, away from his clean-shaven face. His dark eyes barely glanced at the driver, instead he skipped up the stairs to the house and disappeared inside. The driver got back into the car and in a second she was gone, the car effortlessly gliding away.

So that was de Molay. Although there was nothing terribly striking about him Jonathan could see that he was the sort of man women found attractive. Perhaps it was the eyes, or the way he walked or the way he held himself. Charm, that was what he had, and it was possible to see that with one glance. Maybe it was the eyes, dark and intense, the sort of eyes that could disarm anyone. His face was tanned and lined, but it was hard to put an exact age to him.

Jonathan was hungry but the idea of going home didn't even occur to him. He settled down in his car, tilting the seat to make himself more comfortable, knowing that de Molay wasn't the sort of man to stay in for a quiet night at home. The clouds were flecked with pink as the sun disappeared, the temperature falling with it. The surface of the river sparkled with a thousand lights, the fantasy palaces of the riverside reflected in a blazing glory on the rippling water.

As the hours passed Jonathan saw the expensive cars gliding up and down the small street. Fashionable young things emerged from the anonymous houses in blazes of colour before disappearing out into the night, their voices and laughter carrying down the otherwise silent street.

At last, just before midnight, Jonathan saw the blonde chauffeur emerging from a different car, something more stylish than the Jaguar. She went to the door and a moment later de Molay emerged, in full evening dress. He was alone, and Jonathan could see that there was no one waiting in the car.

Jonathan started the car and moved off after de Molay's red car. He wasn't sure whether to follow them directly or to try to retain some distance. Was de Molay the sort of man who worried about being followed? In the tight streets around Chelsea Jonathan had no choice; he followed them closely, afraid to lose sight of them more than he was afraid of being caught.

He trailed them along the Thames embankment, passing the Tate Gallery and then on to Millbank. The traffic was light and soon they were in Westminster, Big Ben clocking midnight as they drove past. De Molay's car turned off into the maze of streets in the West End, speeding effortlessly between the cars parked tightly on either side of the narrow roads. At last it drew to a stop in a quiet back street, the chauffeur parked and then she and de Molay got out and walked together to one of the blank-faced houses.

In a panic Jonathan parked the car at the other end of the street and then dashed out in time to see them disappearing into one of the houses. He waited a second in case they doubled back and then followed on foot. The street was darkly lit and the old houses were mostly converted offices, with brass nameplates on the doors and yellowing blinds in the windows. He wasn't sure where de Molay and the woman had gone, but moments later another car drew up and a young man and woman emerged from it. It was cold and their breath misted as they laughed quietly to themselves. The woman, dressed in a long grey coat, looked at Jonathan and he turned away as they came close. She passed by and a gust of wind blew her coat open. An enticing glimpse of a long bare thigh made Jonathan's heart beat faster. The couple stopped outside one of the houses and pressed a buzzer on the entryphone; they whispered into it and the door clicked open for them.

Jonathan returned to his car and settled comfortably, cheering himself up with the thought that he was getting closer to Mistress all the time. He was disappointed that the house wasn't her residence, but at least he knew he was indirectly going to find out all about her. Several times cars drew up and deposited people outside the house, young couples, single men and women. Other people emerged from the house, laughing and joking loudly in the street. Some looked drunk, or the couples were snuggling close together with in the cold.

The car was becoming increasingly uncomfortable, and Jonathan's hunger was getting worse. His throat was dry and he realised how unprepared he was for a night of spying. As a child he had often played detective, hunting out the imaginary clues in TV style. The reality of it was tedious and uncomfortable, forcing him to question himself all the time.

The chauffeur emerged first, she walked tall, her heels echoing down the street as she went. Her uniform clung tightly to her body, the skirt revealing her long bare thighs and the outline of her tight round behind. She reversed the car and brought it round to the entrance of the house. De Molay emerged seconds later, laughing expansively, his arms around the shoulders of two attractive young women. They looked in awe of him, snuggling close under his arms, smiling half-nervously with him, their eyes fixed on his. The driver opened the car door for them and they entered, Jonathan saw de Molay slide his hand up the thigh of one of them as she got in.

Neither of them was Mistress. Jonathan's heart had been in his mouth, his blood racing with fear and excitement. It wasn't Mistress, and he didn't know whether to be happy or sad. He sat with his hands clutching the wheel, his knuckles turning white as de Molay's car accelerated away.

It didn't matter that they had gone. Jonathan knew where to look for him now, and he was certain that de Molay would not be calling in on Mistress. He felt tired and dizzy, all keyed up with excitement. He got out of the car, gasping for air, wanting to clear his head.

A car pulled up and another couple emerged from

the night and then disappeared. Jonathan walked up the street, drawn to the place, wanting to find out the truth behind the grey anonymity. It was some sort of club, but he wanted to see for himself what sort of place that de Molay and, presumably Mistress, would go to.

There was no name-plate on the heavy black door, nor anything on the entryphone. He pressed the buzzer and waited, he heard it click to life.

'De Molay,' he said, realising that the person at the other end was waiting for him.

'Yes sir,' a woman said. The relay clicked mechanically and the door was opened an inch.

There was a long carpeted passage and then a flight of stairs, with nothing on the dull cream walls to indicate what sort of a place he had gained entry to. There was only one place to go, forward. There was a door at the top of the flight of stairs, through which he could hear the faint strains of music.

Jonathan pushed through the door and stopped. The music was louder: pulsating, throbbing, electronic dance music. It was dark, and there was someone standing in the shadows by a second door.

'Who the fuck are you?' a woman demanded, emerging out of the shadows. She was dressed in a black rubber camisole that zipped down the front, the zip partially undone to reveal the generous curve of her breasts. She also wore highcut rubber panties pulled tight between her thighs, and black fishnet stockings with anklelength black boots.

'Jonathan de Molay,' he said, smiling nervously. The woman had long blonde hair that was growing black at the roots; she wore it high, leaving her neck and shoulders bare. She was scowling, her eyes narrowed and her scarlet painted lips pursed angrily.

'Don't lie,' she said menacingly. 'This is a private

club, and you're not a member. And you're not Jonathan de Molay.'

'Yes, but I am,' Jonathan said, reaching into his pocket. The door opened and for a moment the music was unbearably loud, he caught a glimpse of what was going on inside, the lights strobing on to naked bodies writhing ecstatically on stage.

'You're not Jonathan de Molay, and if you don't turn round and fuck off there'll be trouble,' the woman warned, her voice cold and hard, as hard as the music blasting from next door.

'No, but I am de Molay,' he said, shouting against the music. Another woman, similarly dressed, appeared on the scene, standing protectively behind the first. Both of them were made up in the same style: rouged faces, brilliant lipstick, dyed blonde hair.

He pulled a credit card from his wallet and passed it across to the women. She slapped his hand, knocking the card to the floor. 'I don't care what you say,' she hissed. 'Get out now!'

Jonathan rubbed his hand, he could feel the skin glowing hot where she had slapped him. 'That wasn't necessary,' he said. He looked at the two women, staring back at him aggressively, their painted faces like masks in the pale light.

He bent down to pick up his card and saw one of them move towards him, he reached for his card and she stepped on his hand, digging her heel into him. The other woman pushed him and he fell heavily to his knees. His hand was pinned down, her heel digging into his flesh. He cried out, his voice lost in the sudden blast of music. He tried to push her off his arm but she stood firm.

He looked up and saw that the door was open and people were crowding round, looking down on him and laughing. The woman lifted her foot and he snatched his hand up. The crowd was laughing louder, jeering drunkenly, the women giggling and clinging to the men.

The second woman was behind him; he tried to get up, to say something against the throbbing electronic beat of the music, but she pushed him over. He went skidding to the floor again, falling flat. The woman was astride him, squatting down over the small of his back. She grabbed his hair and pulled his head back painfully. The first woman was in front, she planted her foot inches from his face and then his head was forced over it.

'Suck!' one of the women commanded, to loud cheers from the audience.

Jonathan tried to protest but his mouth was forced down over the black boot, his words smothered. He tried to get up but the other heel was pressed into his shoulder. He felt dizzy, the music blanking out everything, swirling around him noisily. His heart was racing, and then he knew that he was reacting in the way he least expected. His prick was hard, he was gasping for breath, lost in the swirling whirlwind of sensation.

He began to kiss the boot, pressing his lips eagerly over the shining patent leather, his mouth tingling with the taste. He kissed and sucked, eager now to obey. His mouth passed under the high arch and down the long slender heel, sucking passionately, eyes closed, only dimly aware of the jeering audience around him.

He was turned over on to his back, still kissing the first woman's heel. The second woman released him, she stood over him and pulled her panties to one side, the thin strip of rubber revealing the white flesh of her shaven pussy. She squatted down over him, using her fingers to open herself. Jonathan opened his mouth and eagerly accepted, kissing her on the puffy lips of her pussy, gently easing his tongue into her.

The woman began to writhe over him, pressing herself down hard over his mouth, holding him by the hair and forcing him deeper into her sex. He licked and sucked, biting and kissing, taking her flowing sex cream into his mouth with pleasure. He speared her with his tongue, flicking over her throbbing cunt bud as she moaned and cried with pleasure. The music and the crowd seemed to recede, there was nothing for him but her pussy, her glorious, beautiful pussy that he sucked for its nectar.

He could feel her body convulsing, shuddering repeatedly, filling his mouth with wave after wave of her juice. He lapped harder and deeper until she cried out once more and then she sat down hard, unable to control herself. He struggled for breath, then felt his prick pumping, the ecstatic energy passing through his body and then he let go too.

The woman stood up, her face flushed, and fell into the arms of her companion, who kissed her tenderly on the mouth. Jonathan stood up and the audience applauded, as if the performance had pleased them. Jonathan's face was bright red, and he shrank away from the laughing faces, at the eyes that looked down on him as if he were some lower species of animal.

He reached down for his card and felt his come sliding down the inside of his trousers. It was sick and he felt a wave of repulsion pass through him. It wasn't what he wanted, not at all. The crowd retreated, the door closed and he was alone with the two women, holding each other close. Jonathan paused, but there was nothing to say to them.

He turned and left, feeling low, sick with himself for finding pleasure in such degradation. His hand was still hurting, and he had another heel mark to add to his collection.

'Stop,' a woman said quietly. Jonathan was at the

front door, but turned back and looked. She was coming downstairs, tall and slender, her face pale, with nervous grey eyes and a wide mouth with thin lips. 'Who are you?'

'Does it matter?' Jonathan said, his voice barely a whisper.

'No, not really,' she agreed, coming close to him. She wore a long white coat which hung loosely over her shoulders, and underneath it a low-cut short dress, revealing long lithe thighs clad in black stockings. 'You made a mess of yourself, didn't you?'

'Yes,' he said, looking away from her.

She put her hand out to him. She had long elegant fingers with long red nails, a bracelet loose around her wrist. He took her hand, not knowing what to do. 'Either you get to your knees and kiss my hand, or you suck my fingers into your mouth,' she explained. 'I suggest you fall to your knees, like a good little boy.'

Jonathan looked at her blankly. She was serious, her eyes were fixed in a cold stare, her mouth was closed, not smiling. 'I don't understand,' he said, holding her hand at mouth level.

'I'm taking you home with me,' she said, smiling at last. 'You're not very good as a slave, but I think you've got a natural talent for it. You'll learn, or rather, I'll teach you. Now kiss my hand.'

Jonathan bent down and touched his lips to her hand, all the time his eyes were on her. Was she for real?

'Good, you may call me Mistress Victoria. Now, you've got a car I take it?'

'Yes, outside. What makes you think I'm going to go with you?'

'Because you must, you can't deny yourself. None of us can. A hungry man will always eat, and a thirsty man will always drink. And you will always submit. Now, lead the way.'

Jonathan opened the door and Victoria stepped out into the cold, pulling her coat tightly around her. He led the way down the empty street, aware of the mess he'd made of himself and of the presence of Victoria one step behind him. He opened the car door for her but she pointed to the back seat. He opened the rear door and she got in.

'My name's Jonathan . . . '

'I'll give you a name,' she said. 'Until then you're Boy, do you understand? You're Boy, and I'm Mistress Victoria. It's very simple. Now, drive.'

5

They crossed the river at Westminster, Victoria directing from the back seat. They drove for half an hour through south London, Jonathan relying on her to guide him through the unknown streets. Apart from giving directions Victoria said nothing, and that suited Jonathan, he had no appetite for conversation. He kept glancing at her in the rearview mirror, sitting comfortably in the back seat, her pale face caught like a mask under the passing street lights.

Could he deny himself? She had spoken as if she knew more about him than he did, presuming that he would fall in with her plans, whatever they were. But she didn't know him, not at all. It was a misunderstanding, what she had seen at the door of the club wasn't him, not at all. And if Victoria was basing all her plans on the basis of that single scene then she was mistaken. He wasn't sure that he was even going to stay the night with her, but he had gone too far simply to drop her off in the middle of nowhere.

He was struck by the confident way she had approached him, there was nothing forced about it, it appeared completely natural. In fact she had assumed that he would know how to act. Only weeks earlier Jonathan would have laughed at it all, struck by the comic aspect of being treated like a slave. But that time had passed, and now he felt that he was being drawn into a world where the exotic and the surreal were commonplace. The extraordinary had ceased to amaze.

Victoria lived in an old apartment block at the end of a long winding street far from the nearest main road. The block had lost some of its thirties charm, and in the darkness the squat building looked cold and dingy. The walled courtyard was arranged around a sculpted oval lawn, circled by cars parked haphazardly all around it. Jonathan parked his car in the only available space, near to the entrance of the block, and got out.

'This way,' Victoria said, leading the way across the courtyard. He hesitated and then followed, knowing that he would never find his way back alone.

They walked up granite steps, holding on to the black wrought-iron hand-rail. The block was clean and free from graffiti that Jonathan had expected, with balconies leading to the flats and overlooking the courtyard. Victoria stopped at the third floor and led the way along the balcony, her heels echoing right around the enclosed block.

She opened a heavy blue front door and stepped inside, letting Jonathan go through before she locked and bolted the door for the night. 'Strip off and then on your knees,' she said sternly, turning to face him.

'Can't we just talk?' he said wearily. He had no energy to play games, he felt dirty and confused, the only think he looked forward to was sleep.

Victoria hesitated. In the soft orange light of the hall her eyes lost the hard confident glitter; her skin looked soft and warm, losing the harsh painted whiteness that he had first noticed. 'All right,' she relented. 'There's a bathrobe in there.' She stepped back and opened the door to the bathroom. 'You can wash, I'll make some coffee.'

'Thanks.'

The bathroom was small and cramped, the shower

consisting of a curtain drawn across the enamel bath with a showerhead fed from the taps. There was a bathroom cabinet hanging over a basin, and one of the sliding mirrored doors was open, revealing two shelves packed tight with plastic bottles. The room was crossed by a clothesline with a few towels and some small items of clothing hanging limply from it. Despite the cramped conditions the jet of hot water was soothing and refreshing. Jonathan was glad of the time to clean up, and for the time to himself.

Victoria had confounded his expectations. He had expected to be taken to a fine house in the leafy suburbs, or an expensive apartment by the river. The dingy little flat was none of those things. And no matter how hard she might try, there was no way that he could take her seriously as a Mistress. She lacked the natural ruthlessness that Mistress had in abundance. Victoria simply looked too nice. But although she didn't share the same grand background as de Molay or Mistress, she was still nevertheless part of their scene.

He tried on the terry bathrobe hanging behind the door and found it to be hers; the sleeves extended only to his elbows, and its length barely covered his backside. He put it on and felt silly, but the only alternative was to put his soiled clothes back on. He slicked a hand through his wet hair and stepped out.

'Over here,' Victoria called when she heard him.

He walked down the small hall and into her sitting room. The room was small and still contained many original features: the large square iron framed windows, the high mantelpiece over the fireplace. The ceiling was high, unlike most modern rooms, and decorated with soft pale wallpaper. An art-deco lamp, a dark dolphin balancing a soft white ball of light on its nose, provided the only light in the room.

Victoria was sitting with her legs drawn under her

90

on a sofa, cupping a large mug of coffee in her hands. She smiled when she saw him and he smiled back, drawing the robe around him protectively. 'This was all I could find,' he said, sitting in an armchair across from the sofa, aware of the shortness of the robe.

'It looks very nice on you,' Victoria said, sipping coffee from the mug.

'My name's Jonathan de Molay, I was trying to explain that to the women at the door . . . '

'Is that really your name?' Victoria said, with the same disbelieving tone that Jonathan had heard earlier.

'Yes it is, really it is. It was what I was born with, I had an uncle with the same name, for all I know it stretches back for years.'

'Have you ever met the famous Jonathan de Molay?'

'No, never. To be honest I'd never even heard of the guy before.'

'Seriously? You'd never heard of Jonathan de Molay?' Victoria asked, looking askance.

'Yes, really. Until a few weeks ago I'd never even suspected the existence of someone else with the same name. I mean it's not a common name is it?'

'Certainly not. Is that why you tried to get into the club? To meet the man with the same name as you?'

'To be honest it's not him I'm interested in, it's his girlfriend.'

'His girlfriend?' Victoria laughed out loud, throwing her head back and closing her eyes.

'What's so funny?'

'God, you've got no idea of the sort of lifestyle de Molay leads, none at all. For him there's no such thing as "the girlfriend", that's not his scene at all.'

Jonathan could hardly hide the disappointment he felt. 'What is his scene then?' he asked sourly.

'I can't believe you don't know anything about him,' Victoria repeated.

91

'Look, I said I don't know,' Jonathan said testily. 'You know all about it, explain it to me.'

'Jonathan is into adventure. For him there's nothing worse in life than boredom. Boredom and routine are the things he can't abide. He wants excitement, passion, grand gestures, everything. He's the sort of man that would fly halfway across the world on a whim,' Victoria said, excitedly, sitting up, her eyes sparkling.

'Are you part of this grand adventure?'

'Sometimes. When the mood strikes him he's the most generous man in the world. We're all his friends, his fellow adventurers.'

'And when he's not in the mood?'

Victoria smiled. 'It's better not to know him when he's in a really bad mood. Better to keep out of his way. But we're all like that aren't we? Sometimes happy and sometimes depressed. We all have our moods.'

'He looked like he was in a good mood tonight.'

'Oh, you saw him?' Victoria looked surprised.

'Briefly. I saw him getting into his car with two women, they looked to be in a good mood as well. Is that the scene he's into?'

'What's that supposed to mean?'

'It means what you want it to mean.'

'Don't be like that,' Victoria said softly. 'I hate the conventional. Being ordinary is boring, I hate ordinary. Jonathan's very unconventional, there's nothing ordinary about him, or the people he plays with. If you find that shocking then I guess you must be pretty screwed up.'

'Listen to yourself,' Jonathan said, smiling. 'You picked me up without knowing who I am or what I am, you talked to me about being your slave and then you say I'm screwed up? Come on, be serious.'

'You came though, you're here. I knew you'd come,

92

I could tell. You're part of the adventure now. You've crossed the line. You've stopped being ordinary.'

'Perhaps you're right. Things have been very . . . strange lately. Tell me about de Molay's women friends, is there one that's a bit special?'

Victoria shrugged. 'Don't know. We're all special in our own way. Why are you so interested in de Molay's friends? I would have thought that you'd be interested in him, he's the interesting one.'

Jonathan paused. He didn't want to give anything away. Victoria was so in awe of de Molay that he knew that anything he said would be likely to get back to him at once. 'Just idle curiosity,' he said.

'What do you do? In real life?'

'Nothing, at the moment. And you?'

'Nothing,' she smiled, 'at the moment.'

'Were you joking about making me your slave?'

She shook her head. 'I meant every word. You climaxed when you were humiliated earlier, in front of everybody. You're a masochist, did you know that?'

Jonathan shifted uncomfortably, pulling unconsciously at the robe to cover himself. 'I suppose I must be,' he mumbled. No one had ever called him that before, and it wasn't a word he had ever associated with himself before.

'There's no suppose about it,' she said, her voice becoming stern. 'Those feelings are there, but you haven't come to terms with what it means. I'm going to do that, you'll become my slave. I'll train you, so that you'll learn about yourself, and you'll learn how to act. I'll be your mistress.'

'Is that how you'll get your pleasure? Training me?'

'Partly, but life's a lot more complicated than that. There's a contract. If you stay with me, then you're mine completely and utterly. You'll do exactly as commanded, without thinking. You can never refuse.

If you do then it's over, the contract is broken and you must go. That's the contract. Do you agree to it?'

'Can I think about it?'

'Think about it? Look at yourself,' she pointed to Jonathan's erect prick visible under the robe, 'you don't need time to think.'

Jonathan covered himself quickly, feeling embarrassed because he had tried to hide his true feelings and yet been given away by his body. 'I can't let my prick rule my head,' he said.

'No, it's the other way round. You can't let your head rule your prick. That really screws people up. Now, follow me.'

Victoria stood up and led him out of the sitting room and into her bedroom. It was a small room, dominated by the double bed, flanked on both sides by bedside cabinets with matching reading lamps on them. Jonathan was struck by the sheer ordinariness of her flat, in stark contrast to the life she had been describing. It was so odd, to live a life devoted to the grand gesture yet be surrounded by such a normal domestic environment.

She went over to one of the bedside cabinets and opened the drawer. Inside there was a leather collar with some chains attached; she picked it up and signalled Jonathan to go over to her. He padded over, letting the robe hang loose, his prick standing stiffly to attention. She pulled the robe off and let it fall to the floor.

'You've been well marked,' she commented, running her fingers over his cool flesh, pausing at the fresh heel marks on his shoulder. She turned him round and traced her fingers down his back. 'You've been whipped,' she said, sounding a little surprised.

'Does it still show?'

'It's almost gone, I can just see the last traces. And

you've got quite a collection of heel marks. I'm surprised, I thought this was all new to you. It obviously isn't, is it?'

Jonathan turned to face her. 'It is new, it's all happened so quickly, that's all.' The feel of her fingers over his body, and the way she had lingered lovingly at his wounds was exciting. His prick was hard, and he was breathing unevenly. She was so close and warm, the tight dress displaying fully the shape of her body, her breath hot on his cold skin. He reached out and took her by the waist and pulled her close, pressing his hardness against her.

'No, not like that,' she said, pushing his arms away. 'Bend down a bit,' she directed, and then put the collar around his neck, buckling it securely. There was a single chain hanging from it with two leather cuffs at the other end, a solid bar separating them. She put the cuffs around his wrists and buckled them tightly too.

Jonathan felt a surge of excitement, a mixture of the thrill of recognition and anticipation of what was to come. It felt good to be chained again. It made him feel free, he knew that he was handing himself over to Victoria. Mistress had called it a Pavlovian reaction, and maybe she was right; Victoria called it training but it was the same thing.

'Tonight you'll sleep at the foot of my bed like a dog,' Victoria said, looking up when she had finished binding him. 'This is where your training begins.'

'But . . . I thought that we were . . . '

'Quiet. You don't speak unless I tell you to. You're not here to enjoy yourself, you're here to obey.'

She walked over to the wardrobe and pulled a blanket from it. She spread it on the floor and pointed for Jonathan to lie down. He hesitated, standing by the bed, his prick aching for her touch. He looked at her longingly, hoping that she would relent. 'Here, now!' she snapped, and he went over to the blanket and knelt down on the floor, his hands held rigidly apart by the metal bar between the cuffs.

Victoria turned away from him and began to undress, pulling her short dress high over her head and then folding it neatly. She put it down on a chair in the corner of the room and then walked past Jonathan, not deigning to glance down at him. Next she sat on the edge of the bed and undid her suspenders, humming to herself softly. Jonathan watched her with mounting excitement, tantalised by the slow deliberate way she rolled down her black stockings, the darkness falling away to reveal the soft creamy whiteness of her long perfect thighs. She unclipped her black lacy bra and pulled it off, her small breasts standing firm, dark cherry-red nipples in contrast to the pale softness of her flesh. Lastly she stood and pulled down her panties, letting him see the dark bush between her thighs.

She picked up her lingerie and walked back across the room to place it neatly on the chair. 'Please, let me suck you, let me kiss you,' Jonathan pleaded softly. 'Please, Mistress.'

'Go to sleep, Boy,' she said coldly, walking past him again, her backside swaying deliciously as she did so.

'Please, Mistress, please. What about this?' he gestured down to his hard prick, oozing a silver jewel of fluid. He felt so hard, so keyed up that he knew the gentlest touch of her fingers on him would cause him to climax ecstatically.

'I don't care about that,' she said dismissively. 'You'll notice that the chain is deliberately kept short, you won't even be able to touch yourself if you want to. You can rub yourself on the floor like an animal if you like. It's up to you.'

Jonathan struggled but he managed to stand up, he looked at her sitting on the bed, so desirable, and yet so aloof. He couldn't believe that she didn't feel the same raging desire that he did. The way she had touched him, it had to have been exciting for her, as exciting as it had been for him. 'I can't go through with this,' he said, offering her his hands.

Victoria stood and shook her head sadly. She went over to the drawer again and then came back with something else. Roughly she pulled him from the collar and dragged him back towards the blanket. He was thrown off balance and almost fell to the ground. She forced him back to his knees and then passed another chain around the base of the bed and the collar around his neck. In a second he was secure, on his hands and knees and tied to the bed. 'Don't be so fucking tiresome,' she scolded.

'But Mistress . . . '

'Shut up!' she marched angrily across the room over to the chair in the corner. She picked something up and then came back. He couldn't see what she had in her hand. She grabbed his hair and pulled his head back; she bent over, her eyes close to his. She kissed him on the mouth very softly, her lips like velvet on his, her breath hot on his mouth. Quickly, while he was looking at her wide-eyed and open-mouthed, she stuffed something into his mouth. He struggled but she forced her panties down into his mouth.

She returned to the bed, and left him on his hands and knees, the panties gagging him to silence. His mouth was dry and when he breathed his air was filtered through her fine lacy panties, his breath perfumed with her essence. He tried to move, to pull away, but he was too securely tethered and all he could do was look up at her beseechingly.

'This is the lesson,' she said loudly, turning over to the bedside cabinet once more, 'it's my pleasure that counts. You're my slave, you count for nothing.' She sat on the bed and showed him two long black vibrators that she had got from the drawer. She smiled and then opened her thighs wide, letting him see the pinkness of her sex peeking through the dense black bush. The vibrator looked incredibly black against her skin as she rubbed it slowly up and down her thigh.

Very slowly she pressed it up against her sex, teasing herself with it, rubbing it over the lips to her pussy. She seemed to have forgotten Jonathan, who watched her with something approaching pain. When she pressed it into herself she moaned softly, pressing the length of it deep into herself, half closing her eyes with the pleasure. Very slowly she moved it in and out, smearing herself with her wetness, the black vibrator glistening with her juices. In and out, slowly, deep into her pussy and then all the way out. She was teasing, enjoying the delicious thrill of having it far into her sex. She moved it faster and faster, breathing hard, using one hand to drive it into herself and pinching her nipples with the other.

Jonathan tried to get up, but the chains pulled painfully against the collar and he gave up. He felt like a caged animal, filled with adrenalin and excitement but unable to do anything. Victoria was frigging herself harder and harder, letting out little wordless cries. She swapped vibrators quickly, pressing the second one into her wet sex and then taking the first into her mouth. He watched her, his excitement matched by his fascination. She was sucking her juices off the black hardness, sucking her cream into her mouth and swallowing it with evident pleasure. She changed vibrator a second time and then a third, each time sucking the liberally coated tool clean again.

He tried to say something, he wanted to beg and plead for release, but the gag was stuck fast. He could taste her too, taste her pussy in the panties, but he wanted to swallow her thick sexy cream, to suck directly from her pure pink sex, to press his hardness into her. Victoria ignored him, he wasn't there, he didn't matter. She turned over on to her knees and pressed her backside into the air. She took the wet vibrator out of her mouth and pressed it into her backside, crying out with pleasure as it went in. The second vibrator she pressed into her sex, he could see her concentrating her thrust against her apex, playing it against her throbbing clitoris. She cried out ecstatically again and again, her body convulsing with wave after wave of joyful climaxes.

At last she stopped, exhausted, her face and body flushed with pleasure and satisfaction. She seemed dazed, but when she looked up she smiled proudly. Jonathan gave her one last desperate look of longing but he knew it was futile. He was going to be left in torment all night, there would be no release, the fire in his belly was to be left unquenched. His pleasure counted for nothing: that was the first lesson, and nothing was what he was going to get.

Jonathan had dozed fitfully. At times he couldn't tell whether he was asleep or awake, he felt strung out, adrift in a place beyond sleep and consciousness. The floor was cold and hard, the rough blanket that covered him barely kept him warm. He felt suffocated, panicking and struggling for breath and then forcing himself to be calm. Eventually he managed to force Victoria's panties from his mouth. He spat the damp bundle out and sucked the air violently, as if each breath were his first.

He could talk again but there was nothing to say. Victoria was asleep, her nakedness well covered by a thick white quilt. She looked so peaceful and innocent, incapable of cruelty or passion. She was young, in her early twenties he guessed, and yet she was in control of her feelings, much more so than he was.

He lay back down and closed his eyes. Images of Mistress floated into his mind, memories and fantasy, all that had happened and all that was to come. Her voice was still in his head, and in his heart, calling, taunting, laughing at him. Victoria wasn't his Mistress, but he hoped that she would help him on his way: to train him, to teach him how to be the perfect slave for his one true desire.

Victoria woke up early the next morning. She shifted uneasily in her sleep and then she was sitting up, looking at him sitting at the foot of the bed. She stretched and yawned, pushing her chest forward so that her dark nipples were lifted high. 'Did you masturbate last night?' she asked him.

Jonathan coloured. He felt a rush of anger, but checked himself. 'No,' he said sullenly.

'Good,' Victoria smiled lightly. 'Self-denial is good for a servant. You have to remember that, you deny yourself, giving everything to your Mistress. You're a martyr, giving yourself so that another may live and find pleasure. My pleasure is your reward.'

'But you told me that I can't deny myself,' he snapped back. 'Either I deny myself or I don't.'

'Don't play with words,' she told him. 'You know what I mean. You can't deny your true nature, you can't deny yourself. But self-denial is part of that nature, it's part of you. Now, learn to talk to me properly. You call me Mistress. Do it properly or I'll leave you there all day, chained up like a dog who doesn't know his place.'

'I'm sorry, Mistress,' Jonathan said contritely, certain that it wasn't an idle threat.

'That's better. I want to be bathed now.' She got up and came over to the foot of the bed. She was naked and her body looked soft and warm, still clammy from the night's sleep. Quickly she released the chain that held him close to the bed and then released one of the cuffs. 'Go and run my bath now,' she said, watching Jonathan undo the other cuff and then rub his reddened wrists.

He looked up at her. She was waiting expectantly, confident that he would obey. The cuffs were off, he was free and there was nothing that she could do to force him to obey. But she didn't need force. 'Should I keep the collar on, Mistress?' he asked.

'Yes, unclip the chain but keep the collar on. Now, my bath, I don't want the water too hot, nor too cold. And fill the bath well, I hate bathing in a lukewarm puddle.'

Jonathan got up, his back aching as he did so. It felt so good to stand straight and stretch his muscles. He looked at her and then looked away, ashamed that he has submitting with such apparent docility to her demands. It was degrading, but there was nothing he could do to stop himself. She was right, he couldn't deny himself.

The bathroom looked less cramped in the bright sunshine than it had the previous evening. The sun was filtered through the frosted glass of a window, and the light added space and warmth to the room. The wall next to the bath was tiled with old-fashioned white ceramic tiles that extended halfway up the wall. He turned on the taps and sat on the edge of the bath to watch the hot steaming water splashing out. He tested the temperature with his fingers and turned the cold tap on a bit more.

The bathroom cabinet was filled with bottles and lotions, a bewildering array of shapes and sizes; shampoos, conditioners, bath oils, creams and a dozen other things. He selected a shampoo at random and set it on the side of the bath. The water was too cold, he turned the cold tap off completely. It was important: suddenly he was afraid that the water would be wrong, too hot or too cold or not deep enough . . . Why did it matter? He didn't need to care, Victoria meant nothing to him.

He turned the water off and looked at the still surface. He touched his fingers in and the water rippled around the bath, a pattern of light playing back and forth with the tiny waves and ripples. When he had made love to Caroline he had been fascinated by the way their movements were modulated by the water. Her breasts had bobbed on the surface, her nipples moving gently with the ripples and the waves, and when he sucked them they were wet and warm in his mouth. He remembered that when he was fucking her his body had moved through the water, making it flow and ebb with his rhythm, the water overflowing the bath and pouring over the side with every thrust. She had said that it felt like he was pumping oceans of come into her when he orgasmed, gallons of thick cream that poured deliciously from her sex.

'You're turned on again,' Victoria said, walking into the bathroom.

Jonathan looked up at her and remembered where he was, and that Caroline was far away, much farther than he had ever imagined possible. 'I hope it's the way you want it,' he said, pointing to the water.

'Mistress,' she reminded him. 'I don't want that shampoo. Get me something else, and you haven't put anything in the bath water to scent it. Next time I want it perfumed. Pour in some bath oil and mix it in.'

'Yes, Mistress.' He did as directed and poured a small measure of bath oil into the water. She got into the bath and sat back, closing her eyes as she did so, the water lapping around her breasts.

102

'Good, this is just how I like my bath,' she said, her eyes still closed, her face calm and relaxed. 'Now I want you to bathe me, start with my arms and legs. I'm your queen, remember.'

Jonathan lifted her arm and began to soap it gently, working up a rich lather, smoothing his palm back and forth tenderly. She felt so smooth and soft, her arms so small and feminine in his hands. There was something about water and bodies that made him excited, he always associated it with sex, wet bodies were utterly sexy. He finished with her arms and then lifted her leg out of the water. She looked beautiful, long well-turned legs, from her ankles up to the gentle curves of her backside. He kissed her softly, just touching his lips to her toes, not caring whether she approved or not. She said nothing and he began to wash her, rubbing his hands up and down her thighs, thrilling to the feel of her wet skin.

She sat up and he soaped her back, rubbing his fingers up and down her flawless skin. He massaged her shoulders and she sighed softly, opening and closing her eyes. He took her breasts in his hands, cupping them attentively, rubbing his thumbs over the nipples that were hard and erect. He squeezed and stroked her, kissing her softly on the shoulder, soft fleeting kisses lest she should scold him. She was his queen and he wanted to serve her in the way that he might serve Mistress.

Victoria stood up and the water fell from her body as if she were a goddess emerging from the sea. She faced him and he moved his hands up her thighs. She lifted a leg and he passed a palm under her thigh and then over her sex. The mat of bushy hair was wet and soapy and he could feel the warmth of her pussy. She put a hand out and held on to him, balancing herself so that he could get closer. He rubbed back and forth over her sex, her pussy lips running between his fingers, not pressing deep but knowing that he was giving her pleasure.

'Now clean me here,' she said huskily, her voice low and hot. She turned and bent at the waist, pressing herself flat against the tiled wall, her finger sliding between her buttocks.

Jonathan parted her arse cheeks gently and looked at her dark anal hole, beaded with glistening dewdrops of water. He bent forward and touched his lips to her rear hole and heard her sigh. She bent over more, pressing her backside into his face. He kissed her again, just touching his lips against her hole, exploring her tentatively. He'd never sucked a woman like that before, and now the thought made him feel dizzy with excitement.

'Suck me!' Victoria said, and her voice was pleading. Jonathan recognised the familiar ache of desire, he knew what it felt like. But he couldn't deny her, it wasn't his place, it didn't make sense for him to deny her anything. He was the slave. Now it made sense, sort of. He pressed his face deep between her lovely arse cheeks and lapped at her rear hole, passing his tongue down from her pussy and up over her arsehole. He licked her, again and again so that she was writhing with pleasure. He couldn't resist the temptation any longer, he had to do it. His tongue pressed directly against her anal hole and then slipped into her. The tight sheath of muscle resisted his probing tongue but he pressed harder, going into her arsehole. Her moans and sighs guided him deeper, and he tongued and kissed, sucking her, exploring her.

He was aware that her fingers were playing with her pussy, going in and out with the same rhythm as his tongue. She was lovely, it felt so good to be sucking her from behind while she was frantic, pushing down on his mouth while he spread her backside with both hands. His prick had been hard for hours and the excitement had been welling for too long. He felt her freeze, with her fingers deep in her sex and his mouth glued to her tight arse-pussy. She climaxed and so did he, sighing softly, sucking up the last little drops of water that were falling down over her smooth flesh and on to his mouth.

Jonathan spent the rest of the day being trained, as Victoria insisted on calling it. He spent most of the time on his hands and knees, clearing up, dusting, putting things away, while she stood over him and berated him constantly. He wasn't allowed to get dressed; instead he performed all the household chores wearing only the collar around his neck. Several times she had slapped him, on the face or the back, scolding him for being useless or lazy. She had a hard slap and his face or back would buzz and sting; once he looked in the mirror and saw her hand imprinted on his shoulder, red finger marks in contrast to pale skin.

At times he thought that she was trying too hard, shouting at him angrily and then a second later looking back to see what effect her words had on him. He saw it in her eyes, a look of doubt that she tried so hard to hide. There was something a little desperate in her manner, as if she wanted to be the Mistress but knew that she couldn't quite carry it off.

He obeyed at all times, too tired to argue or try to resist her constant demands. She excited him too, he couldn't deny her that. When she lost the doubt, when she acted on impulse, she could be dazzling. Her eyes would be wide and she would be breathing hard; her accent changed without her knowing, her voice becoming harsher, less assured. And then he would react, becoming more submissive, shying away from her rage but enjoying the punishment when it came.

He spent the second night as he had the first, chained to the foot of the bed, allowing himself to be bound without resistance. The only thing he feared was the gag, but she obviously felt no need for it. Her performance with the vibrators was repeated, and he saw that it wasn't for him at all, she needed it for herself. Knowing that added an edge to the excitement he felt, stimulated by the knowledge that he counted for nothing and that the passion was hers and for real.

She didn't wake until very late the next morning. He had been awake for hours and had sat in silence for her. He had waited patiently, dying to speak, to hear the sound of his own voice again, but he knew that as her slave he had to wait. It was hard to think of himself as her slave, but it was what she had decided, and he had promised himself that he would do as she desired.

Once she was awake he bathed her again, but when he kissed her toes she slapped his face and told him off. Her mood had changed and he wasn't sure why. Was it something that he had done? He could think of nothing, but the doubt that he felt made him aware of just how submissive his thinking had become. It was playacting, just a great big game, one of them would suddenly turn around and say 'I don't want to play any more' and it would be over. But much as he tried to convince himself he couldn't quite believe it. If it was a game why did he want to please her so much?

He cooked lunch and did the housework, this time without her running commentary on his performance. This only made him more convinced that he had done wrong, and that she was waiting sullenly for her moment of retribution. It made him excited, imagining all the things that she could do to him, knowing that at any moment she could whip him or step on him or whatever.

Late in the afternoon she stood up and demanded his car keys. He handed them over obediently, trying to fathom from her eyes what she had in mind. She was dressed in a short grey cotton skirt and a loose top. The skirt looked too tight and stretched over her thighs, revealing the full shape of her backside.

'I'll be back later,' she said casually, 'and when I am I expect the house to be spotless. Understand?'

'Yes, Mistress,' Jonathan said quietly, feeling hurt and disappointment that he was going to be left alone. She ignored him and he heard the door slam when she left. He ran to the window and moments later saw her climb into his car, the skirt riding up as she got in, her long thighs looking elegantly sexy.

When she was gone it occurred to him that she was a stranger, and that he didn't even know where he was. And worse, she had taken his expensive car, and he didn't know where. He felt at a loss, alone with himself for the first time in two days. All the time she was there he was her slave, her presence gave him definition, a role to play. Now that she had gone he was himself again, with no definition and no one to play to. It was disturbing, in the same way that his desire for Mistress was disturbing.

He spoke out loud, wanting to hear himself again, but there was nothing to say, his voice merely sounded flat and lifeless. Would Victoria come back? Mistress had used someone else's house, and there was nothing to stop Victoria doing the same. He ran to the window again, looking out at the unfamiliar surroundings. The block curved around the courtyard, closing in on itself, the patch of grass looking dull and lifeless in the fading sunshine. Once the building might have had some charm, but now the facade of dark reddish brown was anything but charming. Everything looked faded and down at heel.

He went into the bedroom and searched quickly through the wardrobe, listening intently for the sound of a key in the front door. She had a lot of clothes, the hangers were squashed together tightly, bulging out so that it was hard to close the door after he had opened it. On a shelf he found some more exotic clothes, dresses and skirts of black leather and sensuous latex, blousons of shiny PVC. Each garment was sheathed in plastic and carefully laid out. The wardrobe door was mirrored, and he turned away from his reflection, unable to look himself in the eyes.

In the bedside cabinets he found the drawer full of whips and chains, an arsenal of corrective equipment that made him shiver with fear and anticipation. It looked dangerous, every item designed to be used on slaves like him. He closed the drawer and sat disconsolately on the bed, unable to decide on what to do next.

The bed felt comfortable after the two nights sleeping on the cold hard floor. He lay back and closed his eyes, letting himself drift off to sleep. He didn't dream, couldn't. His dreams had all been of Mistress, but now even they were gone, as if the slow movement towards her was displacing the fantastic images that had filled his head at night.

He woke up suddenly, aware that somebody was standing over him. Still dazed he looked back and saw Victoria standing over him, her arm raised high over her head. He watched her bring her arm down, moving as if in slow motion, something black in her hand, a blur that hissed as it moved. He cried out when it came down, a resounding smack filling the rooms, its echo drowned by his cry of shock and pain. Her arm was high again and then down, the strap a breath of fire on his exposed backside.

'Please . . . I'm sorry . . . ' he managed to say, trying to get up. She hit him again, a solid stroke across his buttocks, a white hot slash of pain that pushed him back on to the bed.

'This is not what I wanted!' Victoria snapped harshly, her teeth clenched tightly, a look of absolute anger in her eyes. She strapped him again and again, spreading the red heat over his buttocks and down his thighs. He looked back and saw that the wardrobe door had creaked open, he could see himself lying prostrate on the bed, his flesh marked with thick red stripes over his backside. He liked it. He wanted to scream with horror, with shame, to get away from the horrible feeling of pleasure welling up inside him.

He was breathing hard and he could feel his prick throbbing. He was on the verge of climax, the tension in the pit of his belly building to a peak. The hiss and snap of the strap, the rhythm of correction that Victoria was inflicting was hypnotic. He glanced up at her and saw the desire in her eyes; her lips were parted and she was gasping for breath. With every downward stroke he lifted himself up, arching his back and pressing his arse cheeks up to meet the pain that had turned to bitter pleasure.

She moved closer to him and then reached down with her hand, slipping it under his abdomen when he lifted himself to meet the strap. He was moaning softly, eyes opening and closing, everything was blurred. The picture of himself in the mirror drove him on, making him lift himself higher, aching with pain but also aching with pleasure. Victoria took his hard prick in her hand and squeezed it, moving her thumb over the glans so that he gasped with ecstasy. She beat him and rubbed him at the same time, with the same steady rhythm.

Jonathan gasped, clutching at the bed as if he were falling off the edge of the world. He felt blinded, waves of ecstasy passing through him as he spurted thick wads of cream into Victoria's palm. He collapsed on the bed, overwhelmed with the unexpected power of his orgasm. For a moment he had been out of himself, his body convulsed with joyous surges of energy that had taken his spirit over the edge.

He sighed and looked up. Victoria was still standing next to him, flushed and with beads of sweat like jewels on her face. She let the strap go and held out her other hand to show him the thick pool of semen sitting in her palm and smeared over her fingers. She smiled and then quickly turned her hand over and placed it flat on his stinging backside. She smoothed his come over his reddened arse cheeks, rubbing it into the hot flesh she had marked so well. He closed his eyes and sighed, excited again by the feel of her fingers sliding sensuously over his spunk-smeared body.

6

Jonathan looked up at Victoria. She was talking away animatedly, her eyes sparkling with excitement. She looked so young and normal, just like any other young woman getting ready for a night out. Except that he was on his knees, down at her feet, lacing up her thigh-length patent leather boots to match the rest of her shiny wet-look costume.

'Victoria,' he said quietly, hoping that in her good mood she would allow him to talk to her normally.

She stopped talking and looked down at him, as if suddenly remembering who he was and what he was. 'Yes.'

'Tell me about Jonathan de Molay,' he said, turning back to his task, his breath misting on the shiny surface of her boot.

'Jonathan is the most powerful man I've ever met. I don't just mean money and position, though he's got all that as well. No, he's powerful in himself, in his personality. I've never met a man like him; he can read a person inside out with one glance. He has this sort of power about him, he fixes his eyes on you and you know that he is different, and that he can get a person to do anything. It's funny, sometimes he frightens me, he has something magnetic about him. I don't know, I'm not very good at describing things . . . '

'Tell me what he does.'

'He does as he pleases. There's no such thing as morality as far as he's concerned. Everything he does, he does to the limit, especially when it comes to sex. He explained it to me once, how sex is the door to the soul, how with sex you travel into the interior of the person. When he explained it I felt like it was a revelation, that he had the way in. That's when I get frightened, because he knows what's inside himself, and so he knows what's inside other people.'

Jonathan stopped what he was doing and looked at her in the mirror. 'Why does that frighten you?' he asked.

Victoria laughed nervously. 'Because it gives him power. That's what it comes down to, power. Knowledge is power, and he has knowledge about you that even you don't have. It's hard to explain.'

'Give me an example, all you've given me are words,' he said and then saw the look of doubt in Victoria's eyes. 'Please Mistress, please tell me,' he added softly, a tone of pleading in his voice. Victoria smiled, and he knew that it had worked, it was what she had wanted. That was what went on in her mind, she wanted to be the Mistress, it was the thing that drove her. The other de Molay knew that as well, he was certain of it.

'About six months ago Jonathan was doing some business with an American, some fancy guy from New York. He was sort of on the fringes of the scene, the sort of man that gets a thrill from rubbing shoulders with our crowd. I don't know what kind of business they were doing but gradually he got pulled in deeper and deeper. Someone told me that he and Jonathan were really at each other's throat, that the American had a real ruthless streak and was trying to outsmart Jonathan.' She looked appalled at the gall of the nameless American. 'I really don't know what it was about, but I was at a party when Jonathan announced that he was bored and why not fly to Paris for the weekend? Imagine being able to do that, fly all your friends to Paris on a whim.'

'Were you included, Mistress?' Jonathan asked, knowing full well that she was.

'Of course,' she said, smiling proudly. 'We all flew down together, including this American. It was crazy. It was like a scene from a Roman orgy, people being fucked, people being whipped, bodies everywhere. And Jonathan just standing there and enjoying it, like an emperor holding court. The American couldn't believe his eyes, he'd seen some things at our parties, but nothing ever like this. His eyes were popping out, I remember taking his cock and . . . '

'And then de Molay screwed him in their business deal?' Jonathan suggested when Victoria paused.

'Nothing so simple. Jonathan's got this apartment on the Avenue Foch, a really fancy place that must have cost millions of francs. Once we got there the party just carried on, it was outrageous. When things started to slow down he announced that the real fun would begin. He sent somebody out to the Bois de Boulogne and we all settled back to wait. People were taking all sorts of things to keep going, but just the adrenaline of being there was enough really. Then the person returned with our special guest. She was stunning, about six feet tall, long slender legs, better than any model that ever walked a catwalk, and the most perfect bust I've ever seen. I took one look at her tits and felt so jealous, they were perfect. I wanted to suck her nipples the moment I saw them, and honestly I'd never felt like that before. She came in and did this slow sensuous striptease. I mean you'd think that somebody taking their clothes off would be pretty blasé but this

113

wasn't. She looked really sexy, with thick pouting lips like a schoolgirl and dark oval eyes.'

'And?' Jonathan interrupted.

'She stripped off slowly, peeling off an item at a time and sort of dancing softly. There was no music, the place was in stunned silence, but she had rhythm, like she had the music dancing in her head. Then she turned her back to us for the last few pieces. She unclipped her panties and let them slip to the floor and carried on dancing, moving from side to side so that we could see what a lovely tight backside she had. There wasn't a person in the room, male or female, that wasn't creaming it. The American was out of his head, you could see that he was straining at the leash, he had to have her. I don't know what Jonathan was saying to him, he was leaning over and whispering all the time. Then the lights were dimmed, we could just make the outline of her body. I saw her walk across the room, she had poise, I felt her glide past me. She went straight for the American. I heard him say something, then the two of them were together, we could see the bodies in outline, together, whispering, kissing, sucking.'

'And?'

'Do you want me to tell the story or not?' Victoria snapped. Jonathan looked up at her and saw that her nipples were hard, pressing against the shiny skintight material of the dress that she was wearing. Her eyes were distant, as if she could see back to the time she was describing. 'I felt something brush past and then the lights started to go up. We were all in silence still, wondering what was going on. I looked over and Jonathan was at the lights, turning them up again very slowly. Then I heard a sort of muffled cry, I turned back and couldn't believe what I saw. The American and the guest were in each other's arms, on the carpet, he had her lovely tits in his mouth and was biting her

114

hard. But she had this lovely prick, big and long, Christ, I've never seen a man with a prick that big before. And she was fucking the American, while he was sliding his prick over the prick going into him, if you see what I mean. She looked so beautiful, even with her prick, more feminine than any woman I've ever met. She fucked him so hard, really putting her big prick right into him, and he was sort of moaning and crying. He climaxed once, and our guest carried on, she took his prick in her lovely long fingers and worked it up again, still fucking him. He came again and this time he was sobbing. And then she climaxed too, I remember all the muscles in her back went hard, and she cried out like a woman. After that the American was shattered. We flew back later and he was in a daze, like the people you see who've been in some natural disaster. He sort of fell apart, went back to New York a couple of days later, he's never been back since.'

Jonathan was silent. The story was dark, darker than he had imagined it would be, dark and unsettling. Victoria was looking at him intently, he looked away, not wanting to show the fear that had crept into him. 'You're ready now, Mistress,' he said, sitting back.

'Good, now you can get dressed. I've laid out some things for you. Put them on, you're going out with me as well.'

Jonathan looked at the clothes wrapped in a polythene cover that she had placed neatly on the bed. With the clothes there was a collection of restraints, placed equally neatly on the bed. He swallowed hard and felt the pang of fear growing.

Victoria slid into the back seat of the car, her clothes catching the light of the street lamps and shining in the darkness. She wore a velvet jacket to cover her shoulders, the skintight rubber dress seemed moulded to her body, accentuating the contours of her long legs and firm breasts. The short dress was split at the sides, a lattice of tight straps holding it together, her breasts bulging against the black latex.

Jonathan got into the driving seat, feeling very self-conscious. He was dressed in the clothes that she had brought back from her journey earlier, a pair of backless leather trousers and a leather top that seemed to consist of nothing but straps and cuffs. She had allowed him to put on a long overcoat, but when he sat down he felt naked, his backside totally bare. She looked fabulous with her laced-up boots and fetishist dress, but he felt ridiculous.

He started the car and she directed him back to the nearest main road. She had given him an address in Surrey and told him that they had been invited to a party. He was pensive, the story about the American still fresh in his mind.

He had a vague idea of the place they were making for, and once he had been directed on to the main route to Surrey he drove in silence. His backside still stung slightly, and every time he thought about it his prick would go hard and strain against the tight-fitting clothes. It was confirmation that Victoria did have it in her to be a real mistress. Everything about the encounter had been right; even the smearing of his come at the end had been a fitting and degrading finale to his punishment.

Afterwards he had been suitably submissive, kissing her feet ecstatically, begging for mercy. But she was not Mistress, not the austere bitch that he longed for in his dreams. He was in two minds about what to do, more confused than every before. It was tempting to try to forget the other Mistress, to accept Victoria in her place. She didn't have the indefinable quality of

Mistress, she couldn't inspire him with the same worthless feeling, nor would her words ever echo in his mind, but at least she was real.

He was still mulling things over when something occurred to him. 'Was Naomi on the plane when you flew to Paris that time?' he asked, suddenly making the connection. He remembered Naomi saying that the journey with de Molay had changed her life, and it seemed to fit in with the outrageous story Victoria had related.

'Who?'

'Naomi. She was an air stewardess, she flew with de Molay sometimes.'

'I don't know her name. There was an air stewardess on the flight, I remember the look of shock in her eyes once we were all airborne. Come to think of it she was at the party in Jonathan's flat, she saw the thing with the Yank too. Do you know her?'

Jonathan steered the car on to a motorway, accelerating into the fast-flowing traffic. 'Yes, I met her once. She told me that the flight was where she first met de Molay and her Mistress. Do you know who I mean?'

Victoria paused, Jonathan spying in the rearview mirror, caught the look of doubt on her face. 'No. no idea.'

'Come on Victoria, you don't have to lie. Naomi's Mistress is hardly the sort of person you could miss. I guess she's like a female equivalent to him.'

'There's no one like Jonathan,' Victoria said, looking out at the speeding traffic.

'Please tell me. I have to find her, really Victoria I have to.'

'Why, what's she to you?'

'It's hard to explain. You know what I mean, it's hard to put these things into words. She's in my mind constantly, dominating me even in my head. I have to see her, if I don't I'll go mad.'

'She's the one who whipped you, isn't she?' Victoria said, sounding hurt.

'She had me whipped. Everything's happened to me so fast, I don't know what's going on any more. All I know is that she's at the centre of it. I used to dream about her night after night, until she took even my dreams away. Please help me, I'll do anything.'

'I can't tell you, I wish I could but I can't. I know who you mean, you're right you can't ignore her. She's the real mistress you're after, isn't she?'

'I'm sorry.'

'The bitch. I know I'll never be like her, she's been like that from the moment she was born. Christ, I wish I could be like her sometimes. I'm not classy enough am I? Or not tough enough? Tell me, am I?'

'You're . . . too nice. But I saw part of you today that I didn't think existed. You were a real mistress today, it just seemed to come out naturally, without you having to try too hard.'

'It was good, wasn't it? I know what you mean, it just felt right. But it just sort of flares up like that. You're not the first man who's been my slave. But none of them ever seem to last too long. I should be harder, I know . . . Will you be going now?'

It was a good question. 'I have to,' he said eventually, though he knew that the uncertainty was clear in his voice. If she wanted him, if she made a scene he knew that he would stay, but only until Mistress in his mind grew too powerful to be ignored.

'Will you help me? Just for tonight?' Victoria asked softly. They had left the motorway and were driving along a narrow road, lined with trees on either side and winding tightly left and right.

'Sure. Whatever you want.'

'I'm sorry that I can't help you. Jonathan would go mad if he found out that I had helped you in any way. He's that sort of man. But tonight, just for tonight, will you be my slave again?'

'Yes, Mistress,' Jonathan said, and Victoria squeezed his shoulder to show her gratitude. He felt sorry for her, still so young and not a little out of her depth in the glittering social scene that she was involved in.

'Totally my slave?'

'Yes, Mistress.'

They were lost, driving round in circles until they found the private road they were searching for, its entrance partially shielded by a dense copse. They drove up slowly, peering at the big houses as they drove past, grand houses lit up by soft orange spotlights. Each house was alone, walled off from its neighbours, the architecture different in each case. They found the correct house and turned into a gravel drive leading up through a landscaped garden.

Several cars were in the drive, a number with chauffeurs sitting in the front looking suitably bored. Jonathan searched among them to see if de Molay's blonde driver was there, but she wasn't. He couldn't help wondering if Mistress was to be among the guests. The idea made him feel uncomfortably nervous. He wanted to see her, but not while he was Victoria's slave. It had to be right, he was nobody's slave but hers.

He parked the car and they got out. It was cold and when she made him remove the overcoat he was shivering. Before knocking at the door Victoria clipped the chain back on the collar around Jonathan's neck. At the door she handed an embossed invitation to a young woman dressed in a satin maid's uniform, her breasts partially exposed.

Victoria went in, pulling Jonathan after her. He was embarrassed; the leather trousers were tight at the front but cut away around the backside, so that his buttocks, still marked from his beating, were bare. They went into a large room where people were standing around in small groups talking, a mix of people as if it were any other party. But many of the guests were dressed in rubber or leather, their bodies encased in various types of close-fitting garments. On the floor there were several people on hands and knees, most of them only partially clothed.

'Heel!' Victoria snapped absently, and Jonathan fell obediently to his hands and knees. He crawled after her, the chain pulling tight at his collar, aware that his naked backside was even more visible in that position. They weaved through the room, Victoria exchanged polite greetings with several people on the way. She stopped a waitress and took a glass of champagne.

'Vanessa!' she called, waving furiously to another young woman across the room. They made their way across to her, Victoria rushing so that her boots stamped hard on the floor, the heels rising and falling rhythmically.

'Darling, you look lovely,' Vanessa said, exchanging a kiss. She wore a knee-length velvet cocktail dress with matching black stockings and velvet shoes.

'Is he here yet?' Victoria asked, peering across the room with narrowed eyes.

'Not yet. Is he ready?' Vanessa asked, pointing down at Jonathan. He looked up at her and then away, just as he had been instructed. In the momentary glance he had seen her thin face and worried expression.

'Yes he is. He's mine, I told you,' Victoria said confidently, tugging sharply at the chain so that Jonathan shuffled closer to her. 'Look at his back, you can see that he's been a bad boy today.'

Jonathan felt his face and ears burning with shame.

His skin seemed to prickle, as if he could feel the eyes of the two women on him, burning into him.

'There he is,' Vanessa whispered, Victoria and Jonathan both turned towards the door. A couple were entering: he looked to be in his fifties, lean, grey hair, she was younger, good looking, trim figure. They walked over to meet some people, the men shaking hands, the women exchanging kisses and hugs. They were relaxed, the man looked down at a young woman by the heel of one of the guests and made a comment that had the group laughing.

'Have you got the money?' Victoria asked, getting close to Vanessa and almost whispering. She looked nervous, a little embarrassed.

'I'll give you a cheque,' Vanessa said distractedly.

'Not cash?' Victoria sounded disappointed.

'All right, I'll give you some cash with the cheque. Does he know what to do?'

'He's my slave, I told you,' Victoria said firmly, stroking Jonathan's head.

'Have you told him?' Vanessa persisted, this time she looked down at Jonathan with a questioning look in her eyes.

'Not exactly,' Victoria admitted.

'Look,' Vanessa said, addressing Jonathan directly, 'I need a very big favour. Your Mistress is letting me have you tonight, and I'm giving you to the couple that just came in. Now I want you to do exactly as they tell you, to the letter. Tonight they are your masters, not Mistress Victoria. If they say do it then you do it. Is that clear?'

Jonathan hesitated, he glanced back at the couple, still in conversation with the same group of guests. 'What will they want me to do?'

'I thought you said he was ready?' Vanessa demanded, turning to Victoria.

'Jonathan, you promised me,' Victoria hissed, trying not to look alarmed or concerned. She tugged at the chain, pulling Jonathan even closer to her. His face was by her knee, he could see the tight lacing behind her knee, her flesh pressing hard against the black bands. The sight of her soft white skin against the tight restraining bands distracted him, he felt a spasm of desire and wanted to press his lips against her skin, to kiss her where her flesh pressed against the bands.

'I'll pay him if he wants,' Vanessa said desperately.

'No, I need the money. He'll do it,' Victoria insisted. 'Jonathan do as you're told! Please.'

'I didn't realise being your slave meant that I was going to be passed around,' Jonathan complained quietly, careful not to destroy the illusion of subservience. All the other slaves were silent, sitting docilely on hands and knees, sneaking looks at their master or at the other guests.

'Would you do it for money?' Vanessa said quietly, stepping round, blocking him off from view.

'I'll do this for my Mistress,' Jonathan said, and bent low to plant a single kiss on the tip of Victoria's boot. She smiled, relieved.

'I told you he was ready,' Victoria said, squeezing his shoulder affectionately.

'There is just one thing, please Mistress,' Jonathan said to Vanessa, looking up at her sheepishly. 'I would beg you to do me one small favour.'

'Name it.'

'I want a name.'

'A name?'

'Mistress Victoria will explain. She cannot help me, but you Mistress, perhaps you'd help me.'

'Look,' Vanessa said through clenched teeth. 'I need Alex Courtney more than you can know. If you do well

I'll get the contract I need to stop my agency going under. Do well tonight and you can have any bloody name you like. But don't fuck it up, please don't fuck it up.'

'He's coming over!' Victoria hissed. Vanessa turned and Victoria handed her Jonathan's chain.

'Vanessa, how are you? Courtney greeted her expansively, he stepped forward and took her in his arms, kissing her softly on the cheek. 'And Vicky, how are you?'

'Victoria,' she said coldly, putting out a hand for him to shake.

'Where's Sara-Jane?' Vanessa asked, giving Victoria a cold look. 'I thought I saw her a moment ago.'

'Oh you know Sara-Jane, she's around somewhere. And how is business?'

'Fine, fine. And you.'

'It's looking very good, very good indeed. You've heard I'll be in the market for a new agency for the next product launch. Old Jamieson's good, he's got some bright talent on his team, but I'm after something new, something a little different. Is this your young man?'

'Yes, he's been a bit wild today,' Vanessa laughed, it was a high false laugh but Courtney laughed too.

'It's good that he's got a little spirit left in him,' he said, his voice was low, gravelly. 'Looking at the rather sorry specimens on display today I'd say he looked to be the pick of the crop.'

'Perhaps he needs a firmer hand to really put him in his place,' Vanessa suggested. Jonathan looked at Victoria but she studiously avoided his gaze. He felt the fear returning, the same fear that had been triggered by Victoria's story about the American.

'Vanessa darling, you look better than ever!' Sara-Jane said, joining them.

'Vanessa says that her young man here is in need of a little extra discipline,' Courtney told his wife.

'Is that true, Vanessa?' Sara-Jane asked excitedly.

'He's a handful,' Vanessa mused. 'I'm not sure who to turn to. Why, you wouldn't . . . ?'

'Why certainly, my dear girl. I'm sure that Sara-Jane would have no objection if we took him in hand for a night. What do you say? As a favour to dear Vanessa?'

'Well . . . ' Sara-Jane hesitated, and looked at Jonathan dispassionately. 'Okay, as a favour to you. We were on our way out anyway, why not send a car round for him tomorrow?'

'If you're absolutely sure,' Vanessa said reluctantly. 'I could call for him tomorrow. I did have some mock-ups that I had planned on sending to you via Jamieson, but if I come round tomorrow then perhaps I can bring them with me.'

'You mean by-pass Jamieson completely?' Courtney asked, smiling.

Vanessa agreed. 'You could say that,' she said, she smiled too and then handed the chain over to Courtney.

'I'll see you tomorrow then. Bring the mock-ups, and any other ideas you have for the launch. Bye Vicky.'

Jonathan barely had time to look up at Victoria scowling before he was being pulled away. He could hardly believe what had transpired; it was the most transparent set-up he'd ever been witness to, and the most bizarre. It was as if he had stumbled into a private world where sex had replaced money as the ultimate currency. No, it was worse than that — a world where people were part of the currency. He was what it had cost Vanessa to get the deal that she wanted.

'Stand up now,' Courtney said as they got to the door. More people were coming in, Sara-Jane stopped and chatted quietly with another couple; they pointed to Jonathan and whispered something and then laughed.

They got to the car, a sleek silver-grey BMW, and Courtney opened the rear door for his wife, she slipped into the back seat and waited for Jonathan. He looked to Courtney for instructions, and Courtney smiled. Sara-Jane patted the seat next to her and Jonathan got in.

'We've not far to go,' Courtney said conversationally, starting the car and pulling away gently.

Sara-Jane was sitting sideways in her seat. She was wearing an emerald ball gown with a black velvet bodice that cupped her breasts; the skirt was split and drawn to one side so that her long thighs were only partly hidden by the full net petticoats. Her hands were gloved, long arm-length velvet gloves that matched the black velvet of the dress, and her fingers looked black against the tanned skin of her thighs. She was smiling, looking at Jonathan directly, her eyes glittering like the diamonds that dangled from her ears.

'Did you enjoy your spanking today?' Courtney asked over his shoulder as he drove the car at speed down a narrow country lane.

'Yes . . . Master,' Jonathan admitted, avoiding Sara-Jane's eyes.

'We don't bother with that master and servant stuff,' Courtney said. 'I'm Alex and my wife is Sara-Jane. What's your name? Your real name, not a slave name.'

'Jonathan.'

'And why were you spanked, Jonathan?' Sara-Jane asked, touching his bare shoulder with her fingertips. He looked round. She had crossed her legs and her thighs were bare, beautiful long thighs made sexier by dark petticoats.

'I fell asleep instead of doing what I was told,' he

said. It felt strange to be talking about it to strangers, even more strange to be talking so normally, without the master—slave etiquette that Mistress and Victoria demanded.

'Really? So you were taken by surprise,' Sara-Jane said excitedly. Jonathan nodded. 'That's the best way, it's the only way it can really work. Most of this master and servant business is too ritualised to be any fun. There's nothing spontaneous about it, it's too cold-blooded.'

'That's why we don't really go for that scene too much,' Alex added.

'Then why take me for the night?'

'Because after the master—slave stuff you're probably not going to turn out to be too timid when it comes to good sex. And of course using our friend's slaves we are guaranteed a constant supply of interesting partners.'

'Do you like your mistress?' Sara-Jane asked.

'Victoria's all right . . . ' Jonathan stopped. 'Have I just blown it?'

'So you're not Vanessa's young man at all?' Alex asked. The car slowed almost to a halt and then he turned it on to a gravel drive that led to a large cottage.

'Have I screwed up her chances?'

'Not at all. I should have guessed that you belonged to Vicky. I'd never seen Vanessa with a slave before. Still, full marks to her for initiative. You haven't blown her chances at all, Jonathan, in fact she's gone up in my estimation.'

They got out of the car and Alex led the way to the cottage. It was dark and Jonathan couldn't really get much idea of what the house was like. They stepped inside and Sara-Jane took his hand and led him into a reception room.

'Drink?' she offered, going over to the bar. It was

a bright room, with a low ceiling, but the walls were soft peach and several light watercolours added to the sense of space.

'Scotch please.' Jonathan walked over to the bar, conscious all the time of the strangeness of his clothes.

'This is always a bit difficult I imagine,' Alex said, also taking a drink from Sara-Jane. 'But just relax, you're among friends here.'

'Thanks. It's an odd feeling for me,' Jonathan said, turning to face Alex. 'I'm new to this sort of thing. I'm not really used to being a slave, let alone a slave that's handed out for the night.'

'Forget about being a slave,' Sara-Jane advised softly. 'Tonight just be yourself. Relax. We won't beat you,' she looked at Alex, 'will we?'

He shook his head. 'No, I don't think so. I'm bored with that game, I want to try something else. Something we haven't done for a long time.'

'The water game?' Sara-Jane suggested hopefully.

'Sure, why not?' Alex agreed. 'I tell you what, Jonathan. Why not get out of those clothes?' He stepped forward and gestured for Jonathan to follow him. They stepped out of the room and Sara-Jane followed close behind. After a few steps Jonathan turned to look over his shoulder, Sara-Jane had put out her hand and was rubbing him softly over the bare backside. She smiled confidently, and pressed her hands more firmly over him.

'I bet Vicky had a lovely time spanking you,' she said wistfully. 'It's so false usually. But catching you by surprise like that must have been wonderful.'

Jonathan carried on walking, not certain if Alex knew what his wife was doing. His prick was hard and bulging tightly against the leather trousers; he looked down and saw the length of it etched in leather.

Alex led the way down a short flight of stairs and

along a narrow passage. They passed through a door and then into a large bathroom. There were no windows but discreetly placed lights illuminated the room so that it didn't feel confined in any way. The room was dominated by a large circular sunken bath. It was as big as a pool, with steps leading down into the shallow water and white tiles all around the edge.

'Why don't you get comfortable?' Sara-Jane suggested, pressing her hand over the bulge in Jonathan's trousers, her finger tracing the outline of his prick. Jonathan looked up and saw Alex smiling encouragingly. 'Let me slip out of these things,' she said, walking over to a chair in the corner. Alex followed her and when she turned her back to him he undid her zip and she slipped out of her gown and then kicked off her high heels.

'Don't you think she looks lovely?' Alex said, stepping back towards Jonathan. He looked excited, his eyes darting from his wife to Jonathan and back again.

'Yes, very lovely,' Jonathan agreed. Sara-Jane had kept her bra and panties on. They matched the green colour of the ball gown, and the lacy bra pushed up her breasts invitingly.

She walked back to Jonathan and touched his prick, lovingly squeezing it with her fingers. 'Why don't you slip those clothes off?' she said huskily.

Jonathan pulled his top off with difficulty; the leather bands were tight against his skin but once it was loose he pulled it over his head and let it fall to the floor. The trousers had a zip down one side and he pulled it down slowly, aware that both Alex and Sara-Jane were watching.

'Sara, why don't you slip into the water now,' Alex suggested.

Sara-Jane walked over to one side and entered the water slowly, still wearing her bra and panties. There were only three steps and the soapy water reached just above her knee. She smiled when Jonathan finally pulled off his leather trousers and his prick stood hard and firm. She stood in the water and splashed herself with both hands. The panties and the bra turned a darker colour when wet and in seconds were almost transparent. She dropped forward on to her hands and knees and used one hand to splash water all over her. Her skin glistened under the lights, the drops of water like tiny jewels glowing on the surface of her skin.

Jonathan walked to the edge of the bath, excited by the way she was posing in the water, arching her back and pressing her backside up. The water was sliding down her legs suggestively, the panties were transparent and he could see the darkness between her thighs. She turned and smiled to him, pressing her backside higher.

'Hasn't she got a lovely rear?' Alex said proudly.

Sara-Jane took hold of the panties and pulled them up, pulling the thin damp garment into her crotch, so that her arse cheeks were fully displayed to best effect.

'Lovely, absolutely lovely,' Jonathan said softly, half to himself. He wasn't sure what he was supposed to do next, but he knew what he wanted to do.

Sara-Jane reached out and picked up a long thin bar of soap and then very slowly, sensuously, soaped herself between the thighs. The damp panties were soon covered with thick white lather, a white cream oozing down her thighs. She had her eyes half closed and she moaned softly, rubbing the bar of soap up and down between her arse-cheeks and between her thighs.

'Bugger me Jonathan, please, fuck me in the arse,' Sara-Jane said breathlessly, pulling the panties down so that her rear side was bare, the panties a wet line between her thighs.

'Yes, fuck her in her arse,' Alex agreed. He too was breathing fast, his eyes were fixed on her, eyeing her greedily.

Jonathan stepped into the water, he fell into it, vaguely aware of the warm soapy feeling of it against his skin. He was behind her, holding on to her waist, her skin smooth and glassy under his hands. His prick was hard and he pressed forward, rubbing it tantalisingly between her buttocks.

'Please Jonathan, I want it inside me,' she urged weakly, looking over her shoulder, the ends of her long hair dripping wet. She leaned further back and took his prick in the tip of her fingers and guided it against her wet arse hole. He pressed in gently, forcing himself deep into her rear hole. He felt her tense up, holding her breath while his prick slid slowly into her wet hole. The lather dripped down her thighs and was smeared all over him too, a thick cream that felt like velvet against the skin.

'You feel good,' Jonathan said softly, closing his eyes to enjoy the pleasure to the full. She was tight, her rear passage closing around his prick, a warm and loving embrace. Very slowly they began to move together, pulling apart and then joining again. The water flowed around them, moving up and down with the rhythm of their bodies. Each time he thrust into her he felt himself falling through space, powerful waves of ecstasy flowed through him. She moved under him, with him, her body responding to his motion, pushing herself up to meet his downward thrusts.

'That's it, fuck her hard in her arse,' Alex urged from the side of the bath.

Jonathan knew that he had little time. She felt too good, the feeling was too intense. He pressed harder and harder, his abdomen slapping furiously against her gorgeous round arse cheeks, the water lapping around

130

them like a second embrace. He seemed to go deeper into her with each thrust, she was crying and moaning, her voice rising and falling with his body. It felt like heaven, her arse gripping greedily at his thick prick. Her hand was down between her thighs, playing with her pussy while he held her tightly around the waist, pulling her hard into his impaling prick.

She cried out, a loud cry, almost of pain that trailed into a whisper of pleasure. She froze and cried out again and again. His thrusts were hard and deep, pulling his prick out to the very tip and then plunging deep into her anal hole, the pleasure of penetration making them both catch their breath. And then he froze too, his prick inside her arse hole, pumping his thick cream into her ecstatically.

Jonathan fell back into the water, his prick glistening with soap and come. He stumbled but managed to sit himself on the lowest step, breathing hard, his hands shaking a little. He saw a shadow beside him and shifted over.

Alex was naked, his chest flecked with grey hair, his body a little flabby around the middle, but his prick was long and hard. He stepped into the water and knelt down beside Sara-Jane who seemed frozen into position. Her hair was wet and bedraggled, her face was flushed pink and her lips were parted as she struggled for breath. Alex knelt low and then softly massaged her wet arse cheeks, gently pulling them apart to expose the dark jewel that was dripping a thin line of semen down her thighs. He dabbed gently with his tongue and scooped it up into his mouth, he closed his eyes, savouring the taste of it. He swallowed and then went down again, pressing his face between her arse cheeks.

Jonathan watched, fascinated and excited by the loving way that Alex attended his wife. He was pulling her buttocks apart and pressing his tongue deep into

131

her arse hole and sucking out the come. He had his eyes closed and a look of bliss on his face. He sucked her deep, taking the come, that Jonathan had only just spurted, into his mouth and swallowing.

'No! No!' Sara-Jane cried, and Jonathan watched as she reached climax again, her body becoming rigid while Alex sucked her as deep as he could.

Sara-Jane collapsed in the water, and fell forward, losing her grip on the tiled floor of the bath. Alex helped her up, and pulled her on to the lower step, sitting her next to Jonathan. She opened her eyes and smiled at him, looking a little dazed.

'Did you enjoy that, my darling?' Alex said considerately, sitting further back, the water up to his chest.

'Mmm, gorgeous. Jonathan's prick felt so huge, it felt like he was going to split me in half. I just wanted to scream as he was driving it into me,' she said, looking up at Jonathan and smiling happily. 'This is our water game,' she added. 'Next I want you to fuck me in my pussy, fuck me hard, as hard as you like. And then in my mouth. I want you to come in every hole, I want to feel you pumping inside me.'

'And then I'll suck you clean again darling,' Alex added, looking greedily at his wife.

Sara-Jane moved closer to Jonathan and took his prick in her fingers. He was hard again, excited by the game that Alex and his wife played. In its way it was a ritual, like the games that he played with Victoria and which they thought too stylised. We all play games, he thought, closing his eyes as Sara-Jane's lips closed deliciously over his prick. We all play games.

'Jonathan, Jonathan, it's time to go.'

'Caroline?' he opened his eyes and the world swam into view. He was in a bright room, the window was

132

open and the sun was streaming in. He looked round sleepily and saw Vanessa standing by the bed, she was smiling, looking very pleased with herself.

'It's time to go,' she said, handing him the clothes that he had left at Victoria's flat the night before.

'What time is it?'

'Late. You must have been good last night, very good.'

'They know I'm not your slave,' he said, sitting up and swinging his legs off the bed. He felt tired but somehow relieved, it felt as if something had passed, something important but he couldn't tell what.

'I know. Alex frightened the life out of me by revealing all this morning. He was poker-faced and waited while I mumbled some excuse before bursting into laughter. Guess what?'

'You've got the contract.'

'Yes,' she said, deflated. 'He told you did he?'

'Sure, he told me last night. How's Sara-Jane?'

Vanessa smiled, she came and sat beside him, her eyes flicking over his naked body. 'Sleeping. She and Alex want to see you again. They asked me to talk to Victoria about it, I said I would. Are you going back to her?'

'I don't think so,' he said. 'Now, you owe me something.'

'The name,' she pursed her lips. 'Look, Jonathan de Molay is a very powerful man, I don't want to get on his bad side. I'll give you a name and nothing else.'

'Come on,' Jonathan said impatiently. 'I helped you out, or at least return a favour for a favour. Give me her name and where I can find her. No one need ever know where I got the information.'

'Victoria will know, and I can't let her have that power over me. I agreed with her last night, I'd give you a name and nothing else. It's what you asked for.'

133

Jonathan pulled his clothes on angrily. 'Look,' he said, 'if you don't help me I'll go downstairs and talk to Sara-Jane. I'm sure she'll tell Alex all about your unhelpful attitude.'

'You wouldn't,' Vanessa said uncertainly.

'Try me.'

'Jessica Calder-Read,' she said stonily.

'And?'

'I can't give you her address. I'd have him and her on my back. I could kiss this contract goodbye. Please, Jonathan, please.'

Jonathan buttoned up his shirt. He couldn't understand the big deal. All he wanted was an address, yet both Victoria and Vanessa were terrified of de Molay. 'All right,' he relented, 'don't give me her address. Tell me where I can find her, where I can bump into her by accident. No one need ever know.'

Vanessa sat on the bed pensively. Several times she ran her hand through her long brown hair, brushing it back so that it shone in the bright sunlight. 'She has a studio at Jamieson's,' she said at last.

'What's that?'

'It's a design company. Jamieson, Stewart and Grainger. It's her hobby, she dabbled in it at university and sometimes she likes to pretend to be a designer. Her family bought into the company, so she comes and goes as she sees fit,' she said sourly.

'Good,' Jonathan smiled. It was one big step closer to Mistress, one very big step. 'Take me back to Victoria's to pick up my car and then I'll be gone. And no one will ever know what you've done for me.'

'But they'll know what you've done for me,' she smiled.

7

Jonathan could hear the steady beeping of his answering machine even before he had opened the door to his flat. He ignored the mountain of post piled at the foot of the door and went directly over to the answering machine, suddenly certain that Mistress had called while he was gone. He pressed the play button and leaned against the wall anxiously, the tape whirring noisily as it began to rewind.

The tidy stillness of home was a reminder of how wild things had become in his life. It was a reminder too that real life was well ordered, neat and tidy, with nothing out of place and nothing to disturb. In its way that was appealing; the contemplative silence of the flat was what he needed for him to sit down and work things out in his own head. He knew it was the logical thing to do, but he didn't want to. In his heart the only thing he wanted was Mistress.

The tape stopped and switched to play. He held his breath for a second and then exhaled heavily with disappointment. The first message was from work, someone asking for details of a set of computer files. Jonathan fast forwarded to the next message. It was the same person asking the same thing. The third message was apologetic, telling him to forget it, that the files had been found after all.

Jonathan walked back disconsolately to the front

door, leaving the tape on play. He bent down to pick up the post when he heard Caroline's voice on the tape. She was asking how he was and for him to give her a call. And then another call, the same message, this time with a note of added urgency to her voice. He listened in silence to her voice, call after call, asking increasingly plaintively for him to call her. She knew that he was slipping away, moving further and further away from her, and there was nothing she could do about it. She knew it and so did he, there was nothing he could do to stop himself either.

The tape stopped and rewound itself, Caroline's voice still hanging in the air, pleading for him to call. But he couldn't do it. There was no point in calling Caroline, no matter how much it pained him not to. The thing with Mistress was far from resolved, and as long as it wasn't then he could never get her out of his mind. To go back to Caroline like that would be unfair, and unworkable.

He sat by the phone and dialled Jamieson, Stewart and Grainger. It rang once and was picked up by a receptionist.

'Jessica Calder-Read please,' he said with a confidence that he didn't feel. The name sounded strange on his lips, as if he had no right to call her by it. She was Mistress, her other name wasn't for him, it meant nothing, evoking no response and no emotion.

'I'm sorry sir,' the receptionist replied, 'Jessica's not taking any calls at the moment. Would you like to leave a message?' Jonathan paused, not sure what he ought to do. 'Hello sir? Would you like to leave a message?'

'No, no thank you. Can you tell me, is she in the office today?'

'Who's calling please?' the secretary asked suspiciously.

'Just a friend. It's all right, can I call her later?'

'She's going to be busy all day. Would you like to leave a name? I can tell her you called.'

Jonathan put the phone down. She was there, and the secretary knew that Mistress would want to know who had been calling for her. He glanced at his watch. It was still early; he had time enough for a shower and a change before going to see her.

Jamieson, Stewart and Grainger occupied a smart new building by the Thames, not far from Tower Bridge. It looked vaguely oriental, a pagoda of red brick with a roof of ribbed brown tiles that fitted closely together. On one side of the building there was a balcony overlooking the river. A man was standing there, gripping the green handrail and looking at the barges that were moored a little way up towards the bridge.

Jonathan pulled up in the only space in the car park and stopped. There were windows all around the building, and he could see people sitting at computers or drawing tables, people on the phone or gathered together and talking. It looked busy; the young men and women all had the kind of intense look that they worked hard to achieve.

Mistress wasn't really part of this crowd; Vanessa hadn't been exaggerating when she said Mistress was playing a game. He wondered why she bothered; she had everything, what could she possibly get out of associating with these people?

He walked through the double doors into reception. A young woman sat behind a desk; she was immaculately made up, with long blonde hair with darker highlights falling like gold over her shoulders. She smiled routinely when she saw him.

'I'm here to see Jessica Calder-Read, please,' he said, smiling. The reception was only a screen away from the entrance, a coconut plant stood forlornly pointing the way in.

'Do you have an appointment?' the woman asked, glancing down at a list on her desk. She looked doubtful, but when she looked up from the list she was smiling again, an empty smile that conveyed nothing.

'Not exactly, but she'll see me I'm sure,' Jonathan said.

'I'm afraid that Jessica isn't here at the moment. I'm sorry about this. Perhaps if you'd made an appointment . . . '

'That's impossible,' Jonathan said coldly. 'She's here, I know she is.'

'I'm sorry sir,' she said, not sounding at all sorry, 'but she left just a few moments ago. If you'd like to leave a name or card then I'm sure we can arrange an appointment.'

'I know she's here,' Jonathan insisted. 'I called earlier, I was told she was here.'

'You called earlier? You must have spoken to me. Did you leave your name?'

'No, but you said that she was busy and wouldn't be taking calls all day.'

'I'm sorry if there's been any misunderstanding, but Jessica did leave a few moments ago. Perhaps someone else can help you?'

'No,' Jonathan snapped, 'it's got to be her.' He looked at the receptionist with rising exasperation. Did she know something? Was she part of the same group, another Victoria or Vanessa? She had long red fingernails, and delicious-looking red lips. He could see her standing over him, another dominant woman enforcing Mistress's commands. He had to see Mistress.

'Are you all right?' the receptionist asked nervously.

Jonathan realised that his attention had wandered,

he had blanked out for a moment, lost in fantasy. 'I've got to see her,' he said, 'even if it's only for a moment. Please, let me talk to her.'

'But I've explained to you,' she said glaring at him impatiently, 'she went out. She won't be back today. I don't know when she'll be back again. Look, can't you deal with one of the other directors?'

'No, it's got to be her,' Jonathan repeated, but the receptionist had already picked up the phone and was talking into it quietly, all the time fixing him with an angry stare.

'Sorry, can I have your name please?' she asked, speaking up.

'Yes, tell her that it's Jonathan de Molay.'

She repeated the name to the person on the phone and then her expression changed, her eyes widened and she smiled nervously, brushing her hand through her long hair. 'I'm terry sorry, Mr de Molay,' she said putting the phone down briskly, 'there's been some kind of misunderstanding. Jessica isn't here at the moment but Mr Jamieson will be along in a second. I really am terribly sorry.'

'Think nothing of it,' Jonathan said generously.

'No, I'm sorry. I didn't realise who you were,' she said contritely.

Jonathan waited by the entrance impatiently. He caught sight of his reflection in a window. He was trying to appear detached but his face gave him away; he looked jumpy and nervous. He forced himself to relax. He had to if he wasn't going to screw things up completely.

It wasn't Jamieson that came to meet him but someone else. 'Hello, Mr de Molay,' she said brightly, shaking his hand, 'my name's Jeannette. If you follow me we'll go up to Frank's office.'

'Bye . . .' the receptionist said softly, but Jonathan

ignored her. He nodded curtly and Jeannette turned sharply on her high heels and led the way into the building proper. She wore a smart black skirt and jacket, with dark stockings and matching shoes. She was tall and walked with a certain poise and style, balancing confidently on the high heels, the shape of her long legs marking a fine line down from pert backside. Her skirt had a small slit down the back, and as they ascended the stairs he could see the dark band at the top of her stockings and just a tiny glimpse of her pale thigh.

It was just a single flight of stairs that opened out on to a spacious foyer, the light streaming through the tinted glass windows all around the building. There was a low buzz of conversation. One end of the foyer led to a set of open-plan studios where a group of young men and women were gathered round a bank of computers and monitors and were deep in discussion. Jonathan paused for a second then carried on, following Jeannette, crossing the foyer to a group of three offices. The name on one of the doors was Jessica Calder-Read, printed in an oblique and stylish font on the nameplate.

'I hope you have a pleasant visit sir,' Jeannette said, stopping by Jamieson's office. 'If there is anything at all you require please ask for me.'

'There is just one thing,' Jonathan said.

'Yes sir?'

'When will Jessica be back?'

'I'm afraid she won't be back today sir, you've just missed her,' she said sadly, as if she shared in his disappointment. 'I think she's not due back until next week,' she added, 'but no doubt you'll see her before then.'

'Yes, thank you, Jeannette,' he said. She smiled, looking pleasantly surprised.

He didn't knock, but went straight into Jamieson's office. It was the way the other de Molay would have acted, and there was no way that Jonathan was going to act any differently. The moment the door opened Jamieson was up out of his seat, stretching out his hand in welcome. The words he had in mind were frozen though, his mouth was opening and closing wordlessly, confusion etched in the wrinkles under his eyes.

'Jonathan de Molay. Frank Jamieson I presume?' Jonathan shook the offered hand firmly and looked Jamieson in the eye before sitting confidently in the seat in front of the desk.

'Who are you?' Jamieson asked warily, sitting heavily into his seat. He put a hand on the desk, close to the telephone, though his eyes were fixed on the stranger sitting in front of him.

'Jonathan de Molay, as I said. I see there may have been some misunderstanding here. You were thinking of my friend, the *other* Jonathan de Molay.'

'The other Jonathan de Molay?'

'Yes, you see we happen to . . . ' Jonathan heard the office door open and immediately saw Jamieson's expression change from simple confusion to outright horror. He turned to the door and saw a young woman entering. She had dark chocolate-coloured skin, a round face with dark oval eyes and pouting lips that were painted a deep scarlet and looked sensuously glossy. Her black hair was pulled tightly into a bun that made her face look stern, yet this was belied by the sultry look in her eyes.

'No, there has been some misunder . . . ' Jamieson stopped, became silent, slumping back down into his seat with a sense of defeat. The young black woman had a long white overcoat draped over her shoulders, and as she stepped away from the door and into the office she let it fall away, revealing her body underneath.

She was dressed only in a leather harness that crossed her body, thin bands of stiff black leather that were buckled across her, and tightly linked steel chains that hung from the buckles. Apart from that, and her high heels, she was naked, her dark breasts ringed by leather and steel, her ample nipples pressing through steel rings and the dark bush of hair between her thighs obscured by a band of leather buckled under her crotch.

She stepped forward with poise and dignity, her dark eyes fixed on Jonathan. She knelt down in front of him and bowed her head, he could see the soft flawless skin of her back and the way the leather pressed tightly into her soft flesh.

'Charlotte,' Jamieson said quietly, his voice quivering, 'there's been a mistake.'

'Mistake?' she looked up angrily, her eyes flaring.

'Yes,' Jonathan said, and he couldn't help smiling. 'I'm the wrong de Molay, I'm afraid.'

'What the hell does that mean?'

'I'm sorry Charlotte, I didn't know,' Jamieson muttered, looking away from her searching gaze.

'I'm sure the other Jonathan de Molay would have approved,' Jonathan added. 'And I approve of course.'

'You don't count,' she told him contemptuously. 'Well Frank? What's going on?'

'I am Jonathan de Molay,' Jonathan asserted, turning for a second back to Jamieson. 'Look, here, I've got evidence.'

Charlotte took the cards that he offered and looked at them and then at him. Several of the cards had his picture on them as well as the name. She handed the cards back to him and then he gave them to Jamieson. 'You see, Jonathan de Molay is my real name.'

'These prove nothing,' Jamieson said after a while, though not with any degree of confidence. He looked tired and confused, his hand hovering near the telephone all the time.

'You don't need me here,' Charlotte said, picking up her coat and draping it casually over her shoulders again. Her anger seemed to have subsided; she looked at Jonathan curiously, looking him over, as if she were trying to work out who or what he was. He smiled to her but she was stony faced. She turned and left, closing the door after her, though Jonathan was certain that she had wanted to slam the door and storm off.

'What do you want, Mr de Molay, if that's your real name?' Jamieson said, suddenly regaining his composure.

'It is my real name, and you know it is. I want to see Jessica Calder-Read and I want you to arrange it.'

'Don't be ridiculous.'

'What's ridiculous about it?'

'Why did you come here? Who sent you?'

Jonathan made no reply, instead he smiled mysteriously. Jamieson was like an open book, his face reflected his passing thoughts, the flash of anger, the sudden feeling of confidence and finally the doubt. It was the de Molay name — Jonathan realised that it had a certain power and that it could be used to advantage. 'Well?' he challenged.

'I will speak to Jessica this evening.'

'No,' Jonathan said, his confidence growing as Jamieson's diminished, 'call her now.'

'Now?'

'Yes, tell her that I am here and that I would like to see her here, tomorrow if possible.'

Jamieson picked the phone up and pressed a single key. He held the phone under his chin and tapped his fingers impatiently on the desk. 'Hello, Naomi? Yes,

143

this is Frank Jamieson, may I speak with your Mistress?'

Jonathan's heart was suddenly racing, pumping wildly. Naomi was on the telephone, poor beautiful Naomi, with her sad eyes and submissive nature. Lucky Naomi, she was where Jonathan ached to be, beside Mistress.

'I'm sorry, Jessica,' Jamieson said weakly, 'but I've got quite a sticky situation here. There's somebody here claiming to be Jonathan and asking to see you . . . Yes, he just turned up out of the blue waving lots of documents in the air . . . I see . . . Then what should . . . How? . . . Tomorrow? . . . Yes, I understand . . . I'm sorry about this . . . Hello? Hello?'

'Well?' Jonathan demanded, feeling hopeful and excited yet tense and nervous. She had been on the phone, he wished that he had simply grabbed the phone from Jamieson's hand just to hear the sound of her voice. But that would have been too sacrilegious, too disrespectful.

'Tomorrow. She told me to tell you to be here for her tomorrow.'

'What time?'

'Ahhh . . . Before lunch, just before lunchtime. I get the idea that she may treat you to lunch. Yes, that must be it.'

'In that case I will see you tomorrow, Mr Jamieson.' Jonathan stood up and shook Jamieson's hand. He noted the look of relief in Jamieson's eyes and then left. The receptionist sat bolt upright as he passed; she had applied some more lipstick and her smile was rather more desperate as he walked straight past, ignoring her goodbye.

It was getting dark and it had started to drizzle softly when Jonathan saw Charlotte emerge from the office.

144

She was wearing the same long white coat that she had earlier, but this time it was belted tightly around her waist and the collar was pulled up around her neck. He waited for her to proceed a little way from the office before he stepped out of his car and walked briskly after her.

He had waited in his car all afternoon, pondering all that had happened. It was too easy, far too easy to be believable. And Jamieson was no liar, that was obvious. No, Mistress was never going to appear at the office the next day. And Jamieson's comment about her taking him for lunch was as ridiculous a notion as any that he could think of.

'Hello,' Jonathan said, catching up with Charlotte.

She turned to him and then carried on, her heels echoing down the narrow street that ran between two warehouses that had been converted into smart new offices. 'What do you want?' she said as he carried on walking with her.

'Just to talk,' he said quietly. 'Look, this rain's going to get heavier. I've got a car. Where are you going? I can give you a lift.'

They stopped together; the rain was already falling much faster. 'Why should I go anywhere with you?' she asked.

'You know who I am, it's not as if I'm a stranger.'

'Yes, I do know who you are.'

'You've spoken to Jamieson?'

'Of course.'

The sky became a swirl of grey and black and then it cracked, an electric blue vein crossing its surface and then the thunder roared above them. The rain swelled, falling diagonally and sounding like the sizzle of fat on a fire. 'Where's your car?' Charlotte said, pulling the collar of her coat tightly around her.

Jonathan took her hand and they ran back the way

145

they had come, crossing the deserted street as the thunder cracked again. They got into the car and sat silently, catching their breath, watching each other warily. Drops of water were dappled over Charlotte's face, sliding down from her hair over her smooth dark skin. Wet skin and sex, the two were destined to be associated forever in Jonathan's mind. He suddenly felt a stab of excitement that made him catch his breath. Charlotte looked beautiful: her pouting lips were flecked with tiny droplets of water and her skin seemed to glisten in the semi-darkness.

'Well? What did you want to talk about?' Charlotte asked, her voice breaking the heavy silence punctuated by the peal of thunder moving away from them.

'Jessica won't be coming to meet me tomorrow, will she?'

'And Frank thought he had you fooled,' she said, smiling.

'He's not very clever, is he?'

Charlotte shook her head. 'Not very clever, and not there for very long either. It's only a matter of time before Jessica and Jonathan have him in a retirement home and they'll be running the company.'

'Is he clever enough to realise that?'

She shrugged. 'If he doesn't know it then he's the only one. But that's not what you want to talk about, is it?'

'I don't know what I want to talk about to be honest. Jessica won't be meeting me tomorrow, so who will?'

Another shrug. 'Look,' she said quietly, 'I don't know you and I don't really want to get involved in this. The rain looks to be easing up, I'll be going . . . '

'No, please don't. Where do you want me to drop you off? I can take you wherever you want. Please.'

'Fulham, take me there.'

The traffic was heavy and slow-moving, the heavy rain slowing things even further. Charlotte settled back in the passenger seat, loosening her coat and kicking off her shoes. 'It's all right, I don't have my fetish gear on,' she said sarcastically when she caught him peeking at her.

'Sorry,' he said sheepishly. 'I just wondered, that's all.'

'That was Frank's idea, not mine.'

'But you went along with it, even though the old man appears a bit frightened of you.'

'Yes I think you might be right,' she laughed. 'He's got an inkling of an idea of what Jessica and Jonathan are like, so he's doing his best to keep up, but most of the time he doesn't know what's going on. I feel sorry for him really.'

'How did you get into all this? You look so . . . so . . .'

'Normal?' she suggested.

'Yes, so normal. Not, perhaps that's not the right word.'

'No, I think it is,' she said. 'People like you aren't normal, you're extraordinary, different, sometimes very different.'

'And what are you then?'

She pursed lips, thinking it over. 'I guess I'm one of the extraordinary people as well. You see, I think that great passion and everyday life don't go together. Normal life, routine, that kills passion, which is why we're different.'

'You didn't answer my question,' he pointed out. 'How did you get involved in all this?'

Charlotte looked at him sideways for a moment, then turned away again. She rubbed the mist from the passenger door window and peered out into the rain-soaked street. 'It was at university,' she said, just when Jonathan had decided that she wasn't going to tell him. 'I was living with my boyfriend at the time; he was a student at the same university. One day we were invited to a fancy-dress party and when I couldn't decide what to go as he said he'd pick the outfit for me. He chose a latex catsuit for me, complete with stiletto boots and a whip. I just laughed, I thought it was meant to be a joke. But when I put it on it did make me feel different, very sexy, very hot.'

'What did he go as?'

'Can't remember. All I remember is entering that room and everyone going quiet, everyone. They were all looking at me, and I mean really looking. This thing was tight, it looked like it had been moulded onto me, it felt like I was naked yet giving nothing away. The girls were furious, their men just couldn't take their eyes off me. I felt so good, so powerful, and it was a new feeling for me. I'd never been powerful before, I'd never known what it was like to feel so strong. I remember that I felt like I was on air, I spent the whole party surrounded by men, ordering them about, making them do stupid things just because I felt like it. I must have been half drunk, one of the guys there was annoying me so I beat him with the whip, just a couple of playful strokes across the back. I felt so hot, my nipples were fixing to explode, they were pressed right into my catsuit, all the men were pointing at them they were so big. And when we finally got home my boyfriend just begged me to sit on his face. The catsuit had a zip that went right between the legs, I squatted over him and undid the zip, really slowly and then pulled the opening apart so he could lick me properly. He sucked like I was the best thing he'd ever tasted, going deep into me. I climaxed again and again. It was the best sex we'd ever had.'

'And that's how you got into this scene?' Jonathan asked after Charlotte had fallen silent.

'What?' She looked lost. 'No, not exactly. We both

sort of put it down to one of those things, you know, too much drink and a bit of dope at the party. But a couple of weeks later I came home and he was all agitated. You know how it is when someone wants to say something but won't. I eventually got it out of him, he seemed really embarrassed, a bit ashamed actually. One of the men at the party had been going on and on about me and I think this had made Stuart jealous. They had some sort of row and then this guy told Stuart that he would pay for me to humiliate him. Those were his words, he wanted me to humiliate him. I thought it was a horrible idea but Stuart seemed quite taken by it. In the end he talked me into it . . . '

'Or you allowed yourself to be talked into it,' Jonathan suggested.

' . . . Or allowed myself to be talked into it. I had one condition, that Stuart first get my costume back for me and that he be there as well. Stuart and the other guy agreed to it at once. And that was it, I dressed up like a dominatrix and strutted up and down the room abusing the two of them. I made them beg for mercy, shouted at them, they both wanted to kiss my boots so I let them. I sat on the other guy's back and beat him with the whip. I stripped the two of them off too. I just felt so in control, my word was law. I beat the other guy with the whip until he climaxed, he was crying like a baby, weeping and thanking me at the same time. When he was gone I made Stuart tongue me again until I'd come a dozen times. With the money I got I went out and bought myself my own fetish clothes. I was hooked on it, hooked on the pleasure, on that feeling of pure blinding pleasure.'

'And you're still hooked,' Jonathan concluded.

Charlotte reached across the car and felt his hard prick. 'Yes, and so are you I guess,' she smiled. 'You could say I worked my way through university.

149

Students and lecturers, male and female, they all loved me and it paid for my studies. I enjoyed every second of it. And still do. Stuart is Frank Jamieson's son, and he loved the idea of me beating his father, that's why he got me the job there.'

'And have you?'

'No, never. Like I said, I feel sorry for the old man. He's surrounded by devious scheming people, he's got enough to handle without me. Turn off here, and then second left. It's the first house on the corner.'

Jonathan did as directed and pulled the car to a halt outside a tall Victorian town house. 'That might be true,' he said, 'but Jamieson's still terrified of you.'

'He shouldn't be. Look, can you cook?' Charlotte said, turning to face him.

'Yes, I suppose so,' Jonathan admitted, thrown off balance by the change in tack.

'Good, I can't be bothered to cook tonight, you can do it for me,' Charlotte said confidently. She got out of the car without waiting for Jonathan to reply and crossed over to her house.

It was a tall white house, part of a terrace that stretched along the length of the road. Jonathan followed, through the wrought iron gate and up the stone steps to the heavy back door. They went in and she led the way through the hall and up a flight of stairs. Her flat was on the first floor and she opened the door and let him go in first.

'In there,' she pointed him to the kitchen then she disappeared into another room.

The kitchen was unobtrusively modern, with lots of space and everything stylishly integrated. There didn't seem to be very much in the way of food, and so he sat and waited for Charlotte to return. It was the oddest invitation to dinner he'd ever had, but it was like Charlotte, very direct and very difficult to resist. He could see why she had made such a successful mistress at university. Where Victoria had to try hard, Charlotte's manner came naturally. That was what counted, accepting what came naturally. And that's why Jessica was so important, there was nothing false about her at all. She was a mistress instinctively and without a doubt.

'Well? What are you going to make?' Charlotte wanted to know, returning to the kitchen. She had changed and was wearing a long satin robe tied tightly around her waist.

'There doesn't seem to be very much in,' he explained, getting up and going over to the fridge. He opened it and showed her how empty it was; the shelves were largely bare and what was in the cabinets looked far from fresh.

'I hardly ever eat in,' Charlotte shrugged. 'Improvise, do what you can, I'm not very hungry anyway.'

'Why don't I call for a takeaway?' he suggested.

'No,' she said after a moment's thought. 'I want you to cook for me. And you can tell me all about you and Jessica.'

'Have you got any rice? I'll make some rice and stuff, is that ok?'

'Sure. Now, about you and Jessica?'

Jonathan started on the food, gathering all the ingredients he required. 'There's not really anything to say about me and Jessica. I got this weird phone call in the middle of the night. I listened to one woman beating another woman, punishing her for daring to look at Jonathan de Molay. That was the start. I've been trying to get close to Mistress ever since.'

'That's all there is to it? A wrong number and now you're hooked.' She laughed and her laugh was infectious, Jonathan laughed too.

'I still find it hard to believe just how much my life has changed,' he said. 'Everything was so ordinary before, now everything that's bizarre appears completely natural.'

'It sounds like you've got a lovely little obsession on your hands. You shouldn't fight it, you should nurture that little flower of passion. Most people go through life without ever been touched by passion, or by a desire so strong it outshines everything else.'

'Does that mean you'll help me find Jessica?' Jonathan asked hopefully.

'No, it's your journey, not mine. You have to find her yourself, and you'll have to decide when to stop and when to carry on.'

Jonathan finished making the meal in silence. For a moment his hopes had risen, Charlotte seemed to understand the things in his mind, and he hoped that would be enough to convince her to help him. But it wasn't to be. Perhaps it was a journey and perhaps it wasn't. He didn't care, he didn't want to learn about himself, or to discover the meaning of life or anything else like that. His needs were simple, all he wanted was Mistress.

Charlotte was right though, he hadn't seen it in terms of an obsession, but that's what it was becoming. Every waking moment, and even in his dreams, his thoughts and desires were focused on Mistress. And the more distant, the more unapproachable she became, the more he wanted her.

Charlotte opened a bottle of wine, apologising that it was red when a light white would have suited the simple meal. They ate in the kitchen, the conversation matching the meal. They avoided talking about anything important, but Jonathan couldn't help wondering what was going on in her head. Several times he caught her looking at him with unexpected intensity,

152

and then she would smile and the look would be gone.

'Do you know what to expect from Jessica, from Mistress, when you meet her?' Charlotte said, pushing her plate away. She had both elbows on the table and her robe had become loose so that he could glimpse the dark valley between her breasts.

'Yes, a pretty good idea,' he said, sipping a mouthful of wine.

'I'll show you,' she said, and smiled broadly. 'Go into the next room and strip off. I want you on your knees. You owe me.'

'Why so cold-blooded?'

'What's so cold-blooded about this?' she said defensively. 'When I walked into Jamieson's office, that was cold-blooded wasn't it? Weren't you turned on by it?'

'Yes.'

'You tricked me there, you pretended to be the other Jonathan de Molay. Now it's my turn to pretend to be someone else. I'm going to be your Mistress, the one you adore. Now, do as you're told.'

Jonathan obeyed, his heart racing. There was iron in her voice, a voice that he had to obey, knowing that she would be capable of the strictest discipline. He crossed the kitchen, aware of her eyes fixed on him, no longer smiling.

He went into the sitting room and sat in an armchair to undress. The memory of her soft dark body hadn't left him, she was beautiful, her breasts were tipped with dark brown nipples that had strained against the steel chains. He realised that he was afraid of her, afraid of what she might do to him. It wasn't the punishment, it was his reaction that he feared. He knew that once it started he wouldn't be able to resist, he would yield to her totally, letting her do whatever she wanted. She had it, the indefinable thing that was driving him crazy.

153

In a second he was naked, sitting on his knees in the middle of the room. He was in an ordinary room, a sofa behind him, an armchair to one side, a fireplace at the end. It came to him suddenly, a mad feeling of panic that overwhelmed him. He wanted to get up and run away, to leave everything behind. He wanted Caroline, she was there in his mind too, always watching, waiting.

The door opened and Charlotte was there. She was framed in the doorway, the strong light from the hall throwing her shadow over him. He swallowed hard, his palms were sweaty and he felt nervous. She wore a shiny black bra with steel studs around the open nipples and a zip running down the middle. The bra was matched by a pair of briefs with studs on the side and a zip running down to the crotch. Her boots were thigh length and shiny, the strong light from the hall adding to the glossy sheen. Her hair was brushed back again, making her look cruel and austere.

'It's a much nicer costume this time,' he said quietly, then regretted it. His voice sounded weak and reedy in the heavy atmosphere. She ignored him, looking down her nose at him with studied contempt. He swallowed hard again, his throat was dry but his hands were damp with sweat.

She stepped across the room purposefully, the impossibly high heels of her boots cracking hard on the pine flooring. She passed him and he looked up at her long thighs and pert backside pressing against the plastic panties. He crawled round to follow her but stopped. She would tell him what to do, he would obey.

There was a long black case on the mantelpiece which she opened very carefully and from which she withdrew a long leather strap. She turned to face him and he knew that it was for him.

'Here!' she hissed, pointing down at her heels.

'Yes, Mistress,' he whispered. It felt so good to call her that, a thrill of pleasure passed through him. Mistress, Mistress, Mistress. It was a mantra, a soft passing of the breath that would lead him to heaven. He crawled along the floor, looking up at her wide-eyed.

He stopped and kissed her boots without being asked. He pressed his lips against the pointed toes of her boots, lapping at them like a dog. She stamped her heels hard and he winced, pulling away from her.

'I don't think you've ever been really punished,' she spat. 'Now's the time that you learn what it is to have a mistress. I want you on the sofa, lying on your back. Now!'

Jonathan scurried across the room and lay on his back on the soft leather sofa. His skin was warm against the coolness of leather, but it felt soft and comfortable. He closed his eyes and when he opened them she was standing by him, the leather strap held tightly in her hand.

'This is my best friend,' she said, squeezing it lovingly. 'It does so much for me. It's so loving, so very loving. It loves to stroke people, to touch and caress them.'

'Yes, Mistress.'

Charlotte reached down and touched his prick, it was hard and throbbing. She smiled, wrapping her fingers around it lovingly. Jonathan sighed, the feel of her hand was good, she was stroking him with a warm and loving caress. And then he screamed.

'Silence!' she hissed through clenched teeth. She raised the strap again and brought it down flat on to Jonathan's hard prick. He screamed again, twisting and writhing as the white hot pain flashed like a fire through him. He tried to get up, to push her away but she lifted her heel and stamped him down.

'Please . . . please . . . ' he begged, on the edge of

155

hysteria. His prick was aflame, yet it was hard and throbbing with pleasure and pain. She hit him again, the stinging snap of leather on flesh drowned by his scream.

Charlotte beat him again and then dropped the strap to the floor. She lifted her heel and pressed it down on his chest, the point digging into him. He opened his eyes and saw her slowly unzipping her shiny panties, the zip sliding under to reveal the dark patch between her thighs. She moved round, her heel passing over his face and he kissed it passionately, as if trying to put out the fire that was burning inside him.

'Now I'm going to fuck you,' Charlotte promised, her voice hot with desire. She was astride him and held his reddened prick in her hand. She sat down slowly, guiding his hardness deep into the warmth of her pussy.

Jonathan sighed, she was wet and the sensation of his prick sliding into her was heavenly. Waves of pleasure pulsed through him, the heat of his prick was salved by the thick cream from her delicious pussy. She began to ride him, moving back and forth over his prick, pressing her backside down onto his abdomen. He was gasping for breath, driven to the edge of insanity by the waves of ecstatic pleasure pulsing through.

'I'm going to fuck you all night . . . ' Charlotte whispered, she closed her eyes and sighed, moving faster and faster over him.

'Yes, Mistress . . . Yes . . .' Jonathan moaned, he froze, he was on the edge ready, aching with want. He opened his eyes, she was on him, a beautiful demon sucking his strength and energy.

Charlotte raised her hand and dealt him a blow across the face, the slap resounding across the room. He called out, touched his lip and drew blood. She closed her eyes and rode him faster, moving with the rhythm that she wanted, for her pleasure. Jonathan knew that his pleasure was incidental, he didn't matter. His body was aflame and his lip was bleeding, but that was good, it was what she wanted. He felt her gasping for pleasure, manically bucking up and down over his prick. She climaxed, screaming uninhibitedly, her voice strangled with pleasure. He lifted himself into her and froze, his thick spunk shooting deep into her pussy, merging with her creamy emissions.

'Now suck me clean,' she whispered, slowly dismounting. 'And then I want you on your knees.'

'Yes, Mistress,' Jonathan obeyed, and for a moment he didn't know who she was, whether she was Jessica or Charlotte or Victoria. She was Mistress, that was all, and he loved her.

8

'Who will I meet if I turn up at your office today?'
Jonathan asked Charlotte as they stepped out of her
house.

'I don't know,' she said, pulling the heavy oak door
shut. It was a bright but cold morning and she wrapped
her coat around her tightly.

'Jamieson never told you?'

'No,' she said, walking down the steps one at a time
to the pavement, 'but it's hardly likely to be Jessica,
is it?'

'No, I guess not,' he said morosely. He knew it
wasn't going to be Jessica, but he still felt a twinge of
disappointment.

'Look,' Charlotte said, turning to face him. 'I don't
think we ought to see each other again, OK? Things
can get complicated, and I don't want that. So, let's
just leave it at that.'

'Sure, if that's what you want,' Jonathan said, taken
aback by her request. Without thinking about it too
much he had assumed that he was her slave, that she
had somehow taken possession of him in the way that
Victoria had.

'Yes, it is what I want. Bye.'

He watched her go, the long coat wrapped tightly
around her blown by the breeze. His body ached all
over, she had been a ruthless and strict Mistress, more

severe than he had ever imagined possible. But she had taken him out of himself, so that the blinding white heat of pain had become pleasure, and it had felt so good he wanted to scream.

He felt cold, his hair standing on end. He was alone, more alone than he had ever been. There was nothing for him to do and nowhere to go. There was time now for him to take stock, to sit back and work it all out in his mind; where he had been, what he had done and where he was going. But he didn't want to. He felt constricted, suffocated. If he sat down to think then the conclusions were going to be frightening, he knew it instinctively.

The streets were full of people going to work, hurrying along purposefully, their faces set against the sharp breeze, their bodies locked like armour. That was what he had been, he saw his reflection in their faces and in their movements, moving fast, not letting anything get in their way. To what purpose? Was it really less meaningful than chasing a fantasy?

He lost track of time. At some point he found himself down by the river, looking into the murky waters of the Thames. The eddies and pools of the water drew him, he watched it lapping against the embankment, sometimes moving slowly, sometimes rushing, always impossible to gauge its depth. People jogged past, wearing brightly coloured tracksuits, their faces flushed and set hard with grim determination.

He followed the river until he recognised the streets around him as being close to where de Molay lived. It hadn't been intentional, but now that he was close he couldn't help but be curious. In a sense he was still no nearer an understanding of what his namesake was like. That he was powerful was clear, but not much else.

Jonathan walked briskly towards de Molay's house.

There was no plan, just a desire to see the house, to try and get some sense of the man from it. He rounded a corner and a car swept past him, long and sleek, flying away on a current of air. The blonde chauffeur was at the wheel, her face impassive, her long hair swept back over her grey uniform. Jonathan caught his breath, he almost felt weak. There in the back of the car was de Molay, partly obscuring a second passenger, a woman. It was Mistress.

He turned and broke into a run, a mad panic of a run. The car had turned the corner and was moving out on to the main road along the embankment. Jonathan ran with all his strength, his feet pounding the ground, propelling him forward. His breath came hard, he was gasping painfully, his lungs aflame. The car accelerated out into the traffic and was gone in a moment, swept away in the blur of movement.

The car was gone and Jonathan stopped, almost collapsing as his legs gave way under him. He bent over double, clutching his chest and stomach, aching from the unexpected exertion, his legs were twitching and he felt weak at the knees. There was no time to waste. He turned and forced himself into a slow jog, his face clenched grimly. There was still time for him to get to Jamieson's office before lunch. That was where Mistress and de Molay were headed for. It had to be that, he felt sure of it.

Jonathan drove with no sense of danger, his car speeding through narrow side roads to avoid the traffic. He swerved to avoid another car pulling out, and was gone by the time the other driver had even wound down his window to shout and swear. His chest was burning all the time, several times he fought back waves of nausea that had him retching violently. But he fought it back, he fought it all back, compelled by the image of Mistress in the back of the car with de Molay. He had only glimpsed her, a fleeting shadow of a glance but it evoked all the memories, all the phantoms of desire in his heart and mind.

Time was dragging, no matter how fast he drove it was still too slow. He couldn't think straight, everything was fogged. Mistress and de Molay were together, they were going to Jamieson's office, they were going to meet him, they were . . . There was no room for doubt. The car was going too slowly, he pressed the accelerator flat and the car roared. The parked cars were a blur of colour. He crossed a junction without stopping, oblivious to the screech of brakes as cars swerved to avoid him.

And finally he was there. He swerved into a corner, jumped out of the car and broke into an exhausted run. The sweat was pouring from him, running down his face and back, his clothes sticking to him. He felt cold though, the sweat pouring from him was icy, as if his frozen being was melting.

He pushed into the building and went up to the reception desk. He fell forward with both hands, leaning across the desk, wheezing heavily. 'Mistress . . . I want to see Mistress . . . '

'Mr Jamieson will see you in a moment,' the receptionist said coldly, pulling away from her desk with an unconcealed look of distaste.

'I don't want to fucking see him!' he roared angrily. The receptionist shrank from him, stepping back into a corner. 'Where's Jessica? Where the fuck is she?' he demanded at the top of his voice.

'She's not here . . . honestly, she's not here . . . ' she whispered shakily.

'I'm sorry, Mr de Molay,' Jamieson said, appearing from nowhere. 'Jessica Calder-Read has no wish to see you and has asked me to tell you that. She has also instructed me to inform you that if you do not desist from your unwelcome attentions she will consult a solicitor.'

'Don't give me that shit!' Jonathan raged furiously. 'Where is she?'

'She is not here,' Jamieson said stiffly.

Jonathan moved towards him, fists clenched, breathing hard, blinded with anger and rage. Jamieson knew. He knew everything; where Mistress and de Molay were, where they lived, what they did. He was on the inside and Jonathan was on the outside looking in. 'Tell me! Tell me where they are!' he demanded.

Jamieson stepped back, his eyes suddenly wide with fear. 'Please, calm down Mr de Molay . . . '

'Shall I call the police?' the receptionist asked, moving quickly to the phone and picking it up.

'No, there's no need for that, is there, Mr de Molay?' Jamieson said softly.

Jonathan looked at him for a moment. All the anger and disappointment welled up in that instant. He wanted to weep. His life was been wrecked, there was nothing left. Mistress had infected him, like an unseen and debilitating virus. His life wasn't his own, she controlled him, even when she was far away. 'I just want to see her . . . ' he whispered, his voice quivering weakly.

'I understand . . . ' Jamieson said softly. 'We've all been in love before. You just have to forget her, that's all. I know it may be painful, young man, but in time you'll forget her. You'll find someone else, someone who'll love you in the same way.'

'You don't understand,' Jonathan said, shaking his head. He wanted to laugh and cry at the same time, to fall on the floor and weep uncontrollably and laugh hysterically. 'You've got no idea what's going on,' he said finally, 'none at all.'

162

'I think you ought to leave now,' Jamieson said more firmly.

Jonathan hesitated but there was nothing else to do. The receptionist still looked shaken, her eyes were wide with fear and she looked drained of colour. He turned and left, feeling empty. He stepped outside and looked up. Charlotte was at a window looking down on him. She waited for a second, stony-faced, and then disappeared from view. She had known, she too was on the inside, part of the hidden world that he could only dream of gaining access to.

He got back to his car and collapsed. He slumped over the steering wheel, completely hollow and totally numb.

There was always alcohol. When the thoughts became too painful, when it all got too much, there was that. It was the only escape that Jonathan had, escape from the thoughts of all that had been and all that might have been. His drink-filled days and nights, and he had become a man without time, were punctuated only by the ring of the telephone which always reawakened his dying hopes.

Most of the calls were from Caroline. He listened to her guiltily, letting her speak to his answering machine. He felt too ashamed to speak to her, dimly aware that he had let himself down in a way that was unspeakable. She was the only link to his old life, to the time before Mistress had shattered everything. And it was painful. It hurt to think of Caroline, and to think too of who he had once been.

The call from Charlotte came unexpectedly. For the first few seconds he had sat blankly listening to her talking to the tape. Then he realised it wasn't Caroline, the voice finally connected, and he scrambled for the phone before she put it down.

163

'I thought you were out,' she said, sounding surprised when he cut off the answering machine.

'Yes . . . Yes I was, I only just came in,' he lied unconvincingly. He felt glad to hear her voice, almost light-headed with joy.

'I know we said we'd never see each other again, but I thought you wouldn't mind doing me a favour.'

'Anything, anything at all,' he said eagerly.

'I'm having a party at my place in a couple of days and I was sort of hoping that you'd help me.'

'Help?'

'Yes.' She paused, as if looking for the right words. 'Helping. Like serving drinks and that sort of thing.'

'Oh,' Jonathan said disappointedly. 'You want me to be a waiter.'

'Well, it's a bit more than being a waiter. More like a servant. It's one of *those* sort of parties.'

'Yes, I'll do it,' he agreed, trying to sound as if he were only doing it as a big favour. 'By the way, about that day at your office . . . '

'The day you made a complete idiot of yourself?' She made it sound almost forgivable.

'Yes, that day,' he smiled to himself. 'What happened afterwards?'

'Everyone said you'd made a complete idiot of yourself,' she laughed.

'What about Mistress?'

Charlotte hesitated, he could hear her sucking in her breath. 'She was told all about it.'

'And?'

'Nothing. That was it,' she said, and then added, 'I can't tell you any more, Jonathan, I simply can't.'

'But that's not fair,' he protested.

'I'll see you in two days then,' she said, ignoring him curtly. 'Be there at about seven. Bye.'

'But Charlotte . . . ' Jonathan said, and found himself speaking to the dialling tone.

He looked around the flat for the first time in days and saw what a mess the place was in. Empty bottles and discarded food littered the floor, piling up in corners in haphazard patterns. He rubbed his face, felt the rough stubble on his chin and the sticky eyes. Charlotte had told him nothing, but he suddenly felt elated. He was back in with a chance. Through Charlotte he was going to get to Mistress, he just knew he was.

Jonathan arrived at Charlotte's early, giving in to the feeling of excitement that he'd felt from the moment she had called him. Excitement mixed with trepidation, certain that her party was going to prove to be important in some way. It was a feeling, a hunch more than anything else.

'I'm glad you're early,' Charlotte said, showing him into her bedroom.

'Good, I was afraid you'd be angry.'

'No, it gives you plenty of time to try your uniform on,' she smiled.

'Uniform?'

'Oh, didn't I tell you?' Charlotte asked innocently, smiling broadly, her dark eyes sparkling mischievously.

'No you didn't,' he said suspiciously.

'It's your maid's uniform. You have to wear it.'

'A maid's uniform? No, no,' he stepped back from her, shaking his hands to emphasise the point.

'But it's such a pretty uniform. Black satin with pretty white petticoats and frilly white knickers . . . '

'No.'

' . . . And black seamed stockings and suspenders. It's even got a pretty little cap to go with the wig I've got you.'

'No. Absolutely not.'

Charlotte stood with hands on hips looking at him, her lips pursed to show her disapproval. Jonathan wasn't sure whether she was joking or not. If she wasn't he knew that he risked a sound spanking or caning.

'In that case you can wear a white shirt and black trousers. It won't look half as good as the uniform,' she added sourly.

'Thanks. I'll be good, I promise,' he said, wanting to please her now that he'd got his way. He still wasn't certain whether she had been joking or not, there was no laugh of triumph from her that she'd duped him. And if it hadn't been a joke then he knew that she had only relented because she wanted to, not because of his protestations.

'You better be good,' she warned. 'I've got some good friends coming round tonight and I want everything to be the best. I won't be forgiving of any mistakes. I'll thrash you in front of everybody if I have to.'

'Yes . . . Mistress,' he said, and felt a thrill run through him.

'Good, that's how you address my guests as well. It's Mistress and Master and complete deference. Remember that.'

'I understand.'

'Go and check that the caterers have done a good job while I get dressed.'

'You don't want me to dress you?' Jonathan asked hopefully.

'I'm a big girl now,' she teased, cupping her large breasts so that her nipples pressed against the velvety material of her dress.

'Yes, Mistress,' he said, backing slowly out of the room as Charlotte slipped out of her dress. He lingered by the door for a moment, eyeing her beautiful dark body, her delicious breasts tipped with chocolate-coloured nipples that were already hard and erect.

Reluctantly he left her and went into the kitchen. The food was still in silver trays ready to be served, each course carefully prepared to be at its best. It smelt good, making Jonathan realise how hungry he was and also that the food wasn't for him. The furniture in the sitting room had been rearranged, the dining table had been moved from the kitchen and extended, all eight places were set. He dimmed the lights and lit the candles.

'Well, how do I look?' Charlotte asked.

Jonathan turned to find her standing by the door. She was wearing a simple black dress made of shiny black plastic buckled at the sides. Her flesh pressed against the buckles at the side, and it was plain that she was wearing nothing else underneath.

'Lovely,' he said softly. He wanted to get down on his knees and kiss her heels to show her just how much he loved her. She looked stunningly sexy, as if the dress had been stretched over her body, every curve and ripple of her flesh, from the roundness of her belly to the fullness of her breasts was displayed. The glossy material reflected the candlelight, the slinkiness of each step exaggerated by the liquid play of light on dark.

'Is that all?'

'You look stunning, Mistress,' Jonathan breathed, he stepped towards her his heart pounding with desire.

'The door,' she said, stopping him in mid-flight. 'Get the door. And don't forget to take their coats.'

'Yes Mistress,' he said disappointedly. He moved past her and she deftly felt his prick, smiling when she felt how hard he was.

He opened the door to a trio of women, standing

together and laughing loudly on the door step. They walked in without being asked, two of them still laughing while the third was silent.

'Your coat, Mistress?' Jonathan said deferentially to the first, a tall woman with short brown hair that matched her rather longish face.

'Obviously not the hired help,' she said, turning to the second woman, shorter with long fair hair.

'What's your name?' the first one asked, turning so that he could take her coat.

'Jonathan, Mistress,' he said. The third woman caught his eye, she was still silent, her face blank. He also noticed that where the other two were made up she wasn't. Her pretty eyes were free of eye liner and her pouting lips unglossed.

'Charly darling, we're not early are we?' the second woman asked as Charlotte joined them.

'No, Elizabeth, not early,' Charlotte smiled, 'just the first. And Christine, how are you?'

'Well, you know us,' Christine replied, taking Charlotte by the arms and kissing her softly on the lips. 'Always the first to arrive and always . . . '

'. . . The last to leave!' Elizabeth said in unison then broke into a high-pitched giggle.

'And what have we got here?' Charlotte asked excitedly, pointing to the third woman standing unnoticed in the corner.

'That's number seven,' Elizabeth said, looking directly at her sternly.

'Number seven?' Charlotte said, looking at Elizabeth dubiously.

'Yes, number seven. Lady Claudia Mitton, but the little bitch doesn't deserve a name.'

'And she is a bitch,' Christine added venomously. 'Which is why we like to have her fucked like a bitch. It teaches her manners, doesn't it?'

'Yes, Mistress,' Claudia said, her soft voice only just audible. She seemed to shrink away from the eyes that were fixed on her.

'Shall we go inside?' Charlotte said, taking Elizabeth by the hand and pulling her towards the sitting room. The three women walked away, talking excitedly, their voices vying to be the loudest.

'Shall I take your coat?' Jonathan whispered, stepping close to Claudia who was rooted to the spot.

'I suppose so,' she replied hesitantly, her voice was a whisper, nervous and light, and her clear blue eyes were fixed on the ground. Jonathan put his arm out for her coat but she made no move to slip it off.

'It's OK, I'm sure your Mistress won't mind,' he said.

'No, they won't,' she agreed. She waited a second more then turned her back to Jonathan and slipped off her knee-length cashmere jacket.

'It's OK, I understand,' Jonathan said comfortingly, taking her coat. He could see why she had been so reluctant. She was naked underneath apart from a tutu that spread from her waist in layers of stiff white frill. She had her back to him still, smooth and flawless, her white skin soft and inviting. Her face had flared pink with embarrassment, and she brought her hands to cover her eyes.

'Number seven!' a voice cried impatiently from the front room. A look of panic filled Claudia's childlike eyes, and she forgot her embarrassment at once. Quickly she stepped out of her shoes and then ran barefoot to her Mistresses, moving with the elegance and style of a dancer.

Within fifteen minutes all the guests had gathered, and their excitable conversation and gentle laughter soon filled the flat. They looked relaxed and comfortable, totally ignoring the incongruous presence

169

of Jonathan and Claudia. After drinks they sat down for the meal, which Jonathan served with meticulous efficiency. There was too much to think about; what to serve, whom to serve to, which side to serve on. He had never noticed before how much was involved, but he carried it through with silent concentration. He was ignored, totally invisible, conversation went on around him, they sat back to make way for him to serve with scarcely a glance in his direction.

If they ignored him it was hard for him to ignore them. If he did anything wrong, spilt the wine or dropped the food, then he would suddenly become visible, an intruding and unwelcome presence. And it was hard to ignore the women, dressed stylishly in party frocks, or like Charlotte, in outrageously seductive designer costumes that showed their bodies to best effect.

Claudia was made to stand in a corner, her back straight and her arms at her side. Aside from the initial introductions she was totally ignored, not even earning an occasional glance from the assembled guests or her Mistresses.

'What about number seven?' Charlotte asked when there was a lull in conversation.

'Oh yes,' Elizabeth sighed, as if Claudia's well-being were an unwelcome inconvenience.

'Get your boy to bring a bowl,' Christine said, waving a hand in Jonathan's direction majestically.

Charlotte nodded and Jonathan obeyed. He found a plastic bowl in the kitchen and took it back to Christine. She scooped some food from her plate into the bowl, aware that she was being watched by the other guests.

Charlotte was concerned. 'Are you sure you've got enough left? I can get Jonathan to see if we have any scraps left in the kitchen.'

'No, I'm fine honestly,' Christine smiled, 'must look after our figure anyway. Here,' she handed the bowl to Jonathan, 'put it down in the corner.'

'Yes, Mistress,' he said obediently.

Claudia stiffened when he approached her. She lifted her head higher, straightened her back, looked away from him. He hesitated then set the bowl down by her feet.

'You may eat now,' Elizabeth called. Jonathan turned and saw everyone looking on expectantly.

Claudia fell to her hands and knees, scooping right down to lap the food into her mouth. Her back was smooth, her taut flesh twisting seductively, her tight firm breasts scraping the floor. The food was difficult to eat like that, and she had to tease it carefully into her small mouth. The silence was broken with an almost sighing whisper of appreciation around the table.

Jonathan stepped back and saw why. The stiff frills of Claudia's slip had risen up to reveal completely her naked backside. Her back was arched and her round arse cheeks were pulled taut, her long thighs were slightly parted showing that she was clean-shaven between them. The pussy lips were bare and slightly parted, the pink flesh within glistened as she moved gently back and forth to eat.

He stepped back again, unable to take his eyes off Claudia's beautiful backside. He couldn't help wondering if that was how they had fucked her, down on her hands and knees, her back arched and her thighs parted.

The sight of Claudia on hands and knees brought the conversation back to life, as if she had injected some excitement back into the evening. Jonathan served more wine and the mood changed gradually, the laughter was louder, more relaxed and the

171

conversation freer. As he came and went he couldn't keep his eyes off Claudia. She was so open, as if waiting to be taken and used for pleasure.

Perhaps it had been inevitable, but when he finally made a mistake he froze, petrified by the certain knowledge that he was going to be punished for it. He had been pouring wine when Claudia had looked round, and for a moment their eyes had met. Unfortunately the glass he had been topping up overflowed at the same moment.

'Well,' Elizabeth declared, 'it seems that your boy here is enamoured of our number seven. Perhaps he ought to pay us as much attention as he does that little bitch.'

'He will of course,' Charlotte assured her, putting her glass down, 'after he's been taught a lesson.' She turned to Jonathan, her eyes sparkling with excitement, but her face stern and unsmiling. 'You know where the strap is. Bring it here now.'

'Yes, Mistress,' Jonathan said weakly. He didn't want it to happen; he had been trying hard all night to be careful. In his heart he had known all along that the sole reason he was there was to provide Charlotte with a body, a symbol of her dominance. His hands were shaking when he pulled the strap from the case on the mantelpiece. It was heavier than expected and the flat surface cool to the touch.

'The pleasure's yours, Elizabeth,' Charlotte said generously, pointing Jonathan to her. He stood by her chair, offering her the strap as he had offered her the wine earlier. She smiled obliquely and took it, passing her fingers lingeringly over the smooth flat surface.

'I've got a better idea,' Christine said, turning to speak to the other guests.

'I'm not letting you punish him!' Elizabeth laughed jealously.

'No, not that,' Christine assured her.

'Let's all have a turn,' another guest, a thin-faced man, suggested hopefully. There was uproar and for a moment it seemed that everyone had a different idea what to do.

'No, listen,' Christine insisted, they all turned to her. 'Charlotte, we have to admit that number seven was as much at fault as your boy. Why not get them to punish each other? He can beat her first and then she can beat him with the strap.'

Even Elizabeth smiled at the idea. 'But if they aren't thorough I'll make up for it,' she agreed begrudgingly.

'Undress,' Charlotte ordered.

Jonathan did as he was told, self-consciously stripping off. He glanced at Claudia but she was staring straight ahead, giving no sign that she even knew what was in store for her.

'Where do you suggest? Over the arm of the sofa?' Charlotte asked.

'No, across the table would be better,' the man pointed out.

Elizabeth agreed. 'Then we can really judge if they are being good to each other or whether they are doing it properly,' she added.

The guests made way, pulling their seats away from the table so that they could get a more relaxed view of the proceedings. Jonathan wiped the table top and then stood aside nervously.

'Number seven,' Elizabeth snapped, 'come here girl! Be quick!'

'Yes, Mistress,' she whispered, standing nervously in front of the table. She was tall, with small, firm, pear-shaped breasts peaked with cherry red nipples that were sharp points of flesh.

'Bend over, you're going to be punished.'

Claudia bit her lip and her clear blue eyes filled with

173

tears. Silently she lay flat across the table, laying her face and arms flat on the dark polished surface. Her legs were straight and slightly parted, every muscle and sinew was stretched deliciously tight. The tutu was vertical, like an umbrella on its side, and her bottom was stretched tight and round.

'Six strokes, and make them count,' Elizabeth ordered, with a note of warning.

Jonathan stood behind Claudia, holding the strap as if it were red hot. He had never planned on anything like this. He didn't know Claudia, he hadn't even looked into her eyes to try to see what sort of person she was. It wasn't right.

'Go on,' the man urged impatiently. The others nodded, agreeing with his sentiments.

The strap felt heavy and unwieldy but Jonathan lifted it to head height. He could see the dark crease between Claudia's smooth white arse-cheeks, at the tight spot of her anus like an inviting delicacy waiting to be savoured. He brought the strap down hard; it whistled in the air and cracked like a thunderbolt on her soft flesh. She winced, her body stiffened and she bit her fingers. A livid red mark branded her arse-cheeks, spreading across both buttocks with the same red intensity.

Jonathan paused, shocked at the mark he had made across her lovely backside. He wanted to fall to his knees and smother her rear with cool kisses, pleading with his tongue for forgiveness.

'Again,' Charlotte told him, smiling indulgently.

'He's savouring the pleasure of it,' Christine remarked. 'Look how hard he is.'

Jonathan swallowed hard. In the excitement he was almost unaware of how hard his prick had become. His face reddened guiltily. He lifted the strap and brought it down again swiftly, aiming it lower than the first stroke. The noise echoed in the room and silenced everything. Claudia sighed, opened her eyes and looked at him pleadingly. The second strap mark was parallel to the first, a hot scarlet brand across her body. She withdrew her fingers from her mouth and breathed heavily.

The third and fourth strokes followed rapidly, burning into her flesh and making her squirm and moan. Was the pain turning to pleasure? Did she long for the smack of impact the way that he had? He knew what it was like, he knew that the pleasure-pain could make you weep with ecstasy.

Claudia cried out with the fifth stroke, a wordless cry that twisted her face and made her close her eyes. She shifted slightly, arching her back, trying to lift her bottom higher. Jonathan stepped back, he could see that the pink flesh between her thighs was glistening, oozing a trail of creamy fluid down her thigh. She looked even more open, her hairless pussy open and ready.

He lifted his arm higher and brought it down at a different angle. Claudia screamed and her body shuddered, her breathing seemed to stop, she was frozen, overcome with tiny shudders that made her eyes roll. The strap had come down between her rear cheeks, stroking fire into her arse-valley, over her tight arse-hole and licking down at her open sex. He stepped back and saw that the very tip of the strap was wet with her juices.

'I think he did well there,' Charlotte commented fairly. While Elizabeth and the other guests were agreeing with her Jonathan surreptitiously brought the strap to his mouth. He touched the end with his tongue, lapping at the little pearl of cream from Claudia's pussy. He took it into his mouth and savoured her taste, letting it sit on his tongue before swallowing it with

175

pleasure. The strap had been warm, and he could well imagine the heat burning into her sex from the punishment he had inflicted.

'Swap round now,' Charlotte directed.

Claudia straightened up slowly, as if every movement was painful. Her face was pale but her chest and neck were flushed pink. Her thighs were smeared with cream that dribbled copiously from her sex. Jonathan lay flat on the table, still warm from her presence. He adopted the position that she had, knowing that it was what Charlotte wanted.

'Beat him well,' Elizabeth warned menacingly.

Jonathan looked at her nervously. She looked too weak to hurt him, and her voice was so soft and gentle, he was certain she was going to earn herself a second thrashing. She lifted her arm, stretching it back so that her breasts pressed forward enticingly. He closed his eyes and imagined that it was Mistress standing over him, clad in black, her eyes burning with venomous disdain.

The pain was intense, a blinding flash of fire that made him clutch at the table. The sound rang in his ears, a vicious snap of leather on flesh. He looked round urgently and Claudia had the strap high again, her nipples like ripe buds offered temptingly. The second stroke cut across the first, biting into his arse-cheeks and making him flinch. It burned, a liquid fire moving through his body.

Each stroke fell hard and heavy, he was breathing hard, moaning softly as she had done. It felt so good, without wanting to he was lifting himself higher, wanting her to beat him with all her might. Mistress could do it, she could make him beg and crawl with desire. Each stroke was a gift that made him ache with want.

'He's going to come,' Christine warned as Claudia

176

brought down the fourth stroke that was aimed between his buttocks. Its lick was like lava and made him cry out loudly, twisting his body like an animal.

'It's all right, carry on,' the man said. He moved closer and Jonathan felt a hand take his throbbing prick.

The fifth stroke fell and Jonathan jerked forward. Claudia was proving herself to be stronger than he had imagined, she was beating him precisely as she wanted. The last stroke fell as his had done, between the arse-cheeks. It burned his arsehole and caught the base of his prick with a wicked bite. He screamed, blinded by the intensity of sensation. His body was seized by a single pleasurable spasm that pulled him over the abyss. There was a pure moment of intense bliss and then he was pumping his seed with long delicious spurts.

'Well, I've got myself a little prize,' the man said, sitting back in his seat. In his hand he held a crystal wine glass. Jonathan looked up and realised that the glass had been used to catch the thick cream from his prick.

Everyone wanted to know what he was going to do with it. He sat back smirking, playing with the glass, swirling it as if it held the finest brandy.

'Number seven looks parched,' Elizabeth pointed out, smiling cruelly. 'Let her quench her thirst.'

'Yes, why not?' Christine and Charlotte agreed.

'But they did punish each other,' the man pointed out, 'maybe they should share the prize.'

'I wish I'd thought of that,' Elizabeth said enviously.

The glass was handed to Jonathan who held it gingerly, looking pleadingly to Charlotte. His body ached, his backside still stinging smartly.

'Share it. Number seven first,' Charlotte ordered.

There was no choice. Jonathan handed the glass to

Claudia who eyed it with a look of horror and humiliation. Very slowly she brought it to her delicate lips, still quivering fearfully. She drank slowly, the thick cream sliding down the glass into her mouth. They all watched as she paused and then swallowed, closing her eyes as she did so.

Jonathan took the glass from her, it was still half full, her lips marked on the edge of the glass. He closed his eyes too, unable to face the embarrassment, and swallowed quickly. It slid down his throat smoothly, the traces of wine still there but unable to completely mask his own taste. He opened his eyes and realised that his prick was hard again.

Jonathan opened his eyes and yawned, Charlotte was awake already, sitting up in bed beside him. He moved closer to her, wanting to feel the soft warmth of her body on his skin. She smoothed a hand through his hair affectionately, smiling happily and letting him nestle up to her.

'You were very good last night,' she complimented him softly.

'Thanks,' he said. It had been a wild night, far more intense than he had bargained for when accepting her hurried invitation. In retrospect the mutual flagellation between Claudia and himself had only been the start. After making him drink his own emissions he had been forced to his knees and made to suck Claudia's aching sex while Charlotte sat on his back and urged him on with the strap on his backside. Later he had crawled between Elizabeth's thighs and sucked her to orgasm while she carried on a polite conversation with the others. The evening ended when the male guests took it in turns to mount Claudia, fucking her repeatedly in the sex and in the arse while Elizabeth and Christine verbally abused her.

'I really am grateful,' she continued. 'Things would never have gone so well without you. Are you sore now?'

He felt his back with his hand; the lash marks from the final whipping he had endured after the guests had departed were still painfully raw. 'Yes, it still stings,' he admitted. But it had been worth it. Charlotte had chained him to the bed and used a short lashed whip on him before riding his raging prick until she had climaxed repeatedly.

'I did learn something interesting last night,' she said softly, running her hand down his back, soothing the soreness with her fingertips. Her voice was warm and loving, uttered with grateful affection. He pressed himself closer to her, kissing her softly on the belly, her dark skin in contrast to the whiteness of his own. 'Something about Jonathan de Molay,' she whispered.

'What?' Jonathan looked up sharply. He no longer associated the name with himself, it had been appropriated, taken from him along with his old self. Now it belonged to someone else and it inspired in him a mixed feeling of fear, loathing and excitement.

'Christine told me. She's heard that Jonathan de Molay has got a new slave.'

'And?' he waited expectantly.

'Her name is Jessica Calder-Read.'

Jonathan was shocked. It didn't make sense. Mistress wasn't a slave, she was anything but that. There had to be some mistake. 'Maybe they're lovers, that's all,' he suggested.

Charlotte smiled. 'You don't understand. We all know that Jonathan and Jessica are lovers. No, the point is that he has found another woman with the same name. He's got a female slave called Jessica Calder-Read.'

'Another double?'

'Yes, in a way. He's sporting her around town like the latest fashion accessory. They're very much in demand, Jonathan and his new toy.'

Jonathan sat up. He had to find her. There were two Jessicas, just as there were two Jonathans. He was going to find her, the double. And then through her he was going to get to Mistress.

'Where are you going?' Charlotte asked, sitting up in bed while Jonathan got dressed.

'Home. I'm going to find her, this new Jessica Calder-Read.'

'Why?'

'Because I have to. You spoke about finding my own path, making my own journey. This is it.'

'I see,' Charlotte said stonily.

'Did you want me to stay?' Jonathan asked, realising that Charlotte was angry.

'No,' she said petulantly. 'But I don't want you getting into trouble that's all. Be careful of Jonathan de Molay, he's a powerful man.'

'Don't worry,' Jonathan said confidently, 'I can look after myself.'

'Can you?' she said doubtfully. 'I may give you a call again, soon maybe.'

'Thanks. Look I'm sorry about this. It's no reflection on you, you do realise that, don't you?'

Charlotte looked at him sadly. The white sheet covered her thighs and waist, but her large breasts were bare, rising and falling imperceptibly as she breathed. Her skin was smooth and dark, like burnt sugar, and looking at her made him want to kiss and suck her all over. She was beautiful, and her large oval eyes, so expressive, watched him with a look of sadness and concern. She was capable of the sternest and most cruel discipline but at that moment all he could see was the gentle and affectionate side of her character.

'I'm sorry I have to go,' he said sadly. He had no choice. He had to finish the journey he had started.

'Good luck then,' Charlotte said, but her smile was forced.

The moment that Jonathan stepped into his flat the phone rang. He ran across the room and snatched the receiver just before the answering machine cut in. 'Yes?' he asked breathlessly.

'About bloody time!' Caroline snapped angrily.

'Ah Caroline . . . ' Jonathan had made a mistake but it was too late.

'Ah Caroline,' she mimicked. 'You bastard, why didn't you answer my calls?' The hurt in her voice was untouched by the shrill electric hiss of the telephone line.

'I'm sorry, Caroline, I meant to get back to you but . . .'

'Forget it,' she said, and for a moment he thought it meant drop dead.

'Please, I really am sorry.'

'Well, stay there,' she said after a decent enough pause, 'don't move. Do you hear, don't move.'

'What?'

'Stay there, I'm coming round to see you,' she said, and he knew her well enough not to argue.

'I'll be here,' he promised, though not with any great enthusiasm.

'You better be,' she threatened and put the phone down.

Caroline was the last person he wanted to see. Things were still too confused to talk about, especially with her. It was easier to talk with Charlotte, or even with

Victoria, than with her. She was too sensible to be caught up in anything she didn't understand.

There was only one J Calder-Read in the telephone directory and he knew that it must be de Molay's slave. He wanted to kick himself. It would have made so much more sense to look for the name himself rather than trying to get through via Victoria or Charlotte. However once he had been given the name and Jamieson's address by Vanessa, common sense had flown out of the window. He noted the telephone number and then sat down dejectedly to wait, with mounting dread, for Caroline.

The door bell rang in less than forty minutes. Jonathan opened the door and Caroline stood on the step for several seconds, looking him over carefully, then dealt him an open-handed slap across the face. 'That's for not returning my calls,' she said grimly.

'Hello Caroline,' he said, rubbing his face calmly. It was only to be expected, the way he had treated her. But still, it was a new side to Caroline.

'I'm sorry,' she said regretfully. She stepped into the room and into his arms, kissing him on the mouth and face, kissing away the slap that had reddened his face.

'It's all right, I deserved it,' he assured her, trying to extricate himself from her arms and comforting kisses. This was the Caroline he expected, loving, supportive, comforting. The flash of anger and the slap were out of character, extreme reactions for an extreme situation. It was a pity, it was the anger and the passion behind it he found exciting.

'How have you been?' Caroline asked, finally letting him escape from her arms. 'Or should I ask where have you been? And with whom?'

'This is very difficult.'

'You can make some coffee while you explain, I'm all ears.'

182

They moved to the kitchen and Caroline sat down while he ground the coffee. Outside the grey morning had brightened up and the sun was filtering through the clouds, casting an optimistic sheen over the city. Mistress was somewhere out there, he thought, out in the city, the key to everything.

'It's like a journey,' he began, then stopped. It sounded too grand, too abstract, to explain what was happening to him.

'A journey?' Caroline prompted, resting her chin on her palm and looking at him dubiously.

'No, forget that. There is someone, but it's different. Not the way we were, not the normal lovey dovey kind of thing,' he said, struggling to find the words that would convey the truth yet not hurt Caroline.

'Who is she?'

Jonathan emptied the ground coffee into the filter and switched the machine on. The smell of fresh coffee filled the room. 'That's not really important. It's not so much who she is as what she is.'

'And what is she?'

'Out of reach mainly. That's not meant to sound flippant. She's somebody that came into my life by accident and has changed me completely. I don't even know who I am any more.'

'That sounds very melodramatic,' Caroline said sensibly, in her best feet-on-the-ground tone of voice.

'I know it does. God, it is melodramatic in a way. I've become obsessed with her, don't ask me how, don't ask me why.'

She fell silent, as if digesting all that she had been told. He poured the coffee and handed her a cup.

'Do you love her?' she asked finally.

Jonathan laughed. Love? There was no place for love or affection, no place even for liking, it was hard and passionate. Power, dominance, submission — these were the important things, not emotions, not love, not tenderness.

'What's funny?' she asked, looking hurt.

'She beats me,' he said soberly, looking away from the shock on her face.

She was appalled. 'Say that again,' she said quietly.

'She humiliates and degrades me. She beats me with a whip. God, she even stepped on me with her pointed heels.'

'Why?'

He shrugged. 'I don't know. The worse she treats me the more I want her. You see, love has got nothing to do with it.'

'I don't believe you,' Caroline declared, setting her coffee down on the table.

'Maybe this will convince you,' he said, turning his back to her. He unbuttoned his shirt shakily, his hands trembling. He felt awful, as if he were punishing the one person in the world who didn't want to punish him. He pulled his shirt off and let her see the red stripe down his back, a thick red track burned into his flesh by Charlotte with a whip.

'I don't understand,' Caroline whispered. She looked ashen, her face had lost its colour and her voice was barely audible monotone.

'I'm sorry Caroline, I didn't want to tell you. If I've hurt you then I'm sorry.'

'Of course you've hurt me. You'd think I'd see that and feel nothing? Why, Jon? Why do you want her if that's what she does to you?'

'I don't know, sometimes I think I'm going mad. I mean it wasn't even her that did this. She doesn't want me, I want her. And I've got to see her again, I just have to.'

'What if she rejects you again? What if she makes it plain that she doesn't want you?'

184

'Then I'll know for sure. Then it'll be out of my system, I'll be clean again, the virus will be gone.'

Caroline stood up and went to the window. She looked out at the city below, at the hustle and bustle, at the traffic and the people on the streets. Jonathan came up behind her and held her arms. Her scent was intoxicating, bringing back so many happy memories.

He kissed her on the back of the neck softly. 'Sorry,' he whispered, and it sounded so feeble, one tiny word hoping to undo the hurt that he had inflicted.

'I still don't understand why,' she said, still facing the window.

'Have you ever been driving on the motorway and been taken over by someone doing a hundred and fifty miles an hour? It happens sometimes, I'm going fast and then from nowhere a woman zooms past in an open-topped car, her hair streaming in the wind. And she always looks so cool, so sexy, do you know what I mean? Dark glasses, brilliant red lips. And she zooms past, going so fast it takes your breath away. When it happens I instinctively want to drive after her, to zoom off at the same speed, just to be with her. Do you see what I mean?'

'I know,' Caroline sighed. 'I see them sometimes too, in my case smart young guys in love with the speed, with the thrill of danger. I get the same feeling, that sudden temptation to throw caution to the wind and just let rip. But I always hold back, too afraid of the police car waiting a bit further on.'

'Or afraid of the brick wall and the explosion of flame that's at the other end. But this time I've given in, I'm going for the ride, hooked on that speed, on that danger.'

'And at the other end?' she asked, turning to face him.

'I don't know, Caroline,' he admitted, pulling her

close. 'Maybe it's an anti-climax, a police car and a warning. Maybe it's the explosion that destroys everything.'

'If you want to stop then I'm still here,' she said, opening her mouth for his kiss. 'But I don't know for how long any more.'

9

Jonathan had learned his lesson the hard way. He listened intently to the phone ringing at the other end, willing himself to be cool and calm. Blundering in without thought for the consequences had got him nowhere so far.

Somebody picked the phone up. 'Hello?' a woman said.

'Can I speak to Jessica Calder-Read, please,' he asked calmly, even though he felt keyed up with excitement.

'You are,' she said, 'can I help you?'

'We've never met,' he said, trying to inject a relaxed tone to his voice, 'but we have a friend in common. In fact we have several friends in common.'

'Such as?' she asked, sounding wary.

'Jonathan de Molay. That's why I'm calling really. You and I find ourselves in similar situations.'

'Yes . . . ' she stretched the word out doubtfully. She didn't sound like Mistress. Her voice was clear, and she was certainly well spoken, but she lacked the innate arrogance.

'My name is also Jonathan de Molay . . . '

'You're joking surely?'

'No, that is my name. And I've no doubt that you are aware that the other Jonathan de Molay has a close friend with the same name as you.'

Jessica laughed. 'Is this a joke?' she repeated then laughed again.

'No, it's not a joke, I promise you. That's what I mean, we are in a similar situation, aren't we?'

'Yes, we are. How extraordinary. This has got to be the oddest coincidence I've ever heard of.' She laughed again. 'Does Jonathan know about this? Have you spoken to him?'

'No I haven't, though I've no doubt that he knows all about me. I have met your namesake though, have you?'

'Mis . . . Jessica? Yes, a couple of times now.'

Jonathan's heart skipped a beat. Jessica called her namesake Mistress as well. 'I thought it might be interesting for us to meet for a drink,' he said, desperately trying to hide his excitement.

'I can hardly refuse an invitation like this, can I?' Jessica laughed. 'Just wait until I tell Jonathan that I've met his double. It'll kill him.'

'Yes, after we've met perhaps,' he added nervously. The last thing he wanted was for de Molay to get involved directly.

'You're right. Better that we meet first then I can spring the surprise on him later, when he's least expecting it.'

'Yes. And I'm sure that it will be a surprise for him,' he agreed, laughing a hollow laugh.

'You bet it will. He's the one who usually springs the surprises, it'll make a change for me to get my own back.'

'Can you meet tomorrow?'

'I'm working late tomorrow,' she said.

'What do you do?'

'I'm a lecturer, and I have some late classes tomorrow evening.'

'What about lunch?'

'Yes, why not? I can't wait, this is so exciting.'

'Yes, yes it is,' he agreed, relieved that she felt as excited as he did. She sounded so very different from Mistress that it was hard to understand what she was doing mixed up with de Molay.

Jessica told him where she worked and they agreed to meet at noon. After he put the phone down Jonathan felt euphoric, he wanted to scream and whoop with joy. Jessica wasn't Mistress, but she was the key.

That night he couldn't sleep. There were too many thoughts in his head, going round and round in circles without conclusion. He had reached the crossroads, that was clear. One way lead to Mistress and the other lead back to Caroline. Maybe he had lost Caroline already, the look of incomprehension on her face when she saw the lash marks was etched into his mind. The look of incomprehension matched the note of anguish in her voice.

The other path was towards Mistress, and it had already been a painful journey. Maybe there was no conclusion, no finishing point to aim for. Every time he thought he was close he found himself further away. But he couldn't stop. An unexpected glimpse of Mistress in de Molay's car had almost driven him crazy. And her voice was there, buried beneath the surface, waiting to trap him when least expected.

Jessica was going to help him. She had to.

Jessica looked more like a student than a lecturer, with her shapeless jumper and ankle-length black skirt. Her hair was tied loosely at the back with a red ribbon, though wispy strands of it fell across her face, making her look girlish so that it was hard to put an age to her. The poor-student look was complemented by the glasses that she wore, small and round with a wire frame, the round lenses suiting her face.

'Before you say anything,' she smiled, shaking Jonathan's hand, 'I don't look anything like the Jessica that you've met, and you look nothing like my Jonathan de Molay.'

Jonathan smiled. 'Well, bang goes my first line. Where would you like to eat?'

'There's a pub just around here that does a nice sandwich. Is that OK?'

'Sure. Lead the way.'

The pub was rather out of the way and so not very crowded. They ordered some food and then took their drinks to a table in the corner. Jonathan could never imagine Mistress in a place so grotty, it was as if Jessica had deliberately chosen it to highlight the difference between her and her namesake.

'What do you lecture in?' Jonathan asked, raising his voice so that he could be heard above the television set blaring above the bar.

'History. Modern. And what do you do?'

'I'm a business analyst, in the City,' he said, making a point of avoiding the past tense. Once he would have said it with pride, but now it was another label, convenient perhaps but nothing more.

'Is that where you met Jessica?'

'No. I got a phone call from her one night, or rather one morning. I guess she got one of her . . . one of her assistants to dial it. Right name, wrong number. What about you?'

'Nothing so haphazard,' she said, leaning back for the barman to put the food on the table. 'A friend of a friend of a friend mentioned me to Jonathan. A day later I was being wined and dined and assiduously wooed. All very odd really. But it was fun, and different in the way that Jonathan always makes things different.'

The door opened and Jonathan felt blinded by the

shaft of light that cut across the bar. It was noisy and dark in the pub, the walls stained brown from the accumulated cigarette smoke adding to the seedy atmosphere.

For a while they were silent, eating and drinking beer. They had come to the end of casual conversation. Jonathan could feel that there was a barrier.

'It's funny that you've never met Jonathan,' Jessica said, looking up from her food.

'Yes,' he agreed, looking into her eyes, wondering how much to tell her. Her face looked so open, large brown eyes, a small mouth with full pouting lips and a small pointed nose.

'I would have thought that Jessica would have taken you round to see him straight away.'

'Is that what he did to you?'

She smiled. 'Not straight away. It was a couple of weeks after my . . . ' she stopped, hesitated. 'A couple of weeks after we met he invited her and a few friends round for dinner. I was sprung on her then, a strange kind of after-dinner treat I admit, but it worked.'

'Do you like him?'

Jessica stopped, put her glass down. He could tell that the question had been unexpected. She hesitated, as if making up her mind. 'Yes,' she finally decided, nodding to herself. 'Yes I do like him. I like him a lot.'

'But you had to think about it first,' he pointed out.

'Well, "like" is not the sort of word one would use in connection with Jonathan. Do you like Jessica?'

'I don't know,' he admitted instantly. 'When you say that you like something it usually implies that you've got some say in the matter. It implies free will, doesn't it?'

Jessica nodded. 'Yes, I know exactly what you mean. I feel the same way about Jonathan.'

'Is that what you call him?'

'What do you call Jessica?' she countered, evading his question with a sly smile.

'Mistress,' he said sheepishly, not at all certain that Jessica wasn't going to burst into derisive squeals of laughter.

'I call her that as well,' she admitted, her smile one of sympathy and understanding. 'And most times I call Jonathan Master.'

They fell silent again. The barrier had been crossed, and now Jonathan knew that he and Jessica were in the same position. They were both prey to the same feelings, both at the mercy of emotions more powerful than anything else in their lives.

'Do you see Jonathan often?' he asked as they walked out of the pub and into the street. He shielded his eyes, the light of the overcast day still too bright after the darkness of the bar.

Jessica shook her head. 'I see him when he decides. Sometimes I don't see him for weeks. Other times I'm summoned day after day. What about you?'

'I want to see her more,' Jonathan said cautiously. 'But Mistress is in control, of course. But I do wish I could see her more.'

Jessica stopped outside the entrance to the university. People were streaming in and out, groups of students laughing and arguing, individuals carrying armfuls of books and looking suitably academic.

'Can I see you again?' Jonathan asked hopefully.

Jessica looked away for a second, pursed her lips and then nodded. 'Do you have any friends left?' she asked.

'No, not really,' he said, recognising the familiar feeling of sadness. Her life had been turned upside down as well, Jonathan could well imagine what sort of influence de Molay had. 'There isn't really room, is there?'

'Can I have your phone number? Maybe I'll call you.'

'Yes, please do that,' he said eagerly. She fumbled in her bag and handed him a notepad and a pen for him to jot down his number.

She turned to go into the university. 'I'll see you then,' she said, over her shoulder.

'What are you doing tomorrow evening?'

She shrugged. 'That depends on Master.'

'I'll give you a call tomorrow, if that's all right?'

'Yes, all right then,' she agreed.

He watched her go, falling into step with all the other people entering the university. The initial excitement he had felt was gone, and in its place he felt a sense of overwhelming relief. His condition wasn't unique, he wasn't the only person in the world suffering an inexplicable obsession. She felt it too, she understood. And understanding was going to bring complicity.

It was still dark. Jonathan reached for the telephone and checked the time with the same motion. Suddenly he was awake, the adrenalin surging through his veins. It was Mistress, it had to be her.

'Mistress?' he whispered hoarsely, swinging himself out of bed. In his mind he could hear her breathing silkily, her lips pursing momentarily as she whispered 'darling' to him.

'Jonathan? It's Jessica.'

'Jessica?' he sighed, the feeling of excitement ebbing as suddenly as it had built up.

'I'm sorry to call you so late,' she said, sounding nervous and uncertain.

'I was going to call you tomorrow,' he looked at the clock again, the digits flashing green in the darkness, 'or perhaps I should say later today.'

'I'm sorry,' she said, sounding more disheartened

than even he did. 'It's just that I need somebody to talk to, and there's no one else. No one would understand what I was talking about.'

'I take it that de Molay didn't call you again.'

'No. He didn't. I got home late and I've been by the phone ever since, waiting for him to call me. It's been five days since I last heard from him.'

'Maybe he's doing it on purpose, just to prove to you that he's the Master.'

'Of course he is,' she agreed, as if Jonathan were stating the perfectly obvious. 'He does it to keep me feeling insecure, to let me know that my feelings are unimportant.'

'Have you called him?' Jonathan suggested tentatively. If he knew how to contact Mistress it was what he would have done. It would have been better to hear her shouting at him than not to hear her at all.

'No, I can't.' Jessica said softly.

'Look, why don't I come over to see you? We can talk about this properly, it's difficult over the phone.'

Jessica waited for a moment before agreeing. She told Jonathan where she lived and it wasn't far from his place. He felt ashamed of himself for thinking of it, but it occurred to him that Jessica's dark mood could prove beneficial. She was tired and emotional, there wasn't going to be a better opportunity to find out about Mistress.

Jessica answered the door dressed in a baggy blue teeshirt and a long loose skirt that almost reached down to her bare fee. She looked pale and drawn, her eyes reddened and swollen. It was obvious that she'd been crying, even though she smiled apologetically.

'I'm sorry,' she said, leading the way into her sitting room. The lights were dimmed apart from a reading lamp in one corner. The walls were lined with books, the serried ranks broken only by exotic cacti or succulents in plain black pots.

'It's all right,' Jonathan smiled, 'I know what it feels like. I've spent a good few sleepless nights of my own waiting for Mistress to call.'

'You know,' she said, sitting at one end of the sofa that occupied the centre of the room, 'I felt better just talking to you today. It's silly, isn't it? But I always felt that I was the only person in the world in this position.'

Jonathan sat next to her. 'I know,' he smiled, 'you thought you were going mad on your own. It feels so much better knowing that there are two of us going mad together.'

Jessica laughed, and he realised that she wasn't wearing her glasses. 'When I tried to explain it to my friends they just didn't understand. You know, I was told that I was being stupid, giving myself to a man like that. I sort of felt like a traitor to myself and to my friends.'

'I know. I showed Caroline my back yesterday, where I'd been whipped. She looked at me as if I were some total stranger, a person from another planet.'

'Is that your friend? Or was she . . . '

'It's complicated,' he sighed. 'Too complicated.'

'I know. I was living with someone when Jonathan turned up on the scene. At first it was so funny, Jonathan was being very old-fashioned, you know; flowers, romance, the whole thing. But it was different, it was what was least expected. And it worked. I couldn't resist really. Jonathan has this way . . . I felt hypnotised.'

'Your friend . . . '

'Gone. His stuff's still here, waiting for him to come and pick it all up.'

'Caroline hasn't gone, yet. She's still waiting for me,

hoping that this is a passing phase that I'll get over.'

'I'm sorry, I haven't offered you a drink, do you want one?'

'Sure. Whatever you're having.' He stretched out while she disappeared into the kitchen.

'What was it like, the first time you met Mistress?' Jessica asked, handing him a tumbler of drink.

'Cathartic? Transforming? Intense? I felt like I had been hit by lightning. For the first time I felt alive . . . Is that too over the top?'

Jessica shook her head. 'Jonathan had me begging for him before he even touched me. Just being with him made me feel electric. But he never touched me, or kissed me or anything. It made me doubt myself, because there had to be something wrong with me, it couldn't be him. I was aching for him, positively aching. And then one night he touched me, just with the very tips of his fingers, across my lips. I'd never felt like that before, just a simple touch had me melting. That's the power he had, he could do that just by looking and tracing the shape of my lips with his fingers.'

'Was it like this?' Jonathan edged close to her and reached with his fingers and delicately rubbed her lips, tracing the pouting shape of her mouth.

'Yes,' she said shakily, suddenly freezing up.

'And then what did he do?'

'He rubbed the side of my face and smiled,' Jonathan rubbed her face softly. 'His eyes glittering,' she continued, closing her eyes. 'He told me that he was the Master, his voice was very low, deep, almost a whisper.'

'And then?'

'Then I stood up and I undressed, while he watched.'

'It's all right,' Jonathan whispered reassuringly. He took her hand and urged her up. She stood in front of him and undid the catch at the side of her skirt and then let it fall to the floor. Her baggy teeshirt came off next, and she threw it into a corner. Her breasts, large and round, were bare, the nipples hard, red-brown disks pressing forward invitingly.

'He looked at my chest and told me that I had very sensitive nipples,' she said, her voice strained. 'He flicked his thumb over each nipple in turn, kind of testing me.'

Jonathan stood up and did the same, very softly caressing her nipples, feeling the pointed teats press back against his skin. She sighed, he felt her shudder unsteadily. 'And then?'

'Then he told me to cup my breasts, like this.' She cupped her breasts, holding them up so that Jonathan could see just how big they were. She had a small frame, her arms were thin and frail, making her breasts look even larger. Her fingers cupped the firm flesh, so that the nipples pointed straight out.

'Beautiful,' Jonathan whispered. He wanted to kiss her, to take her nipples deep into his mouth, to bury his face between her lovely breasts.

'He told me to kiss my nipples, to kiss and suck them,' she continued. She forced her breasts higher and her neck down, her pink tongue flicked out between her lips and touched one nipple and then the next. In the dim light Jonathan could see her nipples glisten, wet from her tongue. She licked again, more slowly, pressing her tongue harder, then she strained a bit more and closed her lips around one nipple. She sucked and kissed, her eyes closed, her mouth working feverishly. Quickly she switched to the other breast, sucking and kissing in the same feverish way. When she looked up her nipples were glistening pink, ringed with a deeper red where she had been sucking hard.

Jonathan sighed. 'And then?'

'Then he rubbed between my thighs with his fingers. To see how wet I was.'

She was very wet, her panties were sticky with warm fluid from her sex. Jonathan lingered for a moment, enjoying the way she seemed to flutter, sighing as his fingers traced tight circles at the entrance to her sex, pressing the wet panties deeper and deeper into her.

Jonathan drew closer, pressing himself up against her upturned breasts. 'And then he kissed you,' he said softly.

'No,' Jessica said, snapping back to reality. She drew back from Jonathan's lips. 'Then he spanked me.'

'He spanked you?'

'Yes. He suddenly started to smack my breasts with the flat of his hand. Short hard slaps all over them. I just stood there, too shocked to do anything.'

Jonathan lifted his hand and brought it down firmly with a loud smack. He hesitated, saw the red finger marks come out against her flesh. She had closed her eyes, her mouth was open, her breathing deep and irregular. He smacked again, her other breast this time, his hand was warming up, the fingers stinging slightly. Jessica ached, her face alternately clenching from the pain and then softening again with the pleasure.

The steady rhythm of the smacks filled the room, a harsh tempo punctuated with her ever louder sighs and moans. She was lifting her breasts higher, holding them up for punishment. Her nipples were glowing red, hard and erect points of flesh that seemed to expand with each slap.

'Oh, Master, Master . . . ' Jessica whispered, her head was held high, her eyes firmly closed. She shuddered, stepped back unsteadily, cried out. She pressed her nipples between thumb and fingers, letting Jonathan aim the force of the smack directly on to them. She cried out again, shuddering repeatedly. He took her by the waist, afraid that she was going to fall backwards. She collapsed into his arms, her body rigid against his.

Carefully he lay her down flat on the sofa. She was still breathing hard, her face bathed in sweat. Her breasts were blazing red, the nipples still hot to the touch.

'He made you orgasm that first time too,' he said, whispering into her ear.

She nodded. 'Yes. We didn't even make love. That was really the first time he had ever touched me. He made me climax, smiled mysteriously and left. I didn't see him again for three days. They were the worst three days of my life.'

'He let you stew for three days?'

'Yes. And when I saw him again I begged him to do it to me again. I felt like a slut. I felt dirty and impure. But I begged him to do it just the same.'

'Does it sting?' he asked, looking down at her reddened breasts, heaving up and down as she breathed. The nipples looked swollen, like ripe berries full of juice, waiting to be picked.

'Yes. It hurts and I love the feeling. It's like everything is amplified, the slightest breeze feels like his caress on my body. I'm alive and it's wonderful.'

Jonathan knelt down beside her and kissed her softly on the throat, passing his hand down from the knee to the heat between her thighs. Her panties were soaking, and a thin film of fluid was sliding down between her thighs. He kissed her again on the throat and then down between her breasts.

She moved round, taking her breasts in her hands and massaging them into his face. He kissed and lapped, breathing in her scent, smothered by her delicious breasts. He moved back and she fed one of her nipples into his mouth. He closed his lips around the nipple and sucked hard. She cried out, holding both breasts for him, letting him feed from her berries as he wished. He sucked hard, first on one and then the other, biting softly and then licking hard. She tasted good, her nipples hot and hard in his mouth. She was squirming, squealing as he sucked harder and harder, using mouth and lips and tongue.

Jessica climaxed again, she arched her back, involuntarily pressing her breast forward still more. She seemed to lose track, when she opened her eyes she looked lost.

'I've got to fuck those lovely tits,' Jonathan said bluntly, standing in front of her while he stripped off.

'It still stings,' she whispered.

Jonathan sat her up and then stood in front of her. She leaned forward and took his hard prick between her breasts, smothering his prick in her soft flesh. Cupping her breasts carefully she moved up and down, letting him press his prick against her. A thin vein of fluid was pouring from the glans and spreading in the valley between her gorgeous round peaks.

As he pressed forward she bent down and gently kissed the tip of his prick, wetting it with her lips. He sighed and pressed harder, delighting in the feel of her tongue and the velvety smooth feel of her skin. Her nipples brushed against him, making her sigh.

Jonathan began to thrust harder and harder. He closed his eyes to let the sensations wash over him. She was there, kissing him on the belly softly while he fucked her beautifully spanked breasts. The feel of his prick sliding softly against her skin was too much. He grabbed onto her shoulder and let the spasms of pleasure pulse through him, crying out as the climax overtook him.

Jessica looked up at him and smiled. Her breasts were dripping with golden jewels of come, sliding down softly from her shoulder down her breasts and falling like icicles from her nipples.

'What would Master do now?' Jonathan asked breathlessly.

'He'd command me to clean up.' She lifted her breasts high again, pressing them together to form a little reservoir of thick semen. Then she bent forward so that it slid down towards her left nipple, passing over the flesh still marked by his fingers. She looked up, holding herself in position and then bent her head. Jonathan watched her suck the semen into her mouth, rousing her nipple with her tongue at the same time. She closed her eyes and he knew that she was going to make herself climax again, swallowing his come and sucking her own nipples at the same time.

Jessica was already up when Jonathan awoke. He waited for a moment, hoping that she was going to come back to bed, but the sounds coming from the kitchen told him otherwise. He dressed slowly, trying to work out the best way of approaching her. He had let himself get carried away the night before, and so hadn't had a chance to really question her about Mistress.

'Morning,' he said, ambling barefoot into the kitchen. She was dressed in a baggy top and long skirt again, hiding her lovely breasts in clothes that were almost shapeless.

'Hi. I didn't want to wake you, but I've got to get going soon. I'm giving a tutorial this morning.'

'How do you feel?' he asked, sitting at the table.

'Pretty good,' she smiled happily. 'You?'

'Yes, so do I. Look Jessica can I ask you a question?'

'Sure, and call me Jessie.'

'Have you ever been to Mistress's place?'

'Sure. Big, isn't it?'

'Yes. That is . . . Look I'll be straight with you, I've never been there. Do you have the address?'

'No, not exactly. I know how to get there, but I don't actually have the address. You're not planning on going round there are you?' she said, sounding utterly appalled by the idea.

'I've got to see her,' Jonathan explained sombrely.

'No, don't do that, don't. If things get really bad then call her.'

'I don't have her number.'

'How many times have you actually met her?'

'Once.'

'Once?' Jessica repeated incredulously.

'And I've spoken to her on the phone a couple of times. But I must see her. She did to me what Jonathan de Molay did to you with weeks of wining and dining. That one night has changed my whole life. Then I was cast aside, as if my life is nothing.'

She sat down heavily, her face screwed up. 'Jonathan, why didn't you tell me this before?'

'What difference would it have made?'

'I thought that you were really involved with her. The way I am with Jonathan . . . '

'But look at the way you are with Jonathan,' he interrupted angrily. 'He's left you for days, hanging on desperately, waiting for him to call. What's so special about that? It's exactly the same as what Mistress has done to me.'

'Have you tried to see her since that one time?'

'Yes. And she made it clear that she didn't want to know.'

'You see,' Jessica said emphatically, slapping her hand on the table. 'She doesn't want you, Jonathan. If she did, if you were really going to be her slave then she would have had you back.'

'No, it's not that way,' he insisted. 'She's just

prolonging things, taking things to extremes. I know she is, she wants me to go through hell to get to her. I know she is.'

'No, Jonathan, go back to Caroline,' Jessica countered softly. 'Look, I've got to go. Can I trust you to let yourself out?'

'Please Jessie,' he implored, 'help me. There is no one else I can turn to. You're the only other person who even remotely understands me. Help me. Please.'

'I've got to go,' she said, getting up. She went to the door and then looked back at him. 'Let yourself out, OK? I'll call you tonight, we can discuss it then.'

Jonathan listened to her go, the front door slamming behind her. He sat glumly at the table, holding his head in his hands. Nothing was working. Maybe she was right, maybe they were all right and he was wrong. Mistress wasn't for him, she wasn't for anyone but herself. Caroline was still there, he hadn't alienated her completely, but for how much longer? It made sense to go back to her, to put everything else behind him.

'What are you doing still here?' Jessica demanded crossly, standing by the sitting-room door, still holding her jacket and bag.

'I'm sorry,' Jonathan looked up, he hadn't heard her return, 'I sort of lost track of time. You don't mind, do you?'

'I did ask you to leave,' she said pointedly, going back into the hall to hang up her jacket.

'I was just thinking things over,' he called to her. It was early afternoon, the hours had slipped by without him realising it. He got up off the floor where he had been sitting, idly flicking through a book while his thoughts had wandered.

Jessica came back, shaking her head sadly. 'Look,

Jonathan, I think you ought to go. There's nothing for you here.'

'There is,' he said, knowing that it sounded pathetic. 'You're here, and you can help me. I'm not asking too much. Last night I helped you, I came straight over when you needed me.'

'That,' she declared stiffly, 'was different.'

'No it wasn't. It's exactly the same. You needed me and now I need you. You of all people should understand.'

'No,' she said, turning to leave the room again. Jonathan jumped after her, he caught her by the shoulder and spun her round to face him.

'Why won't you help me?' he demanded, glaring at her.

'Because I've got too much to lose,' she said, turning from him and going into the kitchen.

'Why is this so fucking difficult?' he demanded, following her into the kitchen.

'Don't shout!'

'I don't see why this is such a big deal? All I want is an idea where Mistress lives.'

'I'm not going to help you,' Jessica said, saying every word slowly and emphatically, as if talking to a recalcitrant child.

Jonathan turned suddenly and slammed his fist into a cupboard on the wall, screaming angrily at the same time. Jessica stepped away from him, looking alarmed. He was shaking, his blood boiling. Why was it so fucking difficult? Why couldn't she tell him? His fists were clenched and he was breathing fire, short hard breaths that fuelled the anger pulsing in his veins.

'Please leave,' she whispered nervously, looking pale.

'Help me,' he said darkly, looking at her through narrowed eyes. His face was set hard, his lips closed tightly, teeth clenched.

'I can't help you. If Jonathan finds out then he'll never see me again. I'll lose everything. That would kill me, I wouldn't be able to carry on without him.'

'Help me!'

Jessica stepped back again, shrinking away from him. Blindly she reached out and grabbed whatever was at hand, her eyes were wide, fixed on him, on the look of anger and rage in his eyes. The bottle shattered at his feet, showering him with warm milk and a thousand splinters of glass. He stopped, stepped back, looked down at the broken bottle in slow motion, then put his hands to his face.

'I'm sorry, Jonathan,' she said softly, apologetically, 'I can't help you. Put yourself in my position. What would you do?'

He looked at her blankly. He was still shaking, but now it was from sheer mental exhaustion. If he was in her position he would have done the same thing, he knew it as well as she did. He would never allow anything to jeopardise his relationship with Mistress, nothing could be that important. 'I'm sorry,' he whispered, 'I don't know what's happening to me. I'm losing control, I'm frightened. I don't know what's going on any more.'

'You better go now,' she whispered nervously.

10

Jonathan steered the car through the entrance and into the enclosed courtyard. In the dull light of the afternoon the dull brick building looked as if it were sweating. The rain had stopped and the cloud had cleared slightly, the light managing to break through the gloom. The oval lawn was ringed with cars, some of them parked with two wheels on the damp grass. There were no empty spaces that he could see, so he drove round again slowly, almost stalling the engine. Somebody crossed the courtyard and got into a battered old Ford, the engine coughed and wheezed cancerously, but it finally came to life and the car backed out and turned. Jonathan pulled to one side to let the car out and then slid into the vacated space.

He switched the engine off and sat forward, resting his arms on the steering wheel and gazing at the drab buildings around him. Coming to see Victoria was crazy. He felt hollow, thoughts and feelings had been sucked out of him, leaving an empty shell of confusion and doubt. Jessica had been his last hope, he had been so certain of her, so absolutely sure. It hurt, the way she had rejected him, letting him down so brutally. And the ingratitude.

Victoria wasn't the person to see. It should have been Caroline. Poor Caroline, selfless but deluded. She didn't know and he hated her for it. Why was she making things difficult as well? He wished that she would leave him alone. For a moment the anger was strong again, a sudden rush of adrenalin that made him grip tightly at the wheel. He felt brutal. He wanted to tell Caroline to her face to leave him alone, to get out, to disappear, to drop dead.

Not Caroline. If he had to turn to anyone he would have chosen Charlotte. He felt closer to her in a way than to anyone else. Perhaps it was because she still remembered her life before her obsession, she was still in touch with her inner feelings, retaining a spontaneity that he found appealing. But he couldn't turn to her. Jessica was a slave like he was, but Charlotte was a mistress, cruel and ruthless. He couldn't turn to her even though he longed to be at her feet again, crawling like a slave to her commands.

There was only Victoria. A self-styled mistress who tried hard but couldn't quite make the grade. She was the only one to turn to. Her illusions were transparent, but he knew enough about her to get his own way. If he closed his eyes, or she was in the right sort of mood, then he too could have his illusions. She wasn't Mistress, but in his imagination everything could be transformed.

He climbed the stone steps to the third floor, trying to remember which door was hers. Victoria was nocturnal, he was certain that she would be up, but guessed that she would be wishing away the hours before darkness. For all her worldliness she had an essentially innocent view of life. Going out and mixing with her fancy friends was the be-all and end-all. Being a mistress was a fashion thing, that was why he could never take her seriously. She tried hard, like a suburban schoolgirl slavishly following the latest fashions in an effort to gain big-city glamour and sophistication.

He stopped outside a heavy blue door, only half sure

that it was hers. He knocked and waited, going over in his mind all that he was going to tell her.

'Yes?' a young woman answered, opening the door an inch and peering round it nervously.

'I'm sorry, I was looking for someone called Victoria,' he said. He heard a voice calling from a back room, impatiently demanding to know who it was.

'Can I say who's calling?' the woman asked softly, holding the door fast.

'Tell her it's the other Jonathan de Molay.'

The door closed again. Victoria had got herself a female slave. Jonathan was intrigued. A few moments passed and then the door was opened again. 'Please follow me,' the young woman said. Jonathan entered the flat.

The young woman turned and went into the front room before Jonathan had a chance to get a good look at her. He followed, noting her long blonde hair and the short pleated skirt flapping around her behind as she walked.

Victoria was lying on the sofa, wearing her long satin robe, legs crossed over, sitting up like a lady of leisure. 'Well Jonathan,' she smiled, extending a hand, 'I never expected to see you again.'

He walked over and took her hand, raised it to his lips and kissed her fingers respectfully. 'I'm sorry, Mistress, I know I broke the contract but I was hoping you would have me back.'

'That's very . . . very . . . ' she paused, raising her eyebrows, looking for the right word.

'Presumptuous?' Jonathan suggested.

She smiled. 'Yes. Very presumptuous. Last time you left very quickly, before I had really finished with you.'

'Yes, Mistress, but I did as you asked,' he reminded her. 'You lent me out for the night. Like a common . . . common . . . '

'Slut?' she suggested.

'Yes. Like a common slut.' They both smiled, understanding each other fully. It was a game for her, and so long as he played by her rules he knew that things would be OK.

'But I've got another little slut now,' she said, waving her hand regally in the direction of the young woman standing silently in the corner.

Jonathan turned to face her and saw immediately that something was not quite right. The young woman was slender, thin arms and face, flat-chested, but with a fuller waist and thighs. Her face was thickly made up, white foundation with red lipstick and blusher on the cheeks.

'This is Billie,' Victoria said, standing up.

'Hello Billie,' Jonathan said, still not certain what it was that was out of place. Billie was standing with arms by her sides, facing the floor, her eyes expertly avoiding his. Her feet were together, knees straight. In her pleated skirt and loose white blouse she looked like a sixth-form schoolgirl.

'Billie's been a naughty girl, and so she's been given to me to take in hand,' Victoria said proudly. She walked over towards Billie, and as she did so her robe fell partly open, exposing her firm high breasts.

'Does that mean you don't want me, Mistress?' Jonathan asked, letting the real fear and anguish seep into his voice. He didn't know how much more he could take. One more rejection was certain to push him over the edge.

'Turn around,' Victoria told Billie sternly. 'I'm not sure yet,' she said, looking back to Jonathan.

'Please Mistress, don't throw me out. I'll be good, I'll do anything you want me to. Please.'

She turned to face him, perhaps noting the desperate tone or the pleading look in his eyes. 'Relax,' she said softly. 'I suppose there are a certain number of possibilities here.'

'There are. Just think Mistress, you can have two slaves. Two. Think of what all your friends will say.'

'On your knees,' she hissed to Billie, who complied without saying a word, dropping to her knees instantly. 'Now you, Jonathan, here, in front of her.'

He stepped forward, still doubtful and afraid. He needed her, more than she could know, more than he had even imagined himself. There had been too many rejections and disappointments. 'Here, Mistress?' he asked obsequiously.

'Yes, strip off,' she ordered, stroking Billie's face with her long thin fingers. Her robe had fallen loose and she was standing between the two slaves, deliberately flaunting her nakedness.

Jonathan pulled his clothes off quickly and then stood before Billie, his limp penis close to her eyes. He felt too full of doubt to be excited, there was nothing erotic about the situation for him. All he cared about was staying with Victoria.

'Now, girl,' Victoria said sternly, 'you've been very bad, haven't you?'

'Yes, Mistress,' Billie mumbled.

'Louder.'

'Yes, Mistress,' she repeated.

'And what happens if you're bad?'

'I'm punished, Mistress.'

Victoria flicked Billie's long straight hair back, making sure that her face was clear. 'Well, this time you're going to be punished properly. And maybe this time you'll learn your lesson. Won't you?'

'Please Mistress . . . not this . . . ' Billie whined, looking up at Victoria sadly.

'Silence!' Victoria snapped angrily. She stepped behind Billie, smiling cruelly to Jonathan, her grey eyes shining intently. 'Lift your skirt,' she ordered. Billie lifted her skirt at the back, bowing her head with shame at the same time. Jonathan started to shift round to get a better look but a cold stare from Victoria dissuaded him.

Victoria lifted her hand and started to spank Billie soundly on the backside, each slap accompanied with a yelp or a sigh that seemed to escape involuntarily from Billie's scarlet-painted lips. Jonathan watched excitedly, his prick springing quickly to attention. Victoria was raising her hand high and then bringing it down flat on Billie's bare arsecheeks. The slap of flesh on flesh hung in the air, like the distant peal of a bell that hums in the air.

Billie was sighing, she fell forward on to her hands and pressed her backside higher. Her eyes were closed but her mouth was open, her lips parted to reveal her straight white teeth. Her hair fell forward and she remembered to brush it back as Victoria had done.

'Now take Jonathan's cock into your mouth and suck him properly. This is part of your training. I want to see his spunk in your mouth before you swallow every last drop. Understood?'

'Yes, Mistress,' Billie moaned, gasping for breath as a particularly hard slap fell down between her buttocks.

'I'm going to sell that pretty little mouth of yours,' Victoria promised, obviously relishing every word. 'My friends will gladly pay for a pretty flower like you.'

Billie inched forward and Jonathan pushed his hard prick deep into her mouth. She closed her lips around him and he sighed, his prick wrapped in the receptive warmth of her mouth and tongue. He stood still, feet apart, hands on her shoulders. She moved back and forth, up and down, taking his prick deep into the back of her throat.

211

'Fuck her properly,' Victoria warned, finishing the spanking with two more hard slaps, 'or you'll be in trouble too.'

'Yes Mistress,' Jonathan replied. He began to jab forward with his pelvis, thrusting his hardness as far as it would go. He thought she was going to gag, but instead she shifted position to take his full length. His rhythm increased, going deeper as well as faster. She was flicking her tongue over the glans and under it, caressing his prick where it was most sensitive.

He closed his eyes, trying to hold back for as long as possible. Victoria was by him, he felt her hand on his shoulder. He craned round and smothered her fingers with loving kisses. Billie was sighing and moaning, making little slurping sounds as she sucked expertly at his prick.

'Come in her mouth,' Victoria said, giving her permission as Mistress.

Jonathan gasped and let himself go, spraying thick wads of come deep into Billie's hungry mouth. He swayed unsteadily, the waves of pleasure dizzying in intensity. Billie gasped too, Jonathan was aware of her hot breath on his prick. He stepped back and opened his eyes.

'She's come too,' Victoria said dispassionately. 'Look.'

Jonathan stared open mouthed. Victoria had lifted Billie's skirt to reveal a long hard prick dripping with thick viscous cream. Billie was a male slave, but with legs shaved and perfect make-up had been transformed into a willing and submissive female.

In his mind Jonathan found it hard to think of Billie as anything but female. The way she stood, the way she walked and moved, even when she was being unknowingly watched, were all distinctly feminine.

212

When she sat down her knees were held tightly together, when she walked her hips swayed rhythmically from side to side. Her smile, when she finally smiled in his presence, was warm and friendly, though she coyly avoided looking at him directly in the eyes.

Victoria had plans for the evening, and Jonathan's unexpected arrival was going to do nothing to spoil them. She decided that Billie was going to dress her, and sent Jonathan home to change into evening dress. The idea of arriving at a place with two slaves to hand obviously appealed to her. Jonathan knew that she saw it as evidence of her prowess as a strict mistress, and that she couldn't wait to tell all her friends about it.

He arrived home and was immediately struck by the peace and solitude of his apartment. It took a while but then he realised that the answering machine was silent, and that for the first time in weeks he had arrived home without a waiting message from Caroline.

Had she finally abandoned him? He couldn't blame her if she had, it was the least that he deserved. But still he felt a pang of sadness and an onrush of guilt for all the bad things he had wished on her. The only decent thing to do was to call her and let her know that he was OK, and that she should forget him totally. The time had come to end it, once and for all.

He picked up the phone and hesitated. She was going to ask him about Mistress, and what happened with her. It was impossible to tell her the truth, he couldn't tell her that he was as far from her as he had ever been. If he told her the truth it was only going to make her feel guilty, and bring her running back whether she wanted to or not.

He dialled a number and waited.

'Jessica?'

'Yes? Who's that?'

'It's Jonathan,' he paused, half-expecting her to put

the phone down. 'I just wanted to apologise for the way I acted earlier.'

'It's OK,' she said, sounding relieved. 'We all have bad times sometimes.'

'I know, but I really am sorry. Still friends?'

'Yes, still friends,' she agreed. 'And I'm sorry too. I was hard on you, especially after you'd been there for me. I didn't mean to appear ungrateful, I'm not. It's just that the idea of losing Master frightened me too much, it made me realise just how precarious our relationship is. You do understand, don't you?'

'Sure. I think I would have done the same in your position. Do you think I can see you again?'

'Yes,' she said doubtfully, 'but not now.'

'Sure, you'll call me?'

'Yes, yes I will, I promise. Just not now.'

'I understand,' he said softly. She sounded doubtful, but he knew that the moment she felt lost, cut off from her master, she was going to come back to him. Fear and doubt, as much as passion and desire, were part of her life, just as much as his.

He put the phone down, promising himself to call Caroline later, in a few days' time. It was no good calling her without a story, without something definite that she could understand. He had been like that before, everything had to be concrete, logical, justifiable. If there had been grey it had been painted black or white, with no room for the colours to merge at the boundaries. He had changed though, certainty and order were things of the past, concepts that had outlived their usefulness and had been relegated to dim memory.

He dressed as ordered and drove back to Victoria's. The panic that had gripped him earlier had receded. He still felt a vague unease in the back of his mind, a nagging fear that life was becoming too complex, and that his grip on reality was becoming tenuous in the extreme.

Billie opened the door to let Jonathan in. She was dressed in a slinky purple dress that clung sensuously to her body. It was padded at the front, suggesting a pair of firm pointed breasts, and seemed to shimmer in the light as she moved. She turned and Jonathan saw that it was backless, Billie's smooth tanned back fully displayed.

'You took your time,' Victoria said, but her angry tone sounded false. She was ready too, dressed in a shiny PVC catsuit that glistened deliciously.

'Sorry Mistress,' Jonathan said dutifully, and although it sounded like he was going through the motions it still made him feel a little better. Victoria looked divine; the bottom half of the catsuit seemed to have been sprayed on to her, tight and shiny, while the top half cupped and lifted her breasts in a half-cup bra that was covered with a thin transparent lycra blouse. The whole effect was to reveal and obscure at the same time, making her look eminently desirable and yet distantly unapproachable.

'Come on, let's go,' she said, glancing at the clock on the wall.

Billie and Victoria sat in the back while Jonathan drove. It was a mild night, a hint of pink still ebbing on the horizon.

'Alex and Sara-Jane were asking about you,' Victoria remembered. 'He even rang me at home to ask about you.'

'What did you say?'

'I lied, told them that I had other things in mind for you. I might give them a call now that you're back.'

'What about Vanessa?'

'She never wants to see or hear from you again.

215

Definitely not in her good books,' Victoria laughed. 'And I thought that she might like you for herself.'

'What about tonight, Mistress?' he asked.

'Tonight you're just my driver, though I might find a use for you. Tonight is Billie's night. She's going to be good for me, aren't you?'

'Yes, Mistress,' Billie replied obediently, her voice soft and low, slightly lisping.

Did she know what Victoria had in mind for her? He remembered his own feeling of shock when it had dawned on him that he was going to be handed over for the night. 'What will she be doing, Mistress?' he asked, hoping that he hadn't crossed the mark.

'I have a dear friend who's a photographer, professional. She's very good, very well known. I promised to supply her with some interesting models. Billie will be the first, and you'll be good. Won't you Billie?' she repeated nervously. 'One more thing, I've just remembered. Earlier I told you to hold Jonathan's come in your mouth, but you swallowed right away. I don't want that to happen again, understood?'

'Yes, Mistress,' she said, giving nothing away of her own true feelings.

The studio was above one of the smart galleries near Covent Garden, the tinted glass exterior revealing nothing of the treasures inside. Jonathan pressed the bell, the relay clicked on cue and Victoria strode in. The lights were dimmed, and although the gallery was fashionably sparse and minimal, the atmosphere seemed too close. The pictures on the walls were covered up, black velvet drapes drawn tightly in front of each other. Jonathan was tempted to march over and pull the drapes open, to expose whatever was hidden.

'I was beginning to lose hope,' a woman said, emerging from the darkened interior.

'Sorry,' Victoria apologised, giving Jonathan a dirty look. 'But we're here now, and I've got someone special to meet you. Fay, this is Billie.'

'Hello, Billie,' Fay said, stepping forward to offer her hand. Billie looked questioningly at Victoria and only then did she shake Fay's hand.

'And this is my driver,' Victoria announced, stepping aside for Jonathan.

'Hello. Have you modelled before?' Fay asked, putting an arm around Billie's shoulder and leading her to the rear of the building.

'No, Mistress,' Billie replied, looking doubtful, turning back to look for Victoria's approval.

'You can call me Fay, I'm sure your Mistress won't mind.'

'It's OK, Billie's yours for the session. You can do as you like with her,' Victoria explained magnanimously.

'I want her to relax,' Fay explained, leading the way up a flight of stairs at the back of the gallery. 'I want her to relax and forget everything else. I want her to be spontaneous.'

'That's how you'll be then,' Victoria told Billie. 'Pretend I'm not even here, if that'll help.'

Jonathan wondered whether Fay was aware of Billie's secret. Was Victoria really trying to pass her off as a female model? Billie was certainly pretty enough, and she had all the right mannerisms, but could she really go through with it?

The studio was on the first floor, and extended the full length of the building. Curtain rails and partitions separated off different sections of the studio. There were lights and cameras everywhere, hanging from the ceiling, or standing on steel frames. The floor was alive with thick cables and power points.

Fay led them all through to one curtained-off section to the front of the building. They passed through a curtain into a darkened space, the backdrop was dull grey against the varnished floor. The centre of the space was occupied by a large black leather chair, with high arms and a padded head rest. It looked impressive, enclosed in a shaft of light that fell diagonally across the studio, like an old-style dentist's chair.

'Why don't you just go and sit on the chair?' Fay suggested. 'You don't have to pose or anything, just sit down and get a feel of it. Become comfortable.'

Billie walked nervously to the chair, as if she were walking out on to a stage for the first time. Her shoes were flat heeled, and as she walked her dress clung tightly to her rounded backside, swaying gently, sexily with every step. She paused at the chair and touched it tentatively, passing her small white hand over the dark gleaming surface. She pressed harder and the chair tilted back, swivelling to one side slightly, creaking as it did so.

'Isn't it lovely?' Fay asked, turning to Victoria who nodded. 'I bought it in Prague last month. It's prewar, German, manufactured in Hamburg I think. It radiates a sort of power, raw, sensual power.'

Billie turned and hoisted herself on to the seat, sitting right on the end of it, holding onto the arms anxiously. Her legs dangled over the end, making it look as if she were being sucked into the black mouth of the chair. Her face was tense, her lips clenched and her eyes were fixed on Victoria.

'Just relax,' Fay said, walking over to her. 'Can you feel it? Have you ever found that there are certain objects, cold and inanimate, which have a power that exists outside of them? It's the essence of fetishism, a transfer of erotic intent to cold unspeaking objects, investing in them all our unspoken passions and desires.

Just relax, Billie, just sit back and let the feel of the thing envelope you.'

'It does have a certain fascinating quality,' Victoria remarked to Jonathan quietly.

Fay disappeared for a moment and Billie made a conscious effort to get more comfortable. She sat well back in the seat, crossing her legs, smoothing one hand up and down the shining leather. The light moved, focusing more directly on Billie, making her skin look deathly white in contrast to the chair.

'Good, that looks much better,' Fay smiled when she returned. She picked up a camera and snapped the first shot, zooming in close, and smiling encouragingly to Billie. It was an instamatic camera and Fay came up to Victoria and Jonathan to show them the picture as it developed.

'No, it's no good,' Fay whispered, turning to smile to Billie, 'she looks too nervous. She's frightened of the chair instead of being in love with it.'

'The lighting's too harsh,' Victoria suggested.

'No, the lighting's fine. It's her eyes.'

'Maybe you ought to build on that,' Jonathan said.

'What do you mean?' Fay asked, looking at him as if she had only just noticed his existence.

'That chair, it's powerful, isn't it? It looks like it's caught her, got her trapped in its arms. It's holding her there, against her will almost.'

Fay twisted her mouth, weighing up his suggestion. 'I wanted to show her in love with the chair, touching it, caressing it, fucking it. Now you're saying that it's the chair that's fucking her?'

'Yes, that's how it looks,' he turned and nodded towards the chair. Billie still looked swallowed up, sinking into the sumptuous padding that was sucking her in sensuously.

'That's good,' Fay agreed. She turned back to Billie.

219

'That's it darling, very good. Now sit up properly, tuck your feet under you, rest your head on the arm, rest your head in your arms. Good. Hold that.'

Billie was snuggled up in the seat, curled up like a frightened animal. Her arms were crossed and resting on the left arm of the chair, her head resting on her arms, her face close to the black leather. Her skirt was too short, her thighs were almost bare, pressing directly onto the leather of the seat. Fay picked up one of her other cameras and moved in, shifting and sliding, stalking her prey with a feline elegance. The camera clicked and whirred, capturing Billie as she moved about on the chair, shifting position as directed, being swallowed by the chair that seemed to grow in power and presence.

As Billie moved her skirt moved higher and higher, always revealing the sharp line of white thigh against glossy black. The thin white line of her panties was visible, pressing deep into her behind, without ever revealing what was between her thighs.

'Red lipstick, I want her lips as shiny and as glossy as the leather,' Fay decided, stopping for a moment.

'I didn't think to bring anything,' Victoria explained apologetically.

'It's all right,' Fay assured her. She disappeared for a moment and Victoria took the opportunity to walk over to Billie.

'Good girl,' she said happily, stroking Billie's face with the back of her hand. 'You look terribly sexy like that. Good enough to eat. In fact if you're good I may let Jonathan eat you later,' she added, smiling wickedly.

'Everybody, this is Marc,' Fay said, coming back into the room and pointing to a young black man she had brought with her. He nodded curtly, and Jonathan noticed Billie pulling down her skirt and blushing slightly. In his hands he carried a make-up box which he carried over to Billie and put down on the floor before her.

'This might get very interesting,' Victoria whispered to Jonathan who smiled back knowingly.

Fay and Marc discussed the various shades of glossy colour available, comparing several against the jet-black seat. At last they decided on a colour and Marc carefully applied it to Billie's lips, his dark brown skin in shocking contrast to her light-drenched skin.

Marc stepped back and Fay resumed taking the shots. This time she had Billie lying right across the chair, her feet over one arm and her back over the other. It looked as if she were being kidnapped, and carried off by the menacing black presence. She had her eyes closed, and her lips were parted, blood red lips against the deathly pale skin. Fay was whispering encouragement, moving back and forth, in and out rhythmically.

'More thigh,' she told Marc over her shoulder and he sprang to life. He flicked Billie's hair back, turned her face slightly with his big strong hands and then carefully edged the dress higher, revealing long smooth thighs. As he stepped away his hand moved over the thigh, touching Billie longingly with his fingers and making her sigh audibly.

'I think he likes her,' Victoria whispered excitedly, clutching Jonathan's arm. He nodded, the chemistry between Marc and Billie was almost tangible. His dark eyes were fixed on her, scanning her body with hungry intensity.

'On your knees now,' Fay ordered. 'On your knees, looking over the headrest, looking to see what's on the other side. Good.'

Billie had both hands on the headrest and was peering over the edge, her back to the camera and her

221

audience. Her bare back seemed snow white, and with the strong white light seemed to take power away from the seat, shining luminously like an icon. The dress was high, reaching down to barely cover her backside. Fay changed film for the tenth time and then began again with the camera, moving in close up and then stepping back quickly again.

Without prompting Marc moved forward and lifted the dress higher, running his hand surreptitiously over Billie's bottom cheeks. When he stepped back Fay nodded, looking pleased. Billie's backside was almost completely exposed, her white panties a tight triangle of material pulled tightly between her full round arsecheeks. The dress looked as if it had inadvertently risen, and that Billie was unaware of her exposed position.

'I've got it!' Fay suddenly exclaimed. She came skipping over to Jonathan. 'I've got it, I've got it! It's the chair, it has this power, this erotic essence that overpowers Billie. We saw that earlier. But now we can see this in another form. In Marc.'

'You mean Marc is the physical embodiment of the essence in the chair?' Jonathan said sceptically.

'Yes it works. Don't you see it? The natural progression. The only way to show the sheer physicality of the thing. To move from object to subject. It makes sense,' she babbled excitedly.

Fay turned back and went over to Marc and began to whisper excitedly to him. He smiled and nodded enthusiastically, looking at Billie who was still perched on the end of the chair.

'Do they know?' Jonathan asked Victoria, suddenly afraid that the whole thing was going to backfire.

'That would be telling,' Victoria giggled.

Marc stripped off quickly, his muscular brown body already bathed in a layer of sweat under the hot lights.

222

His prick was long and hard, spearing upwards from a dense pubic bush that was barely perceptible against his skin. He stepped forward, his back rippling as he walked, feet padding softly on the cold wooden floor.

He put his hands on Billie's waist and she turned to him. There was no feigning the look of surprise on her face, part fear and part delight. Fay captured the look on film, smiling indulgently. She moved up to take several pictures of Marc's strong hands holding Billie tightly by the waist, and then his fingers moved up her thigh, stroking her hard so that she closed her eyes and sighed.

'Press your bottom out darling,' Fay told her and she did as directed, arching her back and forcing her backside apart. The panties were stretched even tighter, a single thread of material between the arse-cheeks, the darker crease around the arse hole clearly visible.

Marc knelt down and began to smother Billie's thighs and buttocks with loving kisses, his thick lips moving quickly and gracefully over the tight flesh. Billie was sighing and moaning, she turned her back to look down on Marc and her face was twisted with ecstasy, eyes half closed, lips apart, breathing hard and fast.

Billie was clean-shaven between the thighs, Jonathan knew that, but he wondered how long it would be before Marc found out the truth. He was rubbing both hands up and down the thighs, palming the arse-cheeks lovingly, kissing and biting as he went.

'Kiss her behind,' Fay shouted, running across the room for some distance shots before running back for the closeups. Her face was intent, beads of sweat pouring from her, her voice sounding hoarse. A weird bird of prey, she circled Marc and Billie, swooping close then flitting away, a necessary adjunct to their exhibition.

Billie pulled her panties to one side, managing

somehow to expose the tight bead of her anus. Marc flicked his tongue lovingly, snaking it over Billie's anal hole.

'He's going to fuck her,' Victoria whispered, as if she could hardly believe it herself.

'Does he know?' Jonathan muttered, aware of the growing urgency of Marc's movements. He had both hands on her arse-cheeks and was pulling them apart so that his tongue was going deep inside her. He lapped and sucked her, his thumbs stroking her between the thighs at the same time.

'I don't know,' Victoria admitted.

'The darkness can't penetrate the light,' Jonathan shouted loudly, making Fay turn away for an instant. 'It can't be done.'

'What?' Fay looked confused.

'They're two different things. Opposites. He's the power, the dark essence from the inanimate object. She's the light, the physical, the pure if you like. It's the universal dichotomy.'

'Good and evil?'

'Yes,' Jonathan agreed eagerly. 'They are the two cosmic principles. Yin and Yang. One cannot penetrate the other. They're too distinct for that.'

Billie sighed and everyone turned to look at her. She had half turned and was stroking Marc's big prick in her hands, making him sigh with pleasure. Her thin fingers were wrapped tightly around his hardness, her eyes wide with excitement and wonder.

'I don't buy that,' Fay decided, turning back to Marc and Billie and recommencing the photographs. 'Too dualistic,' she added, not turning from them.

'Let him come all over her backside,' Victoria suggested.

'What?' Fay demanded, distracted again.

'Yes, yes,' Jonathan agreed. 'It's his essence, let him

spread it over her. The light smeared with darkness.'

'Over her backside? Over her seat?' Fay paused. 'There's some humour there, I think. Something disturbing too. Her seat is going to be soiled, smeared with the essence of his power. Very Freudian. I like that a lot.'

Marc had manoeuvred himself on to the seat and Billie was on her knees, kissing his prick urgently, licking and sucking with a hunger that was real. Marc was clutching the arms of the seat, gasping and whispering wordlessly. Jonathan recognised the look, he felt it too, voyeuristically, the feeling of holding back, wanting to prolong the blissful sensations for as long as possible.

'Billie, back as you were, looking over the edge of the seat,' Fay ordered, her voice loud and clear.

Billie moaned, Marc's prick was deep in her throat, her lips sliding sensuously up and down the glistening length of flesh. Reluctantly she pulled away, sucking the jewels of fluid from the bulbous tip of his prick as she did so. She resumed her pose, stretching like a cat, pressing her backside so that it was tight and round.

'Marc I want you to ride between her backside, I don't want you going into her,' Fay told him soberly. 'When you come I want you to let it go all over her beautiful bottom. I want to see it all. When you come move away if you can. I want some good pictures of this.'

Marc took Billie by the waist and pulled himself up, moulding his body around hers. Jonathan moved to the side, wanting to watch it all, barely able to control his own excitement. The idea that Marc didn't know who, or what, he was fucking, added to the thrill.

'Fuck me . . . ' Billie whispered hoarsely, pressing herself back so that Marc's hardness was lodged tightly between her buttocks. He obeyed at once, grinding his

225

hips up and down, pressing himself tight into her rear valley.

'That feels good . . . ' Billie cried, closing her eyes and resting her head flat against the cool leather of the chair. Marc's rhythm was becoming more rapid, thrusting hard against her. She was moving too, tightening her arse-cheeks as he thrust against her, making him moan and herself sigh with pleasure. Her lipstick was smeared across her lips, and where it had coated his prick it was now spread pink between her buttocks, adding colour to her soft pale skin.

'This is so good . . . ' Marc cried, his body seized with a series of violently convulsions that had him jerking hard against Billie. He released his tight grip on her waist and fell back. The thick cream that he had spurted was dripping and oozing down between Billie's thighs, golden jewels of melting ice that stained the soft white of her skin.

'Excellent, excellent,' Fay repeated excitedly. She had been close, almost between the two sweat-bathed bodies. Marc's orgasm, the shooting spray of come, the agonised look of climax, the pleasure and the relief, were all on film.

'I'm glad you're happy,' Victoria sighed, looking as relieved as Jonathan. 'I told you Billie would be good, didn't I?'

'She was good. Very good,' Fay concurred. 'We'll have to use her again. And you,' she turned to Jonathan, 'you were very good too. You had some interesting ideas there.'

'Thanks, glad to help.'

'Perhaps we can work together some time?' she suggested, smiling happily at the prospect.

'Definitely. I think we ought to get going now,' he said, purposefully looking at his watch.

'Yes, we're going to hit town now,' Victoria decided

excitedly. 'Come on, Billie, you can fix yourself in the car if you have to.'

'Can I see you again?' Marc asked, padding across to Billie who was wiping herself clean.

'I'll see what can be arranged,' Victoria promised him, cutting off Billie before she had a chance to say anything.

Fay took them back down the stairs, eagerly discussing the pictures that she had taken and the full metaphysical significance of it all. Jonathan could see that she took both aspects of her work seriously, trying to combine the sexiness of image with the full depth of meaning.

'I've forgotten my bag,' Billie remembered the moment they were back in the car. 'I'm sorry, Mistress,' she added, still sounding a little dazed by the experience.

'I'll get it,' Jonathan volunteered quickly.

'Be quick,' Victoria told him impatiently.

Jonathan rang the bell and this time he heard Fay asking who it was. She opened the door to him and he walked back upstairs to the studio. Marc was dressed and was putting the make-up away.

Fay had the bag ready for him. 'I did think your ideas were interesting,' she said, handing him the bag, 'And I was serious about working together.'

'I'd like that. You know I do have some ideas I'd like to explore. It's just I'd never considered doing it this way.'

'We can talk if you like. Will you call me?'

'Yes, I promise.' It didn't seem such a bad idea. There were a lot of things in his mind that he hadn't been able to work out. Perhaps it made sense to try to go through them, to talk them over with someone else, to put words and pictures to the vague feelings and intuitions.

'I'll call Victoria tomorrow, when the first batch of pictures are ready. Perhaps you'd like to come over and have a look? They won't be ready for the de Molay gallery for another month, so we've still got time for another session if we need one.'

Jonathan froze. The de Molay gallery. Everywhere he went that name kept cropping up, it had come to haunt him. 'Actually we were going to see Jessica Calder-Read, but Victoria's forgotten her address book and can't remember the exact address . . . '

'Yes, I've got it,' Fay said helpfully. 'Let me write it down for you.'

Jonathan held his breath. It didn't seem possible, but after all the trials and tribulations the address was going to come to him so simply.

Fay returned a moment later with a gold embossed business card, she turned it over and scribbled the address. 'So perhaps I'll see you tomorrow?' she said, handing it over.

'Yes,' Jonathan said distantly, taking the card in his trembling fingers.

11

Jonathan was alone when he woke. The curtains had been drawn and the sunlight was streaming into the room, several distinct shafts of yellow light slicing diagonally across the room. He listened for a while to the sound of running water from the bathroom and guessed that Victoria was being bathed by Billie.

It had been a wild night, and Jonathan hadn't really had a chance to consider what to do next. He had committed the address he got from Fay to memory, like a poem or a mantra, every syllable inscribed in his mind. It meant everything to him, and it made him scared. What if it had all been in vain, and Mistress didn't want him at all?

He closed his eyes and the memories of the previous night came flooding back. After the photo session they had gone to a club, where Victoria made a grand entrance with Billie and himself at her beck and call. However things had begun to change. Jonathan guessed that it had begun at the photographic session. By the end of the evening Jonathan was no longer a slave, indeed he wondered if he had ever really been Victoria's slave in anything but name.

By the time they returned to Victoria's place she was on his arm, holding him tightly, looking into his eyes excitedly. Billie had lagged behind, recognising that her position hadn't changed, and that Jonathan was now her master, a willing equal to her mistress.

Billie had undressed Victoria, kissing her feet, deliriously running her lips all over Victoria. Jonathan undressed himself and took Victoria in his arms, kissing her on the neck and mouth, sliding his hands down her back and squeezing her small round breasts. He felt intoxicated, alive. He slipped his hand down between Victoria's thighs and felt the damp heat, the thick honey running between the pussy lips.

He and Victoria had parted for a moment and Victoria gestured to Billie to get on to the bed. She had obeyed without question, moving lithely, a rare smile on her pretty lips. He kissed Victoria again, and when she slipped from his arms he saw that Billie was lying flat on the bed, her short skirt bulging at the front.

'I want to suck that lovely prick of yours,' Victoria had said hotly, squeezing his prick with her fingers. She took his hands and pulled him over to the bed, smiling greedily, her eyes glittering with unconcealed glee. She straddled Billie and pulled Jonathan, urging him to do the same. He remembered hesitating, not sure that he wanted Billie involved.

'Send her away,' Jonathan had said quietly, standing with one knee on the edge of the bed.

'No, this will be good,' Victoria promised. She had lifted herself a little and pulled Billie's skirt open, revealing the long thick prick underneath. Billie's body was almost hairless, and even the light hair at the base of the prick had been closely cut and trimmed. Victoria took the hardness and pressed at the dark entrance to the pussy. She smiled at Jonathan and then sat back slowly, closing her eyes and sighing softly as Billie's hardness entered her.

He could still see her in his mind, wriggling her hips,

pressing herself down as hard as she could on the prick digging into her damp sex. Jonathan had watched, fascinated by the way Billie's prick disappeared into Victoria's dark pussy, enveloped by her thick wet pussy lips, dappled with her own flowing juices.

'I want to suck you,' Victoria repeated. She had reached out and taken Jonathan's hands and pulled him towards her. He had allowed himself to be manoeuvred, sitting on Billie's chest, his feet on either side of her head.

Victoria had leaned across and kissed Jonathan on the neck and mouth, slowly pushing him back at the same time. Her kisses became more urgent and she moved lower, her hands exploring eagerly at the same time. Jonathan had inched back, making room for her to bring her mouth over his rock-hard prick. Her first kisses were soft and loving, her tongue flicking over his engorged glans, licking him with an almost joyful abandon. He had sighed, lifting himself up, pushing his prick much deeper into her soft receptive mouth.

Her hands had been on his thighs, moving up and down softly, kneading his muscular limbs. He had shifted back again and felt Billie's hot breath between his thighs. Victoria went down again, cradling his balls in her hot hands while sucking his prick deep into her mouth.

Jonathan had frozen at the first feel of Billie's lips under his thighs. Looking back he realised that Victoria had seen him react, and she had started sucking harder, pulling her cheeks over his prick and riding up and down, like a warm pussy wet with honey. The feel of Victoria's mouth on his prick merged with the feel of Billie's mouth under his balls, exploring him eagerly, her hot tongue tracing unknown patterns between his thighs.

Victoria rode up and down his prick, sucking him ecstatically, her tongue licking him expertly under the glans, making him squirm with pleasure, the sensations passing like waves through his body. She reached back with her hands, caressing his backside with her fingers, then slowly pulling his buttocks apart.

Billie began to lick Jonathan between the arse-cheeks, her tongue moving like a hot flame from the base of his prick and up towards his arse-hole. When Jonathan had moaned softly, closing his eyes, and arching his back, Billie had pressed her tongue deep into him. Jonathan could remember the feeling of falling through space. He had no control, his mind was empty. And the pleasure was burning through him, from his rear hole being kissed and sucked by Billie and from his prick being joyfully fellated by Victoria.

Victoria had pressed down hard when he climaxed, letting him empty himself into the back of her throat. She was gently squeezing his balls at the same time, controlling him, emptying him completely. And all the time Jonathan could feel Billie's tongue inside him, injecting powerful ripples of pleasure through him, making the orgasm more intense, more powerful.

'Are you thinking about last night?' Victoria smiled, coming back into the room. Her hair was wet, slicked back over her head as if it had been greased. Her robe was loose, and Jonathan could see that her neck and chest were still patterned with light pink blotches.

'Yes,' he admitted. 'I see that Billie's bathed you the way I used to,' he said, pointing to her chest.

'She's very good with her mouth,' Victoria said, laughing lightly. The sun fell across her face and chest, casting a dark shadow between her breasts, delineating the full shape and roundness of her bust.

232

'I'm going to visit Fay later on, to see how Billie's pictures turned out. Will you join me?'

'I'm not sure,' Jonathan replied evasively. He avoided her eyes, knowing that she wasn't going to like the news he had for her.

'Fay would really like to see you again, I think,' she purred softly, brushing the back of her fingers over his erect prick.

'A word of advice,' he said sombrely, suddenly remembering the near panic he had experienced at the photo session, 'never ever try and pass Billie off as something she's not.'

Victoria giggled. 'It was scary, wasn't it? But it's part of the game, it's not boring is it? Confound people's expectations, that's what Jonathan, I mean the other Jonathan, always says.'

'I'm serious,' Jonathan said, taking her wrist and pushing her hand away from his prick.

'What's wrong?' she asked, frowning.

'I don't know how to tell you this,' he said, exhaling heavily. 'I don't want to hurt your feelings.'

'It's her, isn't it?' Victoria said accusingly, the hurt clear in her voice.

'Yes. I'm sorry Victoria, I like you a lot, but this is something I've got to follow through.'

'Why? What's she got that I haven't? What's so special about her? Tell me.'

Jonathan shook his head sadly. How could he tell her? What could he tell her? She wasn't a mistress, she didn't have the indefinable presence that Jessica Calder-Read had in abundance. Instead he told her the address. 'I know where I can find her now. Can you give me her phone number?'

'No. You must be mad. Do you really think that I'd give you her number?'

'Please?'

233

'Get out!' Victoria screamed, suddenly standing up, her eyes livid. 'Get out! Get the fuck out of here!'

'Calm down,' Jonathan said softly, moving across the bed towards her.

'No!' she said, twisting away from his arms. She stepped back, her eyes wet with tears and her voice cracking.

'Please, please,' he repeated helplessly. He stood up, put his hands out towards her, wanting to take her and hold her close. He felt like a bastard. And he knew that this was what he was going to do to Caroline too.

'No!' she screamed again, her voice on the edge of hysteria. She pushed him back, knocking him on to the bed. He fell heavily, surprised by the unexpected push and the force behind it. She crossed the room quickly, a manic look in her eyes. Everything seemed to slow down. He watched her pull the drawer open, heard her scrabbling for an implement. He sat up, heart racing, winded by the sudden fall.

Victoria stood up straight, her lips pursed and eyes narrowly cruel. In her hand she held a riding crop, long and supple and tipped with a triangle of leather.

'Look, Victoria, I thought we'd got over that . . .' Jonathan started to say patiently. Billie came into the room and immediately slunk into the corner, putting a hand to her mouth and her eyes wide and fixed on the riding crop.

'Don't talk to me like that, you bastard,' Victoria hissed. 'And don't you dare patronise me either. This is what you want isn't it? This is what you want from her . . . '

Jonathan swallowed hard. He didn't feel like playing games, and in Victoria's mood he had no way of knowing how far she would go. Her eyes were hard and steely, expressing her cold anger and rage. He

234

moved back, slowly moving away from her, covering himself with the bed cover.

'What's wrong? Isn't this how you like it?' she taunted, and then grabbed the cover and pulled it quickly, stripping him once more. She flexed the crop, bending it with both hands, and then sliced it through the air.

'I know you're angry . . . ' he began again ineffectually.

'Angry?' she laughed. 'Why should I be fucking angry!'

He tried to say something but she leapt across the room suddenly, lashing out with the riding crop. It whistled through the air and caught him across the back as he turned to avoid it. It stung wickedly and he howled, he scrabbled to get away but slipped on the discarded cover and fell to his knees.

'That's right,' she hissed, 'at Mistress's feet like a bad little boy.'

Jonathan looked up at her, at the dark anger and contempt in her eyes. He deserved it, she was right, it was just what he wanted from Mistress – to be beaten and humiliated. He crouched down from her as she wielded the crop again, hitting him across the back, striking diagonally so that the tip caught his buttocks.

She raised her arm again and the stroke fell lower, directly on his arse-cheeks. He moved, slipped again and was flat on his back. She planted her bare foot on his lower back, pressing down so that her toes were digging into his flesh. He looked up at her and felt dizzy, he caught his breath, felt the fire kindling inside him. She looked fantastic, tall, elegant, fiery eyes, the whip in her hand a natural accessory. Her breasts were loose, and as she lifted her arm and brought it down her nipples jigged tightly.

He lay at her feet and she beat him, each stroke hissing through the air and then snapping loudly on his arse-cheeks. His breath was unsteady, gasping with each stinging whack, inhaling sharply and holding it until the next blow. He could feel his backside being patterned with thick red lines, each stroke like an arrow of pleasure-pain.

He looked round and saw Billie on her knees behind Victoria, kissing her on the feet and calves and between the thighs. He didn't know how long it went on for, the rhythm filled his ears; hiss, smack, a release of breath. The red heat spread down his thighs and round under his balls and into his prick. The pain had long since become pleasure, and he willingly let her beat out her anger on him. It was what he deserved, she was a mistress and he was nothing. She *was* a mistress.

He climaxed, groaning loudly as the power of Victoria's punishment pushed him over the edge. Everything was white, a blinding white light that throbbed in his mind and body. It felt good, so good, to be at Mistress's feet, his body consumed with pleasure and pain in equal measure.

Some time later Jonathan looked up and saw that he was alone in Victoria's room. He got up, his body protesting, smarting all over. In the mirror in the wardrobe door he looked at his back, striped with thin red lines all over his buttocks and down his thighs.

Victoria had vented her anger on him, all the frustrations and disappointments that he had caused had been paid in full. He hoped that she had climaxed too, that the combination of her domination and Billie's tongue had given her total satisfaction.

He dressed slowly, making no sharp movements in an effort to stifle the pain. He opened the bedroom

236

door and listened, not at all sure how long he had lain on the floor. She had been due to go to see Fay, and he wondered whether she and Billie had gone.

'No . . . no I haven't, honestly I haven't . . . ' he heard Victoria saying. He stood by the kitchen door and listened to her, she was speaking on the phone and sounded agitated and nervous. 'No . . . I don't know where he got the address from. It wasn't me, I can promise you that . . . He says he's going to come round . . . I don't know when, soon I should think . . . Don't worry, I've warmed him up already . . . Yes . . . Yes . . . I'll have him out as soon as I put the phone . . . Not ever? But . . . If you say so . . . Hello? Hello?' He heard her slam the phone down and swear under her breath.

He turned and headed for the door. There were only two people she could have been speaking to and he wished that it was neither of them. It was over between Victoria and himself, though filling in the gaps he was sure it wasn't exactly what she wanted. Now it was time to leave, to make a clean break and to let her get on with her own life.

'Bye,' Billie said softly, coming out of the kitchen just as Jonathan opened the front door.

'Bye, and look after her,' he said, smiling sadly. He closed the door, feeling sadness mingled with relief and apprehension.

'You sound happy,' Jonathan said as soon as Jessica answered the phone. 'Does that mean what I think it means?'

'Yes,' Jessica said, her voice almost a sigh. 'He called yesterday evening and I was with him last night.'

'I'm very happy for you,' he added, hoping that soon he would feel as she did.

'I just feel so happy now,' she continued gushingly.

237

'I feel fulfilled, glad to be alive. I guess he needed me to prove a point for him, but at least I was there for him.'

'What do you mean, to prove a point?'

'He was with a Russian aristocrat and they were having an argument, a real old-fashioned intellectual discussion about free will versus determinism. Jonathan's like that, he's very strong on ideas, everything has to have a meaning, even if the meaning isn't logical. He was arguing for a strongly libertarian line about freedom and responsibility, the Russian was arguing the exact opposite. That's why he needed me.'

'Because you're a historian?' Jonathan asked, not quite seeing the point she was trying to make.

'No. They were having a meal. When they finished eating he had me lie on the table, naked, so that they could eat from my body. Fruit between my breasts, honey on my belly and icy cream dripping from my sex.' She paused and Jonathan could imagine her smiling. 'I proved the point for Jonathan. There I was, a person with complete free will, submitting willing to another's irrational orders.'

'How did the Russian react?'

'Stunned silence. Jonathan was very blasé as usual. He kept playing with my nipples, making them stand hard, or pressing banana into the cream pouring from my sex. The Russian looked very embarrassed, he didn't know where to look or what to do. In the end Jonathan took the man's hand and pressed deep into my sex, ostensibly proving a final point but really he just wanted to show that he'd won the argument.'

'Isn't that what he really wanted to do? He wanted to win, not to prove a point or anything else,' Jonathan said coldly. The idea of Jonathan de Molay caring about ideas or intellectual discussions was too far-fetched to believe. Jonathan couldn't visualise him as the sort of man that cared about anything really, except for his own pleasures and desires.

'You only say that because you don't know him,' Jessica countered defensively.

'Actually I called because I need a favour from you,' he said, not wanting to get into an argument about de Molay.

'What?' Jessica asked suspiciously.

Jonathan told her Mistress's address. 'I was hoping that you could give me her telephone number now. I know where she lives, you're not giving anything away now.'

'How did you get it?'

'I just did. Will you help me now?'

'I hope you know what you're doing Jonathan,' she said slowly. 'Jonathan de Molay and Jessica Calder-Read are two of the most powerful and destructive people I've ever met. Really, do you have any idea of what to expect?'

'Just now you said you felt complete,' he pointed out, 'why deny me the same feeling?'

Jessica told him the number, she spoke quickly and clearly, obviously from memory. There was no need to write it down. He was certain that he would never forget it.

'Thanks,' he said.

'Jonathan?'

'Yes?'

'Good luck.'

Jonathan put the phone down and sat on the floor. Now that he had the telephone number and address he realised that he was scared. The final step was frightening, it needed a leap of faith that he wasn't sure he could take. His heart was pounding, thumping hard in his chest so that he gasped for breath. What if Mistress said no? What was left for him then? His life had been shattered, irrevocably, he couldn't go back to who or what he had been. Once consciousness is achieved there is no going back, and he had become conscious of the things deep in his soul, things that had lain buried, like a treasure in his heart, a treasure that was cursed all the same.

He punched out the number, listening to the musical tones that were generated. For the first time he realised that every number was a song and that this was the one he would always know.

'Naomi?' he whispered, even before anyone had spoken.

'Yes? Who's calling please?' he heard her say, and her image came back to him, her sad eyes that had looked at him with an aching desire that could not be quenched.

'It's Jonathan, Jonathan de Molay.'

'Jonathan? How did you get this number?'

'Naomi, I must speak with your mistress, is she there? Will she speak to me?' he asked, managing to keep the feeling of panic in check.

'Please wait, Master,' she said softly.

He waited tensely, his hands sweaty and tiny beads of perspiration breaking out all over his body. He looked around him, at the neat and tidy house, at the light falling into the room, making it shine luminously. The sky was alternately grey and blue, the day hesitating, changing mood with the passing of the clouds.

'They do say a dog will always find his way home,' Mistress said, the familiar note of sardonic amusement in her voice.

'Mistress . . . ' Jonathan whispered, suddenly feeling weak at the merest sound of her voice. He closed his eyes to block out everything but that voice, as pure and as sweet as anything he had ever heard.

'Well, Dog,' she continued, 'you've been very persistent. I'm impressed, I didn't think you'd make it.'

'Please Mistress, can I see you again?'

'Well, darling,' she said, stretching the word out till it ached in the air, 'I think it may be amusing. Will you beg like a dog?'

'Yes, Mistress, on my hands and knees, anything.'

'Will you grovel before me? Lick me between the thighs?'

'Yes, yes . . . ' Jonathan repeated, his prick already hard. Anything, he would do anything for her, anything at all.

'And if I had you tied up and left in a corner, would you like that?'

'Yes . . . No . . . '

'Not very decisive, are you, my little doggie?'

'If that's what you wanted I'd do it, Mistress,' he begged. 'I would do anything for you. Tie me up and leave me in the corner, at least I'll be in the same room as you, I'll be able to see and hear you.' It was agony, she was toying with him, playing with his fears and emotions. He longed to be at her heel, beneath her, under her domination. At least then he was certain of his place.

'But you're so tiresome,' she said, beginning to sound bored. 'You talk too much. I don't like that, not at all. Perhaps I'll have you muzzled.'

'Yes Mistress, let me be muzzled, if that's what you want.'

'Muzzled and then whipped, to teach you the value of silence,' she mused, as if thinking it over.

'Yes, Mistress,' he agreed obediently, forcing himself to say nothing more, despite the thoughts and words swelling in his mind.

'I'll grant you another little audience,' she said decisively. 'Be ready this evening, somebody will call.'

'Thank you Mistress, thank you,' he breathed relief, almost wanting to scream with grateful joy. 'My address is . . . '

'Be ready,' she said and then the phone was dead.

Jonathan sat still, hardly daring to believe his good luck. He was going to see her again, to sit and beg at her feet, to bask in her reflected glory.

He punched the tone pad again, another number, and this time he imagined that the sound it made was sad and mournful. It rang insistently for several minutes before it was picked up.

'Caroline,' he said, 'it's me.'

'Jonathan,' she said, instantly recognising his voice, 'I was going to call you.'

'I've got something to say . . . ' they both blurted at the same instant, then laughed nervously.

'You go first,' she insisted.

'I've spoken to Mistress, I'm going to see her again tonight . . . I just wanted to let you know.'

'I see . . . ' she said.

'I feel like I've been a real bastard to you, stringing you along . . . '

'No, stop,' she said. 'I've got something to tell you too.'

'What?'

'I was going to call you to tell you anyway. I can't wait any longer for you, Jon, I'm sorry, but I can't. I don't understand you any longer, the last time we met just proved it. It frightened me too, to see the way we're splitting apart. I'm frightened of you too and frightened for you . . . '

'No, I'm all right,' he said, trying to stop her going on.

'Let me finish. I don't understand what's going on in your mind. It's alien to me, I can't believe that you're the same man I used to love.'

'Love?' he said, the word causing a knot of anguish to form in the pit of his belly. Why was it that they had never spoken of love before? Why was it that they had avoided the word like the plague until it was time for them to part?

'Yes, love. You always shied away from it, but that's what it was. I must have been the same, too scared of making commitments, too afraid to let emotion get in the way of everything else. Now I can't love you, and you'll never love me.'

She paused, and Jonathan wondered if she were crying, there was a sadness and a tenderness in her voice that struck a chord. For a moment he wanted to forget everyone else, to leave behind all the obsessions and rituals and go running back to Caroline. It was a dream, a misty-eyed memory of what had happened once, long before they were even aware of themselves as real people. 'I'm sorry it had to end this way,' he said sadly, his own voice cracking mid-sentence.

'I hope Mistress is good to you,' she said, exhaling, 'that you get from her whatever it is you're looking for.'

'And you?'

'There's somebody else now,' she said. 'That's what I wanted to tell you. You don't know him, but he loves me, Jonathan, and he's not afraid to tell me so. He makes me feel good, like you used to make me feel. And I can understand him, I can see what sort of person he is, I can look into his face and understand what's going on behind his eyes.'

'Do you love him?'

'He loves me,' she responded a little too quickly. 'He loves me for what I am, not . . . not . . . '

'I understand,' he said softly.

'I've got to go now. Will we ever see each other again?'

'Sure we will,' he said reassuringly, knowing that it was a lie, and that she knew it was a lie.

'Bye, Jonathan,' she said, her voice soft and sad.

'I love you,' he said quietly, but the phone was dead and he wasn't sure whether she had heard him or not.

12

The phone startled Jonathan. He picked it up and listened. 'There is a car waiting for you,' a woman said, emotionlessly.

He put the phone down and stood up. Outside it was dark, the night had fallen suddenly, but it was at least clear and dry. On his way out he caught sight of himself in a mirror, dressed in black, hair brushed back, clean-shaven, eyes clear and bright. It was going to be the most important night of his life, and he wanted to be ready, ready for anything.

The car was waiting by the entrance to his apartment block, a red convertible with the black hood up, the bright red paintwork gleaming provocatively in the pale electric street light. It was one of de Molay's cars. He recognised the driver at once, there was no way he could mistake her for anyone else. She sat in the driving seat, looking straight ahead, long blonde hair cascading over her shoulders, prominent red lips slightly parted.

He took a deep breath and got into the back of the car. It meant that de Molay knew what was going on, and the thought unnerved him. The driver started the car without a word, the sudden acceleration pushing Jonathan back into the leather seat.

'Where are we going?' he asked after a while, unable to stand the brittle silence.

'Wherever I take you,' she replied, her voice icy cool. Her eyes caught his in the rear view mirror, clear blue eyes that stared back at him impassively.

'Have we met before?' he asked, suddenly struck by the thought that her eyes were familiar, that somewhere, sometime, she had stared back at him in the same way.

'You mean you don't remember?' she asked mockingly.

'So we have met?'

'Yes, just the once mind you. But you seemed deeply affected by it at the time.'

'I'm sorry,' he said, shaking his head, 'I just can't remember it.'

'I'm sure that's not true,' she smiled. 'Actually I was rather worried at the time. I'd made a mistake but luckily you didn't notice it. Naomi would have noticed, but she wasn't the one that prepared you.'

'Prepared me?' Jonathan looked up at her, realisation suddenly dawning.

'Yes. I'd had my hair plaited, I had the boots, but then I'd forgotten the most important thing of all – the riding crop. Still the whip served me well, and you were too out of your mind to really notice the details.'

'It was you?' he said, horrified. She had been the imposter, the brilliant blue eyes that had stared at him through the black mask were the same eyes looking at him in the mirror. He had grovelled at her feet thinking she was Mistress, suffering the pain and humiliation willingly, only to find out that she was a stranger.

'Yes, it really was your first time under the heel of a woman, wasn't it?'

'Yes,' he said glumly, his face burning with shame at the memory. It had been an effective first encounter,

246

and in its way it had set the pace for all that had happened.

'I felt so honoured, to be the first to make you submit like that. I look forward to the day when I'm allowed to do it again.'

Jonathan fell silent. There was nothing he could say, the humiliation that he felt that first day came flooding back, redoubled now that he knew who his tormentor had been, and that she longed to beat him again. He looked away from her, away from her piercing eyes. She was an alluring vision, her face in profile, pale skin in contrast to her wide glossy lips painted deep red, alluring but cruel.

He looked out of the window for a time, not seeing anything, lost in his thoughts and in the apprehension building up inside him. It had been so callous, to deceive him like that, to make him think that the woman before him was Mistress. The more he thought about it the worse he felt. It had been deliberately cruel, done in the certain knowledge that it would heighten every feeling of humiliation and degradation. And it had worked, with surgical precision it had cut him to the core.

The car stopped and the driver turned to him, smiling. 'This is the end of the road,' she said, her lips parted over brilliant white teeth.

'Is she there?' he asked coldly, filled with the doubt that had been there at the start of the journey.

'You'll soon find out, won't you,' she said, her smile becoming broader, crueller. Jonathan opened the door and stepped out into the cold night air. 'And next time I'll have the riding crop,' she called after him as he slammed the door shut.

It was de Molay's house, close to the Thames. Jonathan climbed the granite steps to the imposing black door. He pressed the bell and waited anxiously, looking back to see the car disappearing round the corner at the end of the street.

'Naomi,' he cried, entering the bright warmth of the house. He took her hands and kissed them fervently, he felt so glad to see her. She smiled briefly then pulled her hands away, looking back nervously towards the stairs.

'Welcome, Master,' she said softly, her face impassive once more.

'I'm so glad to see you,' he said.

'Thank you, Master. Please follow me,' she said, turning and walking towards the first door on the left.

Jonathan followed, not even bothering to look around him. Naomi's presence was reassuring, and he felt that she was an old and trusted friend. She was dressed in stark black and white, from black flat-heeled shoes to short black skirt to crisp white blouse. Her clothes seemed to reflect the ambiguity of her position, close enough to domestic uniform without being totally obvious.

Naomi stopped at a door and knocked quietly, putting her ear to the door for the reply.

'Do I have to get on my hands and knees?' Jonathan asked her anxiously.

She shook her head. 'That won't be necessary,' she said softly, 'not at this stage.'

Jonathan hadn't heard a reply but Naomi pushed the door open and entered first. He followed her nervously, trembling, breathing sharply, a dagger of sweat sliding down his back.

Mistress was there, sitting on the edge of a leather seat to one side of the large room. He looked at her and felt afraid, the space between them was nothing, her eyes were on him, looking deep into him, seeing everything.

Naomi was walking across the room, and Jonathan was following, though he felt that he was moving automatically, floating across the room, drawn by the power of Mistress's presence. She wore her hair long on one side and swept back on the other, so that her face seemed in profile from all angles.

'I'm here, Mistress,' Jonathan said, his voice uncharacteristically clear and strong. He looked at her, held her eyes for a moment and then looked away, down at her black patent leather shoes. It was an effort, but he controlled his breathing, trying hard to appear calm when in reality he felt close to panic. Mistress raised her hand and Jonathan kissed it respectfully, touching his lips to her long elegant fingers.

'You've done very well,' Mistress said, half smiling.

'Thank you, Mistress,' he said, certain that for once she wasn't laughing at him. Her eyes were fixed on him, but when he glanced at her all he could see was her curiosity. There was none of the outright contempt that he remembered so vividly.

'You did very well with Sara-Jane. She liked you very much, much more than Vanessa I hasten to add. And of course young Vicky is absolutely besotted with you. But you know that, don't you?'

'Yes, Mistress,' he agreed.

'And Charly liked you very much too,' she continued, all the time her smile becoming broader. 'She was very eloquent on your behalf, I might add. She spoke about you in the highest possible terms, you ought to be grateful to her.'

Jonathan made no reply. Mistress knew everything, and she was making it plain to him that she knew. He felt a little sick, a hollow feeling had formed in his stomach and was spreading, making him feel empty. All along he had imagined that he was working blindly towards Mistress, but it wasn't true. He had

249

been played like a fool, manipulated and used at every turn.

'Jessica spoke to Jonathan about you, did you know that?'

'No, Mistress.'

'She was always going to be the difficult one, I wasn't sure how she would react under the circumstances. Did she give you the telephone number?'

Jonathan looked up sharply, Mistress was waiting expectantly, eyebrows raised and lips parted. 'Yes, Mistress,' he said, hoping that he wasn't going to cause Jessica any problems. He had no choice, he couldn't lie to Mistress.

'Yes, she told me that she did. I'm glad to see that you're not willing to lie to protect her. Your loyalty had to be to me,' she paused and looked at him, her smile had gone and her eyes were staring into his. 'I expect complete and absolute loyalty and submission. There's no room for anyone else. Do you understand that?'

'Yes, Mistress,' he said obediently.

'You have been loyal to me. Everyone, from Vicky to Charly to Jessica, attests to that. Has it been a painful journey?'

'Yes, Mistress. Very painful.'

'Would you do it again?'

'Of course,' he replied immediately, not waiting to think about it.

'Well done, darling,' she said, and her voice was at once clear and beautiful yet soft and erotic.

'Mistress, may I ask you one question?' he asked, daring to look at her directly.

'One question,' she said, standing up, 'for the first and last time.'

'That first phone call, was it an accident?'

She looked at him and then laughed, filling the room

250

with the sound of her voice. 'On your knees,' she ordered curtly.

'Please Mistress, please tell me . . .'

'Now!' she snapped.

Jonathan fell to his knees obediently, the sharp sound of her command striking red hot inside him, making him feel weak with sudden desire. Her eyes were flaming, cruel and contemptuous. She wore black stockings and from his position he could glimpse the soft white flesh of her thigh. He remembered sucking her between the thighs, filling his mouth with her taste, feasting on the honey pouring thickly from her sex.

'Have him prepared,' Mistress ordered Naomi, 'then bring him down to the chamber.'

Jonathan fell forward and kissed Mistress's heels as she strode past, her heels cracking hard against the cold floor. She ignored him, striding confidently out of the room, her long legs almost crossing as she walked. Jonathan watched her go, too afraid to call after her, aware that her mood had changed in an instant. Cruel and capricious, Mistress could do as she wished with him.

'We have to get ready,' Naomi said, coming back into focus after Mistress had gone.

'Was it?' Jonathan demanded, looking up at Naomi suddenly. 'I have to know, was it an accident?'

'Does it matter?' Naomi asked softly, taking his hand and urging him to his feet.

'Yes it does, it matters a lot,' he insisted. 'I need to know. Was it an accident or was I deliberately set up?'

'I don't know,' she said, standing close to him, so that he could breathe her scent and feel her warmth. 'What matters is that you belong to Mistress now. Isn't that what you wanted?'

'But it's not what I wanted before all this began. It's not what I wanted when I was woken up in the middle of the night to listen to you being punished.'

'What did you want then?' Naomi asked him, taking his hands and kissing them tenderly. 'What did you want before Mistress?'

'I don't know,' he admitted. It felt wrong. His whole life had been turned upside down and now he didn't know whether it had been fate or cruel deliberation.

'Forget that now,' she said persuasively. 'I have to prepare you for the chamber.'

'The chamber?'

Naomi nodded. 'You belong to her now, she can do what she likes with you. You're Dog now, not Jonathan de Molay.'

'I don't know who I am any more. I thought I had it all worked out. But now I realise that I'm only the one who didn't know what was going on. She made me. I'm her creation.'

'No,' Naomi shook her head, her long brown hair shimmering around her. 'Mistress could never make what wasn't there already. She helped you to form yourself, just as she did with me. That's why we are the way we are, because this has been inside us all along. It just took Mistress to show us the way.'

'Do you ever feel despair?'

Naomi came up to him and put her lips against his, kissing him softly, taking his hands in hers. 'Don't feel upset,' she murmured softly, her breath hot on his lips. 'Whether it was by accident or design, you've been chosen, that's the important thing. Mistress was telling you that, in her own way. Victoria, Sara-Jane, Mistress Charlotte, all these new people, all these new friends. You should be happy, not sad.'

Jonathan looked at her, at the concern clear in her eyes. He kissed her, taking her in his arms, holding her tightly against his body. He closed his eyes and just let the feeling flow through his body – love. He hadn't realised it before, but now it was clear. He loved her, and Charlotte and Victoria and all the others.

Naomi began to undress him, her nimble fingers unbuttoning his shirt, kissing him on the mouth and face at the same time. He was responding, his breathing was faster and his prick was hard. He rubbed his fingers on her face, brushing back her hair so that he could look at her properly. She was so soft and responsive, turning to let him stroke her, her eyes half closed. He reached down and brushed a hand over her breasts, feeling her nipples standing hard and erect under the loose blouse.

In a few moments he was naked, and Naomi was on her knees in front of him, holding his strong hard prick in her fingers and kissing the tip lovingly. Her tongue traced tight circles around the glans, making him sigh as waves of pleasure passed through him. He began to pump his prick far into her mouth and she moved round so that she could take it deeper.

'I have to prepare you,' she said, and he saw her pulling herself away reluctantly, her desire clear and bright in her eyes. She kissed him once more on the very tip of his dome and then stood up.

'Will we ever get to make love?' he asked her, unbuttoning her blouse slowly.

'Yes,' she sighed, 'when Mistress allows us. But not tonight. Tonight is very special.'

'You're beautiful,' Jonathan told her, pulling her blouse open to reveal her pear-shaped breasts, the nipples hard points of red flesh sticking out enticingly. He smoothed a hand over one breast, cupping it gently and then flicking his thumb over the nipple, watching her close her eyes as he did so.

'I must get you ready . . . ' she sighed once more, but made no move to stop him from playing with her breasts. He stooped down and kissed between the breasts, holding them in his hands and pressing them against his face. Her body was scented with a subtle perfume that seemed to inflame him. He thumbed her nipples excitedly, making her sigh and cradle his head in her arms. He sucked a nipple deep into his mouth, almost biting her, and she squealed and then sighed. His hands were exploring her all over, moving up her thighs and under her skirt. She wore no panties, and when he palmed between the thighs she was wet.

'No, please don't do that . . . ' she whispered as he pressed a finger between her pussy lips. But her voice and body betrayed her, she parted her thighs and fell against his shoulders, her protestation sounding more like an invitation.

Jonathan moved his hand back and forth, enjoying the sticky feel of her honey flowing freely from her sex. He had an arm around her waist, supporting her, as he touched and probed her deep in her sex. He could feel her tensing up and then relaxing again as he played with her, flicking a finger across her apex until she moaned softly.

'Oh Jonathan . . . Jonathan . . . ' she cried, clutching him tightly. He worked harder, his fingers rubbing deeper into her, sliding into her hot wet sex faster and faster. Her breathing was hard, he could hear her catch her breath when he plunged his fingers hard into her. She was swaying, her head thrashing from side to side, eyes closed. He finger fucked her expertly, knowing that he was driving her wild with pleasure. She froze, held him with white knuckled intensity and then shuddered. His fingers were rubbing against her hard sex bud, driving her over the edge into climax.

He looked up at her and she smiled weakly, brushing her hair back into place. Her face looked flushed, her eyes still half closed, her skin glowing pink. She smiled when he showed her his fingers, wet with her juices, dappled creamy white on his fingers and knuckles. He licked each finger in turn, sucking up her essence joyfully. 'You taste lovely,' he told her, finally standing up. They kissed, and he knew that she must be able to taste herself on his tongue.

'Now I must prepare you,' she said, pulling away and glancing up at a clock above the door. She went over to a small nest of tables by the seat where Mistress had been sitting. There was a small package on the table and Naomi picked it up and walked back to him.

'A collar?' he suggested, knowing that it was how Mistress liked to see Dog.

'More than that,' Naomi replied, opening the package and pulling out a number of black leather items. She knelt down again and gently sucked away the drops of silver fluid beaded on the tip of his prick. Very slowly she unrolled the first item and then slipped it over his hardness.

Jonathan watched Naomi fit a leather sheath over his prick, pulling it tight and then buckling a tiny catch under his balls. It was at once stiff but soft, so that it made his prick stand out hard and cold, yet it displayed completely the full shape of his prick and balls. It fitted tightly, and he guessed that it had been made specially to fit him.

Naomi stood up and stepped back, admiring her handiwork. He looked down at himself, at the sleek black weapon emerging from between his thighs. She touched him, tracing a finger from his balls and up the full length. It felt different, one step removed from direct contact, yet still deliciously sensual.

'Now the collar?' he guessed when Naomi removed the second item from the package. She nodded and he bent down to allow her to put it around his neck. It fitted snugly, without chafing or pulling uncomfortably. The hard saddle leather was studded, with heavy steel studs that added weight to it. There was a single ring at the front, and when Naomi produced the long steel chain from the package he bent down for her to attach it but she shook her head.

'Not there,' she smiled. She reached down and he realised that there was also a ring hanging from under his balls. She clipped the chain on to it and stepped back. 'Now we're ready,' she smiled.

Naomi went first, holding the chain and pulling him along gently. He followed, enjoying the strange feel of having his prick harnessed and attached to a chain. He felt a thrill of pleasure when she tugged with the chain, knowing that he was at her mercy, and that soon it would be Mistress, *his* Mistress, that would be in command.

Naomi led him across the hall towards a flight of steps that led down into a lower storey. He glanced back at the house, and saw that he hadn't noticed the grandeur of his surroundings. He didn't care, the surroundings were meaningless to him, mere surface details that hardly impinged on his consciousness. He remembered how impressed he had been when he had first gone to Mistress, he remembered the feeling of intrusion as he had entered the grand house filled with even grander paintings and fine *objets d'art*. But the feeling had been dwarfed by his meeting with Mistress, that was what was important, nothing else.

'This is the way to the chamber,' Naomi explained, stepping down the stairs.

'Naomi,' he said quietly.

'Yes?'

'Thanks.'

'For what?' she asked, stopping to look back at him.

'Just for being there I suppose. What you said earlier, about my new friends, I hadn't seen it that way until you pointed it out.'

She smiled and carried on down the stairs. 'It's a strange life, I know,' she said, 'but it's extraordinary. We have what millions of other people will never have. We have understanding.'

The stairs led down into semi-darkness. It was cool without being cold, the stone steps ending in a long narrow passage way. Naomi carried on, leading Jonathan through a cellar stacked high with wine. Sound seemed dead, as if it had ceased to travel forward.

They stopped at an archway at one end of the wine cellar, a rough wooden door blocking their way. Naomi smiled, her face partially in shadow but her eyes piercing in the darkness. Jonathan fell to his knees instantly, his heart pounding and a knot of excitement pulsing in the pit of his belly. Naomi opened the door and went in, Jonathan following on hands and knees, the chain tugging gently at the leather covering between his thighs.

They entered a long dark room, it was a chamber, just as Mistress had said. The light was dim, but casting a soft unfocused glow on everything. The walls were of bare stone, and in various places Jonathan could see that manacles and bars had been added. The place seemed deliberately isolated, the atmosphere as far removed from real life as possible. It was the sort of place where anything could happen, and it made Jonathan both nervous and excited.

Mistress stood against the wall closest to the door,

one arm up against the wall, hand flat against dry black stone. Her hair was loose now, cascading over her shoulders and down her back. She wore long black boots, shining glossily in the weak light, extending from six inch heels up to her bare thighs. The other hand was at her side, encased in a shiny black mitten made from the same glossy material as her boots, leaving her long fingers, tipped with brilliant red fingernails, free. Her breasts were encased in a glossy plastic shell, seemingly moulded to her white skin, the nipples extruded and glinting in the pale light. The plastic shell was part of a top made of rubber, skintight and ending in a high collar around her neck. Around her waist she wore a skirt made of the same material, cut very short so that the folds of rubber barely extended to the top part of her thighs.

Jonathan swallowed hard, and felt a dagger of desire shoot through him with lightning impact. Mistress looked divine, her face was stern, cheeks drawn in a little, lips pursed disdainfully, eyes full of pure contempt.

'So this is my alter ego,' a voice said.

Jonathan turned and saw de Molay looking at him. He was naked and leaning against a high wooden post set in the ground at the other side of the room.

'This is Dog,' Mistress said, her voice cold and hard. 'This is your other self. Retribution for all your sins will be made on his back. Whenever you're beastly to me, he'll suffer in your place.'

'Is that my name then? Dog,' he laughed, pushing himself off the post and walking across the room. His body was well defined, taut, muscular, his chest patterned with hair tinged with silver around the nipples.

'You didn't expect me to follow your example, did

258

you?' Mistress asked archly, nodding towards a corner. Jonathan looked across to where Mistress had indicated and saw someone standing there, partly shadowed. It took a second for him to recognise who it was, but then he saw that it was Jessica. She was standing with hands on her head, legs together, skirt pulled up and her panties down at her ankles. Her backside was naked and even in the dim light Jonathan could tell that she had recently been spanked; her buttocks were marked red and pink all over.

'No, and it would have been silly of me even to think that you would, Jessica,' he said. 'Have you ever considered the true possibilities of having our doubles with us?'

'Which possibilities? They're endless, aren't they?'

'Consider this, the true meaning of masturbation is to make love to oneself. If Dog is my double, then by having sex with him I'm performing the purest form of masturbation possible. I am really making love with myself.'

'I'd like that,' Mistress said, smiling excitedly. 'And of course I'd have to make love with myself at the same time, to match your pleasure with my own.'

Jonathan froze when de Molay touched him. 'He's not very well trained,' de Molay said, turning back to Mistress.

'He needs a touch of the rod, I think,' Mistress said, standing up straight. She marched across the room, her heels clicking hard with every step, sounding like gunshots in the near silence. She went over to a set of drawers and pulled one open. She seemed to linger for a moment, rubbing her chin while she looked and then selected an implement.

'If he's a dog then he's not very well trained, is he? Not at all canine,' de Molay continued, standing up straight again.

'In that case he also needs reminding that he's a dog,' Mistress said, her back still to Jonathan.

'Pretend that it was I who was at fault,' de Molay suggested, joining Mistress.

'In that case Jonathan, I'm going to take great pleasure in punishing you for your impertinence,' she agreed, turning to face Jonathan. She had a long thin cane in one hand and a vicious-looking black whip in the other. 'First let's remind Dog of his species. Naomi, wet him.'

Naomi had been standing behind Jonathan, she knelt down instantly and took his arse-cheeks in her hands and gently pulled them apart. Jonathan turned to look at her but she had already bent down low and was licking him, wiping her tongue from under the leather harness and right up over his anus. She wet him liberally, smearing him with her spit and then pressing her tongue into his backside. Jonathan closed his eyes. The pleasure was intense and unexpected, making his prick quiver in the leather sheath. Naomi was sucking and kissing greedily, and he could feel his anal hole closing tightly around her probing tongue.

'That's enough,' de Molay said sternly, and Naomi stopped at once.

'Maybe now you'll remember that you're a dog,' Mistress said harshly, marching across the room, whip hanging loose in her hand.

Jonathan flinched, afraid of the whip that would surely bite deep into his skin, making him scream like an animal. But the blow never came; instead Mistress pressed her knee into his back and reached down behind him. He could feel the warmth of her body so near, she smelt wonderful, making him ache with desire and with pleasure at being so near to her. He tried to twist round to kiss her heel but couldn't reach.

He cried out suddenly, and Mistress pressed down

harder with her knee. She had taken the handle of the whip and forced it deep into his arsehole. The sudden pain had been intense, but Naomi had done her job well and Mistress was able to stuff the handle deep into his rear. She stood up and immediately he scrabbled round to kiss her boots, fervently seeking forgiveness for all his sins. The whip hung from between his thighs, the ribbed handle held tight between his arse-cheeks.

'Now that he's got a tail I doubt that he'll forget what he is,' Mistress told de Molay, smiling proudly.

'Very good, Jessica,' de Molay said approvingly, 'and his punishment?'

'I want him on the whipping post. Naomi, see to it.'

Naomi pulled the chain sharply and Jonathan cried out, he shuffled after Naomi quickly, not having time to fully understand what was going on. She made him stand up and then took his hands and lifted them above his head, putting them into suede cuffs attached to the top of the wooden post.

'Will this hurt?' he asked quietly, afraid of the punishment to come. He could feel the whip hanging from his rear, the thin leather strands reaching down to his knees. It was a tail, and Mistress was right, it was a reminder of just how little he mattered to her.

'Silence!' Mistress barked sharply, and both Jonathan and Naomi were startled. Jonathan tried to turn back but couldn't, his arms were too tight and he had to stand almost on tiptoe. He could make out Mistress walking towards him, a sleek shape in the corner of his eye, a tall lithe figure, her body swaying sexily as she walked, like a feline goddess.

'Well Jonathan, you've been a bad boy haven't you,' Mistress said teasingly, her voice softly insinuating, like a teacher talking to an errant child.

'I'm sorry, Mistress . . .' Jonathan said nervously.

'Silence, Dog!'

'No I haven't, Jessica,' de Molay said, sounding both defiant and playful at the same time.

'Jonathan, don't try my patience,' Mistress warned.

'Why not?' de Molay demanded with mock impudence.

'This is why not,' Mistress said coldly.

Jonathan screamed out loud with the sudden biting pain as the first stroke landed across his backside. It stung viciously, like a red flame across his flesh. He tensed up immediately, he heard the cane whistle through the air and then it struck again.

'Stop making so much noise, Jonathan,' Mistress scolded. She raised her arm again and brought it down hard.

Jonathan held his cry, gritting his teeth and letting the lightning flash through him before subsiding into a white heat of pain and pleasure. His breath was irregular, and his arms ached from being stretched, but the spark of pleasure was growing. His prick was throbbing, pressing against the constricting heat of the leather sheath. Every movement of his body caused waves of pleasure to pass through him. Every time he tensed he could feel the tail between his thighs, the handle pressed deep into his rear, a hard and painful presence that only added to his pleasure.

Mistress gave him two more strokes of the cane, each one perfect in execution, striking a different lattice line across his bare flesh. He collapsed, hanging painfully from the wrists, his body limp before the cruel power of Mistress.

'Let me fuck you,' de Molay whispered coarsely, his voice hot and low with desire.

'Well Jonathan, you obviously take well to being punished like this,' Mistress told him, the amusement in her voice tinged with excitement.

'Let me fuck you, now,' de Molay murmured darkly.

'Cut him loose,' Mistress told Naomi.

The cuffs were loosened and Jonathan fell to his knees. His body ached unbearably, he could feel the red stripe marks raised on his backside, etched into him. He crawled round and saw Mistress and de Molay kissing. Their mouths looked tight, her arms around his neck and his holding her by the shoulders. They kissed passionately, sucking at each other's breath, faces twisting and turning in unison.

'Fuck me here, Jonathan,' Mistress whispered, 'standing up, right now.'

They kissed again, and as they did so de Molay bent down low for a second and then came up straight. Mistress moaned and held him close, parting her thighs slowly and beginning to rock back and forth slowly. She moaned louder and Jonathan could see that de Molay was moving back and forth with his pelvis, thrusting up and down, pressing his prick deep into her sex.

'Dog, heel!' Mistress ordered, not turning round or stopping what she was doing.

Jonathan obeyed, crawling towards her quickly, his tail slithering along the ground. Her legs were parted, her thighs wrapped around de Molay. He sat back and traced the shape of her boots with his eyes, from the heel up, over the glossy seams at the back, up her bare thighs and into the darkness under the short skirt. He could see and hear de Molay sliding his prick in and out of her sex, and he could sense the pleasure growing in intensity.

'Jessica do the same,' de Molay snapped, hardly taking his lips from Mistress's shoulder and neck. He reached down and lifted the back of the skirt, revealing Mistress's round bottom cheeks.

Jonathan knew what to do. He moved forward and

planted his lips on one of the sharp heels and then began to work his way up slowly. He tasted her heels and the cold glossy surface of the boots, and then the softness of her thigh and the pure white skin of her buttocks.

In a moment he was joined by Jessica, on her hands and knees behind de Molay. For a second Jonathan and Jessica looked at each other, there was a moment of doubt, or perhaps it was shame, but then they smiled.

Jonathan buried his face in Mistress's backside, his tongue lapping up the creamy emissions slipping from the join of de Molay's prick and Mistress's sex, and then scooped it up towards her tight anal hole. He kissed her there, happy that he was going to be giving her pleasure, happy that he was close to her. He pressed forward and his wet tongue slipped into the tight anal ring, sliding in softly, lubricated with the love juice on his tongue.

Mistress moaned, squirmed and pressed her backside in and out, moving with de Molay's rhythm. Jonathan moved to the same rhythm, kissing and sucking when Mistress pressed her arse-cheeks out to him, then lapping at her buttocks when she moved in to take de Molay's thrusting prick deep into her.

Jessica touched Jonathan's hand, and without looking their fingers were entwined. Jonathan knew that Jessica was doing the same, sucking lovingly at de Molay's arsehole, as deliriously happy as he was.

Mistress cried out, her body jerking spasmodically, and de Molay cried out at the same instance. Jonathan could feel de Molay pumping deep into Mistress, both of them sharing a single blissful climax. The effect seemed to jump from one body to the next. Jonathan's cry was smothered, his breath buried between Mistress's beautiful arse-cheeks.

Jonathan felt lost for a moment, overwhelmed by the force of his own climax. He sat back, the taste of Mistress still strong in his mouth. He looked down and saw that the leather hardness was dripping with his own come, sliding viscously down his thigh.

With Mistress standing over him, her body bathed with sweat and come, her harsh cruelty tempered by the ecstasy of mutual orgasm, he felt complete.

It wasn't the end of the journey.

It was only the beginning.

Dear Reader

Oh, to be in April, now that December's here! It's all
right for you lucky lot, ducking spring showers to dive
into bookshops and browse along the offerings from
Nexus; I'm writing this at the winter solstice, with only
the anticipation of mistletoe and party games to keep
me going through the drear.

I will do my very best to enter an equinoctial state of
mind, however: this, my third letter, will appear in the
Nexus books that will be published in April.

And they are a varied bunch.

Ms Deedes on Paradise Island is the second Nexus
novel to feature the totally gorgeous Ella Deedes, *agente*

tres provocatrice. Once again she crosses libidos with the sadistic Texan megalomaniac, Blas Carnel, who has managed to corner the world market in aphrodisiac vanilla and whose base is an archipelago in the tropical South Seas. As she travels from island to island, sampling in typically excessive fashion the various sexual specialities served on each, she closes in on Carnel — until she is captured, punished, and sentenced to death by sexual overload. Does she win in the end? Well, I'm told there's a third Ms Deedes book being written.

Wrong numbers are so seldom interesting. 'Hello, Gran? Gran, is that you? Who? No, I wanted Gran.' Or perhaps 'Takeaway please, I'll have number thirty-two the king prawns kung po style, number forty-one the beef with — what? Well why didn't you bloody well say so?'

In *Obsession*, Jonathan de Molay answers his telephone. The caller has dialled the wrong number. But instead of any of the above, he hears a wickedly silky female voice say: 'Darling. I'm going to punish Naomi for you.'

Obsession is the third book that Maria del Rey has written for Nexus. The first was *The Institute*, which was apparently one of the best sellers from 1991; and the second was *Paradise Bay*. All three are very different, but each in its own way explores the fascination of power differentials: the thrill of dominance, the thrill of submission. From the moment he hears the voice from his telephone, Jonathan de Molay is hooked: he has to find the mystery woman, even though to do so he has to submerge himself in a secret world where everyone is a master, a mistress or a slave. It's one of those books that makes you understand the pleasure in being at both ends of the riding crop.

Violette, April's classic reprint, is by contrast a straightforward bawdy tale, translated from a French original probably written at the end of the last century — and probably by a woman, too. It's a simple story of one girl's introduction into the ways of licentiousness, first with a male lover and then with a noblewoman. There's plenty of boudoir action, and you'll enjoy Violette's adventures if you like corsets and crinolines. Lace me up, Scotty!

Just a moment. Got to do up a few buttons. The editor's coming to look over my shoulder.

He says that the titles to be published next month — May — are: *War in High Heels*, the follow-up to *Spies in Silk*, which continues the story of Britain's secret army of well-disciplined Mata Haris in World War Two; *Queenie & Co*, the first in a three book series about two globetrotting journalists with knockdown looks and knickersdown behaviour; and a new edition of *Blue Angel Nights*.

The editor's gone now. Funny — I'm sure I remember doing up those buttons. You know, sometimes I wonder whether his insistence on my writing a monthly letter wasn't just a pretext to bring me into his office.

If you're a regular Nexus reader you must have seen the questionnaire that appeared in the back of almost every book in 1992. Perhaps you're one of those who replied: the publisher has a bulging folder containing hundreds of completed forms.

The Nexus editors are already using the information, trying as much as possible to tailor the contents of the books to readers' requirements.

Now, the publisher doesn't want me to reveal any trade secrets. He's threatened to do things that even I wouldn't enjoy. But, after I'd spent some time being very persuasive, he relunctantly agreed to let me tell you about a few of the more unusual results.

You're a mixed bunch, you Nexus readers. You come from every corner of the country, you're any age from just adult to senior citizen, and you're as likely to be a wealthy businessman as a penniless student — or anything in between. As expected, most of you are men — but there is a significant minority of women readers, and they have noticeably different requests from their male counterparts.

For one thing, most of you men don't mind at all that Nexus book covers show pictures of implausibly buxom wenches wearing immodest amounts of clothing; in fact, many of you want even more female flesh to gaze at.

The publisher tells me that he'll have to disappoint you. He has to take into account W H Smith's ban on nipples, and the fact that several of his export markets — Canada, for instance — have regulations about shop displays that are even stricter than Britain's.

And we women don't care, anyway. Female Nexus readers — in general — don't like the blatant covers, and would prefer to buy books with subtle illustrations on their fronts.

The section in the returned questionnaires at which I always look first is the question about particular settings or subjects that readers would like to see in Nexus books. You lot really have got some wild ideas, haven't you?

It doesn't surprise me that, in general, male and female readers like the same wide range of interests. But you men are terribly specific! A woman who fantasises about a strict boss/naughty secretary scene would probably write that she's into domination fantasies; a man with the same fantasy goes into detail about the precise colour of the secretary's miniskirt and the height of her heels in millimetres.

And there are differences between the men and women. There doesn't seem to be a single woman reader who wants to read about enemas, for instance, whereas there is a vociferous if small minority of men who seem very enthusiastic about nozzles and tubes.

And while many of the men congratulated Nexus books on being well written, the women tended to think that Nexus authors could do better. We're just more discerning than you chaps, that's all there is to it.

There's loads more I could reveal about the survey, but the publisher doesn't like me to fill up too many of his precious blank pages. I'll keep some revelations for a future letter.

In the meantime, even though the questionnaire isn't appearing in Nexus books any more, I'd still like to know what you think about the books, and what kind of novels you'd like to read. You can write to me at the Nexus office; the address is at the front of the book, on the back of the title page.

Don't be bashful! I'm very hard to shock, as I'm sure you can imagine, but that doesn't mean you shouldn't try.

Bye bye for now, and keep thinking those rude thoughts!

Nexus

THE BEST IN EROTIC READING

The Nexus Library of Erotica – almost one hundred and fifty volumes – is available from many bookshops and newsagents.

A complete list of titles, with prices and information about ordering by post, is available from the publishers. Please send a large, stamped and addressed envelope to:

Nexus book list
332 Ladbroke Grove
London
W10 5AH